Weehawken Free Public Library

49 Hauxhurst Avenue

Weehawken, NJ 07086

201-863-7823

Young Adult Department

THE
DEVIL'S
INTERN

THE
DEVIL'S
INTERN

Donna Hosie

Holiday House / New York

Text copyright © 2014 by Donna Hosie
All Rights Reserved
HOLIDAY HOUSE is registered in the U.S. Patent and Trademark Office.
Printed in Bound in July 2014 at Maple Press, York, PA, USA.
www.holidayhouse.com
First Edition
1 3 5 7 9 10 8 6 4 2

Library of Congress Cataloging-in-Publication Data
Hosie, Donna.
The Devil's intern / by Donna Hosie. — First edition.
pages cm
Summary: "Seventeen-year-old Mitchell discovers a time-travel device
that will allow him to escape his internship in Hell's accounting office and
return to Earth, but his plans to alter the circumstances of his own death take
an unexpected turn when his three closest friends in Hell insist
on accompanying him back to the land of the
living"—Provided by publisher.
ISBN 978-0-8234-3195-3 (hardcover)
[1. Hell—Fiction. 2. Future life—Fiction.
3. Death—Fiction. 4. Time travel—Fiction.]
I. Title.
PZ7.H79325De 2014
[Fic]—dc23
2014002402

For Beth Phelan and Kelly Loughman,
for loving Team DEVIL
as much as I do

Contents

Acknowledgments

It takes one person to write a manuscript but a whole army to take that manuscript out into the world. So, here is the love for *my* Team DEVIL.

First, to my wonderful agent, Beth Phelan, because no one worked harder: thank you for constantly supporting me and Mitchell on our journey through time—and for Americanizing this English writer's spelling before her editor needed to do so!

Thanks to my amazing editor, Kelly Loughman. From our first introduction you have blown me away with your enthusiasm and attention to detail, picking up little things that the rest of us missed. Working with you has been a joy. Team DEVIL, and especially Alfarin, have no greater champion.

Thank you to Kelly Bohrer Zemaitis, Peggy Russell, and Charlotte Evans for your erudite critiquing skills.

To Mike Weinstein (and Bear, of course!), thank you for the supportive e-mails and Middle Earth/Sherlock YouTube links! You've been a tower of strength throughout my publishing journey, and I've learned more from you than anyone else, although those pesky dashes still kill me. . . .

Sincere thanks to Jennifer Azantian for your advice and support.

Thanks to my husband, Steve. You've never once complained about the hours and hours and hours I've spent typing away. You just kept me supplied with wine and chicken fajitas! Best. Husband. Ever.

Thanks to my gorgeous kids: Emily, Daniel, and Joshua for just being proud of Mum, and to *my* mum and dad, Lorraine and Peter Molloy.

And last, but definitely not least, thanks to my Devilish Degenerates of Doom who get onto social media and talk up my books to death. Gina Anstey, Kristin Weiss Devoe, Charlotte Evans, Madeleine Henderson, Connie House, Jennifer Jones Bragg, Anne Fetkovich Ehrenberger, Maria Dotson, Julie Elizabeth Seay, Denise Dowd, and Athena Stewart, I would be nothing without you.

P.S. Raj Khanna, no, you can't retire!

1. Welcome to Hell

"How did you die?"

That's the first question you'll be asked in Hell. Four years ago it was certainly the first question I was asked. I had just walked into a holding area cramped with the recently dead—the processing center I know now to be the HalfWay House—when I was thrown against a wall by another dead person demanding to know. It's a question I've been asked a million times since.

I was too shell-shocked to consider lying. So I told him the truth. "I—I was hit by a bus," I stammered.

Big mistake. Huge. Rule number one in Hell: if you have a crappy death, don't tell other dead people about it. You'll be mocked for all eternity if you do, and apparently that's a long time.

It was a Greyhound bus that did the dirty deed. I was visiting my father in Washington, DC—my parents are divorced—and... splat.

Here is the thing I can't quite get my head around, though. I wasn't crossing the road when it happened, or at least I hadn't intended to. I was just walking down the street, listening to my iPod, minding my own business.

Something distracted me. Something major. I can't remember what it was, and it drives me crazy when I try to think back. For some stupid, dumbass reason, I ran out into the road. I couldn't hear the bus, or the squealing of the brakes. All I could hear was Radiohead through my headphones.

At least my death was instant; I should be thankful for that. Down here, devils wear their demise like a badge of honor, but I bet if they had to relive it, not one of them would choose to bleed to death on a muddy battlefield, or slowly asphyxiate by hanging.

My death may have been stupid, and I may not like talking about it, but at least I can't remember the pain.

A bus, though, I ask you. Of all the ways to snuff it.

I'm seventeen and always will be, but being dead for four years has made me a little more experienced. You can make your death as heroic as you want in Hell, because nobody checks up on you. The only way to know for sure is to look in the devil resources files, which no one ever does because the photographs freak everyone out. So now I say I died doing something brave. Animals, that's the key. Say you died saving an animal and... well, if you end up here— and you almost certainly will—you try it. See for yourself how much love you get.

I work in the accounting department of Hell under the supervision of Septimus, The Devil's accountant and civil servant number one. I'm The Devil's intern so I get a desk in here with The Devil's right-hand man. Like me, Septimus is tall and thin. Unlike me he wears the sharpest pinstripe suits. His dark skin has a reddish tinge to it, like a sunburned glow. He wears small golden hoops in his ears, and his head has been shaved to the scalp. But I think Septimus's most awesome feature is his eyes. They are bloodred. They weren't originally like that, of course, but Septimus has been here so long, he can't remember their original color.

One day I'll have eyes like that. Right now mine are pink. Pink! As soon as a devil enters Hell, their eye color changes. At first the irises turn opaque, the color of foamy warm milk. Eventually, after a year or so, the color starts to reflect the heat that has built up inside, and a hint of rose appears. This intensifies over time, and the spectrum of eye pigment changes from pale pink to magenta to cherry, until finally the irises are bloodred. The only exception to this rule is The Devil himself. His irises are black.

I'm on my way to work right now—and I'm late. Again. Septimus isn't the kind of boss who will rant and rave, because he knows I work my butt off in his office, but I'm just no good with time. Hell is so overcrowded it takes hours to move from one end of the corridor to the other.

I was sure I was wearing a watch when I died, but somewhere between getting hit by a bus and getting checked in at the HalfWay House, I lost it. At least I got to keep my cell phone and my iPod.

And now I'm really late because the alarm is going off for The Devil's morning tea. The alarm is actually a recording of Chopin's "Funeral March." The Devil thinks it's funny.

Yeah, right. My sides are splitting.

What's even worse is that the recording is actually me. When The Devil found out I was a musical prodigy I had to spend a week playing Chopin for the Grim Reapers while they recorded it. I could hardly say no to The Devil, but I was so depressed afterward that I completely lost my appetite. All that recording session did was remind me of what I'd lost. I'm still not used to the fact that I'm dead, and I don't think I ever will be. I breathe on reflex, even though I don't need to. I still feel pain, though nothing can ever kill me again. I never really appreciated living until I stopped doing it.

And do you have any idea how unpopular that music makes me with some of the other devils? They have to hear the "Funeral March" every single day. Talk about rubbing our dead faces in it.

I—along with millions and millions of other devils—work in the central business district, or CBD, of the Underworld. There are nearly seven hundred floors, each with its own balcony and elevator. Flaming torches hang from the walls, so at first glance it looks like the façade of an enormous cruise liner docking in the dead of night. It freaked me out the first time I saw it, but pretty much everything freaked me out back then.

Each floor in the business hub of Hell deals with a specific area of administration or maintenance. The higher up the cave you are, the more important the office. So The Devil's Oval Office—not that he's a democratically elected demon, he just likes irony—and the busy accounting department tower above everyone else on level 1; the heating department is on level 2; and The Devil's fabric selection team has recently been promoted to level 3. Those in true torment work on level 666. This is a new department, reserved for reality TV stars. They clean out the ground-floor toilets.

The rest of Hell is separated into zones, connected by thousands and thousands of tunnels. Our dorms are near where we work, so there are enormous swaths of the Underworld that most of us never get to see.

Now I'm *really* late, because the recording of me playing Chopin has finished. I'd better reach the office by the time "Abide with Me" reminds everyone it's lunchtime.

Finally, I get to the elevator. If I close my eyes, I can pretend I'm an astronaut flying into space. I wanted to do that when I was little: walk in space. Then I was going to be a paleontologist. Finally I settled on rock star. Not like Jon Bon Jovi or even Hendrix, but more alternative rock, like Chris Martin. Someone who plays the piano like a madman.

But then I died and became The Devil's intern. They don't tend to give you that option on career night.

I'm actually walking on tiptoes as I inch toward the accounting office. First I need to get past the Oval Office, and even though I walk past this door several times every day, it still makes me anxious.

I'm at the door when I hear raised voices. It's The Devil and Septimus. I can tell The Devil is in another foul mood because sparks of blue electrical current are zapping across the damp outer stone walls.

The Devil has been throwing tantrums all week, and from the sound of it, he's finally reached the end of his patience. Heaven—or Up There, as most of us call it—has sent another notice, making The Devil scream and rant until he set fire to his gold throne (the seat he extorted from King Louis XVI in return for his head). Septimus must have gone to try to calm Sir down.

4

I don't know why I listen in on their conversations. It's hard not to be inquisitive when you're this close to power, but most of the stuff they talk about in there gives me nightmares.

"Septimus!" shrieks The Devil. "I am vexed, Septimus. One could claim I am in despair."

"What's He done now, sir?" asks Septimus. His accent, which apparently was once Roman, has now transformed into a deep southern American drawl. A lot of accents and languages change in Hell. I guess it depends on who you hang with. All dead people are implanted with a communication translator as soon as they arrive at the HalfWay House. So regardless of the mother tongue, all of us can understand one another. With all the scary stuff that gets screamed around here, I sometimes wish I didn't have the translator.

"He!" cries The Devil. "I'll tell you what He has done, Septimus. He has threatened to stop funding the HalfWay House. That is what He has done. He really has gone too far this time.

"And," says The Devil, continuing to wail, "to compound my misery, Septimus, His letter exploded into rainbows and destroyed another set of my drapes. He is such a vile show-off. Why can't He send a messenger like the rest of us? It's getting to the point where I'm considering the removal of all my furnishings, and you know how much I cherish my drapery.

"Up There is conspiring against me, Septimus," sniffs The Devil. "Without the HalfWay House to triage the dead, our reception area will soon be swamped with poets, librarians, vegans, and charity workers. It's no good, Septimus. It's getting absolutely out of control. Hell is already bursting at the seams. Soon we'll be overrun, and our costs are already astronomical. The Highers created Hell and Up There for a good reason—these dead people have to go *somewhere*. He can't simply refuse to take His fair share."

"I agree wholeheartedly, sir. In fact, I was thinking it might be time to bring the Viciseometer out of storage," says Septimus. "I have been formulating a plan."

"The Viciseometer? That's an excellent idea," replies The Devil. The hairs on my arm suddenly lift with a chill I don't usually experience in Hell. The Devil's voice has dropped. It sounds much deeper, menacing. "You know, I was thinking we could unleash Operation H as well," he adds.

There is silence.

"You don't think that might be a little too hasty, sir?" says Septimus. "We have yet to explore all alternatives. Every scientist who saw the infection spread in those poor dead souls is still traumatized...."

"But isn't that exactly what we want, Septimus?" whispers The Devil, and although I can't see him, just the tone of his voice is making me feel sick. The words tumble from his mouth, as if he has waited a long time to say them.

"I thought you and I were in agreement here. I want Up There so scared, so beyond fear, so traumatized at just the *thought* of what I can do to them that they will go down on bended knee and beg to take more of the dead."

"I do understand, sir," says Septimus gently, "but perhaps you would like to see my plan for the Viciseometer first? I just have a couple of extras to add, but it should be ready within twenty-four hours. Just leave it to me. I have never failed you."

"Then I should allow you to get back to your plan. Don't keep me waiting."

My desk—now.

I run into the accounting office and throw myself into my chair. I grab a stack of papers and try to look busy as Septimus's shoes clip along the marble floor toward our connecting door.

Then a high-pitched voice calls out, "Send in the cherubs on your way out, Septimus. I need amusement to take my mind away from the torment."

I hear Septimus sigh on the other side of the door. "Sir, we don't have the cherubs anymore. Remember, you lost them in a game of chess several thousand years ago. He has them now."

The Devil starts wailing again.

"Perhaps you would like me to send for the chimeras?" says Septimus hurriedly. "I understand they have been learning the art of Irish folk dancing from one of the witch covens."

Septimus walks into the office.

"Make the call, Mitchell."

"Send for the chimeras," I say into the handset, "and better have the leprechauns on standby. Sir is having a very bad day."

Septimus slumps into his office chair and puts his feet up on the mahogany desk.

"It's getting worse, isn't it?" I ask.

"He's proving to be rather troublesome," replies Septimus, "but then He knows exactly which buttons to push and Sir rises to the bait every single time. This time He's threatening to close the Half-Way House."

"Can He do that?"

Septimus shakes his head. "I don't believe so—although I know Fabulara would find it very funny. But even then, He knows that if the dead aren't sorted properly we will have anarchy in administration on both sides. However, it is an undeniable fact that more of the dead are crossing our threshold than theirs."

"So what will you do?" I'm fishing for information, and judging by the narrowing of Septimus's red eyes, he knows it. We rarely mention Fabulara, the Higher who is responsible for Hell and Up There. The Devil is paranoid about the name being said aloud. He thinks it's cursed. But it isn't Fabulara I'm interested in. I want to know what a Viciseometer is, and what Septimus plans to do with it.

"It's going to be yet another long day, Mitchell," drawls Septimus, ignoring my question. "Now, file the laundry receipts and then pop down to maintenance and ask Geronimo if he has a quote for furnace number eight yet. When you've done that, send the quarterly figures to Augustus for double-checking and then ask IT to come and look at my computer—another virus has gotten into it, the Black Death I think, judging by the pus oozing out of the hard drive. Take my suit to the dry cleaners, and then send the ledger for the Masquerade Ball costs to Heather in accounts five."

Now, I can juggle a lot of things when it comes to work, but smoke is rising from my pen as I furiously scribble down Septimus's instructions.

"And when you've done that…" I look up in alarm. Time is running short and I want to grab a shower and a burger or three before I meet Medusa.

"Never mind, perhaps tomorrow," says Septimus hesitantly. "Then you shall go to the ball, Cinderella."

"Does that make you an ugly stepsister?"

"I'm far too handsome," says Septimus as a gong from the Oval Office starts to ring over and over again.

The unmistakable shrieks of The Devil are now bouncing off the walls throughout the entire first floor.

"Septimus! Septimus! Help me! The chimeras are attacking my pelmets. Send for security. Oh, woe is me…*Septimus!*"

Believe it or not, this is actually a typical day in Hell: heat, long hours, The Devil's screaming, heat, wishful thinking, and even more heat.

This is my existence for the rest of eternity.

Because four years ago, on the eighteenth of July, I died and went to Hell, and nothing will ever change that.

2. The Masquerade Ball

The Devil's Masquerade Ball is apparently one Hell of a party and, for many devils, the only highlight of their existence in the Afterlife.

It takes place in an immense rock cave situated between the business district and the accommodation complex, where most devils sleep when they're not being worked to another death. For the Masquerade Ball, the cave is decorated to be an exact replica—although on a far larger scale—of the Salon de Mars ballroom in the French Palace of Versailles. I wouldn't know if this was true, myself. I never had the time to get a passport, let alone travel.

Tickets for the Masquerade Ball are snapped up within seconds of going on sale, and the waiting list for returns stretches into the millions. The rules of entry are simple: each devil in Hell is only allowed to apply once every hundred years. You aren't guaranteed a ticket, but at least you have a chance. Septimus—who has been in Hell for thousands of years—has been to nine balls. The last one he attended was in 1547, which was the year Henry VIII arrived. The Devil was so impressed by the royal parties Henry—or Chopper, as everyone calls him—threw when he was alive that the king was fast-tracked onto the organizing committee.

This year's Masquerade Ball is to be my first. I'm going with Medusa, one of my best friends in Hell. Apparently, I was lucky; to get a ticket after just four years of being dead is unheard of. *Lucky* isn't a word I tend to use a lot now. Medusa has been so excited that she's barely slept. So, because of her, I'm looking forward to it, too. Plus I get to listen to live music all night, which is numbers one, two, and three on my what-I-miss-about-being-alive list.

So, once work is finished, I rush back to my dorm and throw on my rented tux—which has clearly been worn a thousand times, judging by the smell. Then I have to fight my way back through the crowds to the ballroom.

I look—and stink—like a stretched penguin. I devil-watch while I wait for Medusa, taking care not to catch any eyes. I don't like standing out.

The costume designers on level 339 have clearly been working their fingers to the bone creating everyone's masks and outfits. We all get paid for our work, although it's more pocket money than a wage. Most of us spend it on food and cell phones, the only salvations we have left. Those who get tickets for the ball often go without to pay for their outfits.

Except me. I've got best friends who keep me supplied with burgers.

My thoughts of food disappear when a smoking-hot devil sidles up to me. Her slim figure is wrapped in a sequined black dress that falls to the floor and then fans out like a fish tail at the back. It's only when I pay attention to the rear that I notice that the dress plunges to a deep V at the back. It takes a while for me to realize my mouth is open. The girl is pale and her chestnut-colored hair is wound into a complex knotted bun that rests on the back of her neck. Her eyes, like mine, are pale pink, and are just visible behind a black satin mask studded with tiny red jewels.

Pink eyes are very pretty on a girl.

Without warning, a sharp elbow makes violent contact with my stomach.

"Ow."

"Stop looking at my ass."

"Medusa?"

"Who did you think it was?"

"I don't know—it's just—well, you look gorgeous," I reply, massaging my stomach.

"Thank you for that display of shock," says Medusa tartly. "I can clean up pretty nicely when I make the effort, you know."

Medusa is small and skinny. She usually has a wild mane of tightly curled hair—hence the nickname Medusa. She works in the kitchens on level 180, and she makes the best strawberry cheesecake in Hell. Her real name is Melissa Pallister, and she has been dead for just over forty years. She's never told me how she died, but I have my suspicions because of her nightmares.

Not that we sleep together. Let's get that straight. We just have a tendency to crash at the end of each other's beds when we're too tired to navigate the labyrinth of bunks packed into each dorm.

"How about we start again?" I suggest quickly, fearing another blow from my best friend. I take five steps back and then approach Medusa at a slow pace. I place my arm at a right angle in front of my stomach and bow deeply.

"Medusa Pallister, also known as Melissa Pallister, also known as the Queen of the Cupcake, may I have the honor of your hand?" I say, gazing into her pretty pink eyes. Medusa immediately starts giggling.

"What about the rest of me?"

"Do you want me to pick you up and carry you in over my shoulder?"

Medusa curtsies, still giggling. I've noticed that girls giggle a lot, but I never know whether it's from nerves or amusement. Is there an instruction book somewhere that I should know about?

Medusa slips her arm through the crook of my elbow and we go in search of our table. I certainly don't need an instruction book for anything that involves food.

The Devil has expensive tastes, and each year the Masquerade Ball gets more outrageous. This year is no exception. A red satin cloth covers every table, each embroidered in a heavier thread with images of The Devil. The bewildering amount of cutlery that frames every black china plate is made from the finest gold, mined from Aztec mountains thousands of years ago. Trust me when I say this stuff costs millions, which Hell just can't afford.

With everyone in the ballroom masked and dressed in their penguin suits and party dresses, it's hard to distinguish who is who. Older devils mix with the new, and only the color of their irises gives away their seniority.

Have I mentioned my eyes are pale pink? It could be another two hundred years before they start to turn red.

The Devil arrives as the clock strikes midnight. The orchestra immediately commences "For He's a Jolly Good Fellow," and most of the guests enthusiastically sing along. I pretend to sing by mouthing the words until Medusa pokes me in the ribs and glares at me for cheating. The Devil grins and waves exuberantly at his guests. He is tall, with pale skin that looks almost transparent, like parchment paper. His jet-black hair is thick and gelled back from his face. Apart from his black eyes, it's rumored that The Devil's pride and joy is his goatee, which is just long enough for him to curl at the chin. I also know—because of the receipts—that he never wears anything other than Prada.

Medusa nudges me in the ribs once more.

"Will you quit doing that? You have bony little arms that hurt."

"Look who's sitting next to The Devil," she whispers back. "It's Septimus."

She starts waving at the high table. Two bloodred eyes shine back at her, hidden behind a white mask with diamond teardrops. Septimus waves back.

The Devil is soon heckled with cries of "Speech!" He motions that he has no intention of standing up, but the calls are getting louder and louder. All of the dead in Hell know it's in their best interest to stay on The Devil's good side, and no one misses an opportunity to kiss ass.

Someone hands him a microphone. It whistles loudly, causing everyone to wince. Somewhere in the darkness beyond the ballroom, a wolf howls. It sends shivers down my back, as if freezing fingers are touching the bones in my spine. Perhaps it means someone has just walked over my grave?

"Deities, Your Royal Highnesses, lords, gentlemen, ladies, humans, and things that haven't been categorized by social services yet," calls The Devil in his shrill voice. "Welcome to the thirty-nine hundredth Masquerade Ball."

He pauses for dramatic effect as thousands of hands bang their approval on the tables. I don't. I'm too preoccupied with getting thoughts of my grave out of my head. By the time I realize I'm the only one not cheering, it's too late.

"I won't keep you long, as I know you are all champing at the bit to get going—which reminds me, did someone muzzle Cerberus?" The Devil turns around in a panic but is immediately calmed as several civil servants—Septimus among them—nod in unison.

"Excellent," continues The Devil. "We wouldn't want a repeat of last year's entertainment, would we?" He laughs and thousands of sycophants laugh with him. Medusa and I don't laugh, though. I don't think there's anything funny about a rabid three-headed dog tearing dead people to pieces, which is apparently what happened to the devils who arrived too early for last year's ball.

"Well," continues The Devil, "all that remains is for me to thank the committee once again for their tireless work in organizing such a party. I understand Chopper only lopped off one hundred and eighty heads this year, which is a vast improvement from last year. Special mention must also go to Joanne Cartwright, a new…"

I zone out as my thoughts drift back to what I heard earlier between Septimus and The Devil. What is a Viciseometer? I'm sure I've heard of it before. Maybe Medusa knows. She knows everything. Then again, I shouldn't get her involved in this, even on the periphery. The Devil is psychopathic on a good day. Medusa is smart because she asks questions; I'm smarter because I know when to keep my mouth shut.

Eventually, The Devil stops talking, the butt-kissers stop

cheering, and the arrival of roasted potatoes and flame-grilled steak is enough to bring my attention back to the present. After I fill my stomach to the point of bursting, Medusa announces she wants to dance. I'm unwilling to part from my third bowl of crème brûlée but relent when Medusa threatens to pummel me with her elbows. She says she never got the chance to dance when she was alive, but I haven't danced ever.

Since I'm a good friend, I slip one hand around Medusa's waist and, rather stiffly, we waltz around the dance floor. My fingers go searching for the bare skin of her back, but I quickly learn my lesson after Medusa grabs hold of them and twists.

"You may have been a musical prodigy when you were alive, but I am not a piano," she growls. "Leave your hands where I can see them."

"Can we go back and sit down? Dancing is for girls."

"I *am* a girl, Mitchell," replies Medusa, "and try telling The Devil that." We both look over at the master of Hell, who has cleared the dance floor with his moshing.

We sit back down at our table and I pull my bowl of crème brûlée toward me. But I've lost my appetite—thoughts of this Visciseometer thing and Septimus's plan are eating away at my insides. I don't understand why. Maybe it was the tone of The Devil's voice in the Oval Office. It was chilling.

"What's wrong, Mitchell?" asks Medusa.

I stare at her hair. The curls are already starting to escape from the bun she tied them into. I don't know why she bothered. I love her hair. It's different.

"Hell calling Mitchell Johnson," says Medusa in a singsong voice.

I tuck the errant curls behind Medusa's ears. Her cheeks have gone red. She must be hot from the dancing.

"I need to ask you something," I say. "In private."

She laughs at the irony. Okay, so there is no such thing as *private* in Hell.

"Never mind," I say, lowering my voice. "I'll ask you here."

I lean in toward her; she does the same. We're so close our noses are almost touching. My head is telling me I shouldn't share information from the office with Medusa. It's just too dangerous. I don't know what my heart would say, because it's dead.

And that reminder is enough to make up my mind.

"Do you know what a Viciseometer is?" I whisper.

Medusa's face falls a little and I notice that her shoulders slump a fraction.

"It's okay," I say quickly. "Ignore me. It was just something I overheard."

"I thought—" Medusa stops. "It doesn't matter what I thought." She smiles thinly, not wide enough to show her dimples. "I know what a Viciseometer is," she whispers. "It's a legend; a stopwatch, or at least that's what it's supposed to look like. Only two were ever made, apparently, one for Hell, and one for Up There. They're supposed to be really powerful objects."

"But what does a Viciseometer do?" I ask. I knew Medusa would know. She's always got her crazy hair buried in a book.

"A Viciseometer is a time-traveling device," she explains. "But why do you want to know? How did you hear about it?"

I get out of answering by forking two whole profiteroles into my mouth. Then Septimus joins us. I start choking, worried that he somehow overheard us.

"I have to say, Medusa, the kitchen has outdone itself this year," drawls Septimus. "That peppered salmon was to die for."

Medusa smiles but doesn't reply; all her hair is now escaping and she's desperately trying to pin it back.

Septimus leans down, puts a hand on my shoulder, and whispers into my ear, "I don't mean to ruin your evening by talking about work, Mitchell, but I'm afraid I will need you to come into the office tomorrow."

Really? On my one day off all year? "Any reason in particular?" My voice doesn't betray how worried I am. I'd bet everything that Septimus just heard me talking about the Viciseometer, which means I might have gotten Medusa into trouble as well. Why did I listen to my heart? The damn thing isn't there anymore.

"I've had an idea," replies Septimus. "Mitchell, we are going to stop the dead."

3. Septimus's Plan

I don't like being dead, and it's important that you know that.

I get on with existing in the Afterlife because I have no choice. Septimus calls me *stoic*. I admit I had to look the word up. He says it's a good quality, especially in Hell.

I think what he means is that I just go with the flow. I go to work, and I do my best. I hang with Medusa and my two other best friends, Alfarin and Elinor, and I'd like to think they see me as a pretty excellent friend. Loyal, funny, maybe cute in a dorky sort of way...

I shouldn't be in Hell, though, and it isn't fair that I am.

My old best friends, the ones still alive, will be turning twenty-one now. They'll be graduating, traveling, dating, and living.

Living. I have that one word written on a piece of scrap paper. It sits in my wallet, scrunched up and faded from being unfolded and read all the time.

And living is the one thing I will never do again.

I just exist.

So if Septimus's plan is to stop the dead, I am totally in, because seventeen-year-olds shouldn't die.

Because once you're here, there is no way out.

The morning after the ball, I wake up in my dorm and immediately rub the crusty remains of sleep from my eyes. It takes me a while to focus my brain. I could lie here for another few hours easily, especially as the other two hundred and sixty dudes I share the dorm with are all at work and for the first time—ever—I have the place to myself. I think back to last night and smile. Then I think I could be having a night like that every day if I were still alive, and my smile disappears. For a few hours I felt as if I were alive again. A fun, pretty girl keeping me company, great music, a ton of food...

Yeah, for a few hours I felt alive. And now for the rest of my existence I'll be reminded that I'm not.

I make a pact with myself. *No more maudlin thoughts today.* I have a day off work—finally—and I intend to hang with Medusa, Alfarin, and...aw, crap. I don't have the day off work at all. Septimus asked me to go in, didn't he?

Okay, five more minutes...

Three hours later, it's Medusa who wakes me up. She has a pillow in her hands and she's thumping me around the head with it.

"I'm getting up.... I'm getting up...."

"Septimus sent me a message!" *Whack.* "He is waiting"—*whack*—"for you"—*whack*—"Mitchell."

"I'm getting up, I'm getting up. Now stop hitting me, you maniac." My feet are already on the floor.

Whack.

"What was that for?"

"You insulted me."

Whack.

I wrestle the pillow from Medusa and start to smack her with it. Her yellow T-shirt rides up her stomach and I can see her tummy ring glinting like a new coin. It has a pink diamond hanging from it. Medusa got it to match her eyes.

Whack.

Medusa grabs a pillow from another bed and lays a padded right hook across my jaw. She plays dirty. I was distracted by the sight of her skin.

"Cheat."

"You're pathetic."

"We'll call it a draw."

"No way, loser. I owned you."

My honor as a man is being called into question. This demands just one response.

Second death by pillow fight.

Ten minutes later we collapse onto my bed. Feathers are floating around the dorm room like elongated snowflakes. Being dead doesn't cure allergies, and it isn't long before I'm sneezing, wheezing, and scratching at the hives on my neck.

Medusa is still mocking me as we arrive on level 1.

The boss is already waiting. Septimus is still dressed in the clothes he wore to the Masquerade Ball—including the mask. He's lounging in his big black leather chair with his feet up on the desk. Then we hear the snoring.

"He's asleep," says Medusa fondly. "We should have gotten him some coffee before we came."

"I'll have a hot chocolate while you're at it."

"Get your own, hive boy."

"Ah, the sounds of young love," says a deep voice. Septimus pulls off his mask and stretches.

"Ugh," we both reply, although I notice that Medusa's cheeks are suddenly red. I resist the urge to stick my finger in one of her dimples.

Septimus starts chuckling. "Mitchell, thank you for coming in this—" He stops speaking and looks at his wristwatch. "Is it the morning after, or the evening after before the morning?"

"Uh..."

"I think Mitchell left his brain in the ballroom, Septimus," says Medusa, throwing a punch toward my kidneys.

"Well, while you work that little riddle out," says Septimus, winking at Medusa, "how about we have a little chat about my plan?"

"You seriously think you can stop the dead from getting into Hell?" I grab a chair and wheel it over to Septimus's desk.

Septimus shakes his head. "We'll never be able to stop the dead, Mitchell, and I apologize if I gave you that impression. The Bloody Mary cocktails were aiding and abetting my imagination last night—I'm sure that frightful woman puts something illegal in them. Alas, if there is one guaranteed event in life, it is the impending arrival of death." Septimus exhales a long sigh, which has nothing to do with tiredness. "However," he adds quickly, "I do believe that with the correct tools, we can stem the mass migration to these particular transcendental shores, and together we can start leveling the playing fields of death once more."

"You've lost me."

"You were lost years ago," quips Medusa.

"Don't you have something important to do?" I ask, unleashing an elastic band in her direction. "Girl things, like doing the dishes, or cleaning?"

"Are you sure you two aren't married?" drawls Septimus. "The pair of you sound exactly like my wife and me, before the joyful release of death finally separated us once and for all."

"I would rather marry a skunk," replies Medusa. "Better hygiene."

"Hell will freeze over before I get married."

Why am I feeling hot and shaky? It's probably because I haven't had any breakfast. I forget that Septimus has asked me here for a reason, and I start to mentally plot my day around meals. It immediately makes me feel better.

Septimus stands and stretches. "I know it's your well-earned annual day off, Mitchell, but I need you to collate a list for me."

I push thoughts of corn dogs out of my head.

"What kind of list, boss?"

"Responsible devils. People we work with on a daily basis who can be trusted absolutely. Don't go for CEOs, they're all corrupt. Start with department deputies, or even better, their executive assistants. Preferably devils who have been dead for at least two hundred years. They won't have the same longing as the newly dead."

"Longing for what?"

"What do you know about the Viciseometer?" asks Septimus. My boss isn't just looking *at* me, he's staring so hard it's as if he's seeing *through* me.

And I realize he knows that I know.

Medusa answers before I get a chance, "It's an urban legend," she blurts out, her eyes darting between me and Septimus.

"Most legends have their foundations in a truth, Medusa," says Septimus.

"Are you saying it's real?"

"As real as you or I," replies Septimus. Medusa whistles through the gap between her two front teeth. "The Viciseometer has been used to go back in time to introduce the wheel; fire, of course, to the cavemen; and even the recipe for Coca-Cola. Alas, it has also been used to reveal the secret of atomic fission, and it was also responsible for sowing the seeds for cabbages—truly the most heinous use ever recorded." He shudders. Septimus hates vegetables.

"Back to this list, Septimus. How many names would you like on it?" I ask. As much as I adore Medusa, I'm the one Septimus called in to help him.

"I think a shortlist of twenty names should suffice," says Septimus. "Now, if you will both excuse me, I need to check on our lord and master. He is usually rather delicate the day after the Masquerade Ball and that does not bode well for anyone."

"I'll e-mail the list to you, boss."

Septimus pauses by the door. He has a strange look on his face. I get the impression he wants to say something long-winded, like a warning, but all I get is, "Thank you, Mitchell. I won't forget this."

"No problem, boss."

"And I'm sure I don't need to remind either of you that discretion is paramount."

"Absolutely," I reply.

Once Septimus has gone, Medusa skips over to my desk and sits down on the edge. Her skinny legs dangle over my wastepaper basket. I have a sudden urge to dunk her like a basketball, and the thought makes me laugh.

"Can I help you with the list?" she asks.

"If you want."

"What about Dominic in banking?"

"He's a moron who gets lost in his own department."

"What about Patrick in the legal department? I've worked with him and he's very diligent."

"Patrick has the IQ of a peanut."

"Why are you writing Patty Lloyd's name down?"

"Because she works in the library, so she must be smart."

"And the fact that she looks like Marilyn Monroe has nothing to do with it?"

Medusa and I continue to bicker for another fifteen minutes. I'm so weak from lack of food I can barely grip my pen.

"I hope Septimus lets us see the Viciseometer," says Medusa. She was playing with the combination of the safe; now she's spinning in a circle in Septimus's chair. "Just imagine all that power. You could do anything."

"It does sound seriously cool. I wonder what Septimus is going to do with it."

"What would you do with it, Mitchell?"

"Get myself a plate of fries and a triple cheeseburger. Then I'd go back in time and repeat the order a million times."

Medusa throws an empty soda can at me. She's a lethal shot, especially when I'm the target. It bounces off my nose and then lands in the recycling bin.

"Pack it in, Melissa!" I yell. I rarely call her by her real name, but I'm getting annoyed. I can feel my shoulders starting to seize up with tension, and my head aches from where I've been grinding my back teeth. Another hundred years and I'll have magenta eyes and dentures.

"You have no vision, that's your problem, Mitchell," says Medusa. She jumps off the chair, grabs my pen, and writes down fifteen names in quick succession. They're inspired choices and exactly the kind of people Septimus is looking for. Medusa is wasted in the kitchens. I don't know how I got this job ahead of her. She's so smart, sometimes my head hurts just trying to keep up.

"Thanks," I mumble.

Medusa grabs my hands and pulls me up. I'm at least a foot taller than she is, yet sometimes I feel really small in her company. Today is one of those days. My hands are hot and sweaty and covered in ink. Totally gross, but she doesn't seem to mind.

"Do you know what I would do with the Viciseometer?" Medusa asks. She isn't meeting my eyes; her concentration is fixed on interlocking our fingers in some kind of game.

"Go back in time and get stretched out on a rack to make you taller?" I suggest.

It was meant to be funny, and she does smirk. I still get a punch to the stomach, though.

"I would do what every devil would do, stupid."

"And what would every devil do?" I ask.

She lets go of my hands, although I find I don't want her to.

"I would change my death, of course."

4. The Peasant and the Warrior

Medusa helps me finish the list of twenty names, but now my head is buzzing. Is it really possible to change your death? Or even better, go back in time and stop your death completely? Now, *that's* a thought I'm not going to shake easily.

Everyone looks without seeing in Hell. It's just the way it is. Every steaming, dark corridor is a crush of people. Some are crying; some are screaming. Most are silent, and that's just as depressing. Everyone is trying to get somewhere, all the while knowing they can't ever leave. Devils are buffeted and jostled as we search for our next source of food, our one reminder that we can do something other than work. I don't even like the burger bar that Medusa and I are now heading toward, but it's the nearest food stand to the CBD. Because I'm young and tall, I can push my way through more easily than most. Medusa follows in my slipstream, holding tightly to my T-shirt so we don't get separated. Back on earth the same distance would take five minutes; less than two on my skateboard.

Here in Hell it takes over an hour.

"So tell me more about the Viciseometer," I say as we fight our way through the crushing crowds. We're meeting our other two friends, Alfarin and Elinor. We're running very late, which means there may not be any food left after Alfarin has been let loose on the place. A cause for concern if ever there was one.

"What's going on, Mitchell?" asks Medusa thickly. She's chewing four pieces of gum. Her first attempt at a pink bubble ends when I pop it all over her face.

"I just want to do a thorough job for Septimus, and I think it's important that I know everything there is to know about the Viciseometer, that's all."

"Kiss-ass." Medusa is annoyed at me because now she has gum in her hair. Her curls are wild today. The humidity and heat of Hell wreak havoc on everyone's hair, mine included. Even though my blond hair is cut short, there are times when I look like an albino hedgehog. Today Medusa's hair makes her head look ten times bigger than normal.

Alfarin and Elinor are already sitting down at a table in the burger bar. It's littered with empty boxes and greasy wrappings. Their gleaming red eyes shine across the room as they wave us over. When I think about the amount of food we consume, I have to thank the Highers for decreeing that the dead don't gain weight. Can you imagine how much worse Hell would be if everyone was fatter? We'd be in a state of permanent sweaty gridlock, although Medusa could stand to gain a few pounds, especially on her elbows. A nice bit of padding for when she punches me.

Alfarin, son of Hlif, son of Dobin—new introductions always get the epithet—has been dead for a thousand years. He's a Viking prince. He's shorter than me, about five feet ten inches, but his bulk almost matches his height. He's also younger than me in alive years because he died during his sixteenth winter, but everyone thinks he's older because he's like a man-mountain. Alfarin has this funny accent, like Arnold Schwarzenegger in the *Terminator* movies, and half of his face is covered with a long, golden beard that Medusa and Elinor like to braid with beads. And he totally lets them! Alfarin worships Elinor with a passion, but as clingy as she is with him, she *just wants to be friends*. The phrase every guy loves to hear.

Elinor Powell died in the Great Fire of London in 1666 when she was nineteen. While official records placed the number of deceased in single figures, the truth is many of the dead were simply incinerated as the medieval city burned. There were no bodies left to count, and Elinor became one of the forgotten dead. There are a lot like her here. Every disaster, natural or otherwise, causes a flood of dead refugees. Terror in life just becomes terror in death. Elinor is the eldest of six children. Two of her brothers are also in Hell: Michael and Phillip, although they don't bother with Elinor much because she's a girl. Their loss, my and Alfarin's gain. We assume the other three siblings—John, William, and Alice—went Up There, but Elinor never stops looking for them. She was killed on her nineteenth birthday after the blazing roof of her home collapsed on top of her.

That has got to suck. It's bad enough dying when you're young, but to croak on your birthday is just sick. We get to the table. Medusa and Elinor immediately hug and giggle. Alfarin and I bang knuckles.

"Dude."

"My friend."

I think you'll agree our greeting is cooler. It has nothing to do with the fact that if Alfarin were to hug me, my bones would be pulverized into mush.

I grab the last remaining burger on the table and cram it into my mouth.

"We saved it for ye, Mitchell," says Elinor. She lowers her voice and leans forward. "We had to. They've run out of food."

"What!" I exclaim. "What do you mean, they've run out of food?"

The food in Hell is sourced from the living, by any means necessary. The Devil sees nothing wrong in the living going without to keep order in Hell. Famine and plague are not acts of Up There, as some people and insurance companies would have you believe, but instead are acts of The Devil.

And Hell never runs short.

Medusa shushes me.

"The kitchens are having problems with their sourcing," she

whispers. "There are just too many devils to feed, so they're delivering fewer supplies and meals to the rest of Hell...."

"So much for everything ending when ye die," says Elinor sadly.

I stare at her. The oldest in our group doesn't look well. Elinor's skin is pale and it has a greenish tinge. She is so pretty, though. Long red hair falls all the way down her back, and she has a smattering of freckles around her nose. Like those of all of the devils who have been in Hell over four hundred years, her irises flame with a bright red fire. When Elinor is not biting her nails, she will nervously paw at the base of her neck. She's doing that now. The back of her neck is like her security blanket.

"How was the ball?" asks Alfarin, changing the subject. "Did my Viking kin bathe in the entrails of the heathen Saxons?"

"It was all right, I suppose—"

"Oh, listen to you trying to be all cool," interrupts Medusa. She leans over the table toward Alfarin. "Mitchell danced!"

Elinor squeaks like a mouse. I think she's laughing. Alfarin just shakes his head as his bushy eyebrows join in a frown.

"Tell me it isn't true."

"Medusa made me."

"Dancing is for the womenfolk. Men drink beer and fight."

"Hey, you've been on the end of Medusa's fists. It was either dance or end up in Hell's casualty unit."

"What was the music like?" asks Elinor, biting her thumbnail. "And what did everyone wear? Did they like yer dress, M?"

Medusa and Elinor have taken to shortening each other's names. So Elinor is now *El*, and Medusa is now *M*. I keep waiting for them to shorten my name, and the second they do I will shoot them down in flames. You know my first name is Mitchell. Not Mitch, or Mitty, or, Hell forbid, Chell. My name is Mitchell. Mitchell Johnson in full. No middle name—my parents didn't see the point.

I like my name; it's succinct, strong, masculine. But I know it's only a matter of time before Medusa and Elinor start calling me M.J.

Just the way my mother did.

She got everyone calling me that when I was little. I liked it at first, but after a while it started sounding babyish so I asked people to stop. And everyone agreed—with the exception of my mother. I was always her M.J.

Only now do I realize I should have appreciated that a bit more than I did.

So I never want to hear the name M.J. in Hell. That's a part of me that will always live. In Hell I'm just Mitchell Johnson. Four syllables and nothing more.

My *no maudlin thoughts* policy isn't working out too well. I think learning about the Viciseometer has put me a strange place. I'm now hovering between this new existence and the longing for what has been snatched from me. I try to force a smile at my three friends. Medusa is stroking my back; Alfarin's face is so furrowed his bushy eyebrows are in danger of disappearing under the folds of skin on his forehead; Elinor has just gone the color of raw rhubarb.

Is it always so hot in Hell? Of course it is; I see the heating bills. They're one of the reasons Septimus is so worried. Hell is on the verge of bankruptcy, and with so many new devils arriving, the cost of running the Afterlife is insane. Right now The Devil's moods swing from deliriously happy to just delirious. We're approaching the end of the financial year, when The Devil goes through the budget with the finance team, and let's just say the last time they met, the furnaces in Hell weren't fired by wood and coal that day. Then all that melted dead flesh and bone ended up breaking the furnace and that just incurred more costs. Everyone on the budget team was put back together and healed, but it was a mess that made even Septimus puke his guts up. And now my boss is under pressure to stop the dead....

And then it hits me. This is Septimus's plan. He's going to send a team of devils to the land of the living with the time-traveling device. They're going to stop future devils from becoming... well, devils. With fewer dead, the costs will go down. It's like downsizing, before a person is employed.

Septimus is a genius.

"Mitchell, Mitchell."

Medusa has stopped stroking me like a puppy and has resumed slapping me between my shoulder blades.

"He looks very hot," says Elinor.

"But not in a way that is attractive to the peasant women of Ye Olde England?" asks a nervous Alfarin.

"For the billionth time, Alfarin, El doesn't *like* Mitchell like that. He's way too feminine for her," answers Medusa. Every word is matched with a thump on my back. "El wants a real man, with muscles, don't you, El?"

Elinor is blushing so furiously I'm amazed she hasn't combusted. She mumbles something about being thirsty and races off to buy some drinks with the few Hell coins left on the table.

"The peasant Elinor is as glorious in movement as one of the Valkyrie," sighs Alfarin. "Why, if I were to steal but one kiss from those delicious red lips, I would gratefully remove one of my own arms and present it to Thor himself as an offering of my thanks."

"I think El would probably settle for flowers and chocolates, Alfarin," says Medusa. "Less messy."

"You should also think about not calling her a peasant, Alfarin. Girls don't dig that sort of thing."

"And what would you know what girls like, Mitchell?" says Medusa with a smirk. Her pretty pink eyes are wide with interest. "You're hardly Casanova."

"Well, apart from the fact I don't know who Casanova is, I can tell you I am way more successful with the ladies than you give me credit for."

"Our friend Mitchell is quite correct, Medusa," says Alfarin. "You do him no honor to doubt his manhood in such a way. Why, just seven moons ago, the buxom wench Erin Fenshawe swooned on top of Mitchell and had to be pulled away from his lips by my great-aunt, Dagmar."

I nod emphatically at Alfarin's defense of my...what did he call it? Manhood?

"Oh, please," says Medusa dramatically. "He was having an allergic reaction to the feathers Erin had stitched onto her sweater. She thought he had died—again—and was trying to do CPR on him. If that girl had a brain cell she'd be dangerous."

Elinor reappears with four large sodas. I down mine and then Medusa's in quick succession. I need the sugar rush to help calm my frayed nerves.

Frayed nerves? Where the Hell did that phrase come from? I'm turning into an old woman. What is wrong with me today?

"So what's the plan?" asks Elinor. She sounds so eager that not one of us continues the argument. Elinor is the quiet rudder that steers our ship away from the rocks. Without her, we would be lost.

"I want to go to the library." The words run out of my mouth before I realize I'm saying them.

"Did you just say *library*?" asks Alfarin. His enormous mouth is open.

"When did you learn to read?" asks Medusa.

"There's just something I want to look up," I reply, "and there's no point in sitting here if there's no food."

Alfarin and Elinor are the first to get up and leave. They love the library. Both arrived in Hell without much of an education, which comes down to their own times rather than choice. In the hundreds of years they've been here, they've absorbed nearly every book in the place. If ever I need a question answered, I go to my own personal oracles, so I can kind of understand their incredulity at my wanting to go to the library. I just won't tell them why—yet. I smile as I watch Alfarin attempt to help Elinor with her cardigan. As he opens the door for her, he pulls it so hard it bounces back off the wall and the glass shatters into a thousand glinting crystals.

"Alfarin, you brute!" yells Pedro, the manager of the burger bar. "That's the third door you've smashed this month. You're barred."

Alfarin is muttering about not knowing his own strength, and Elinor takes his arm to console him. He immediately brightens and the two of them walk ahead, leaving Medusa and me to follow them down the torch-lined passage to the elevators.

"What are you planning?" whispers Medusa.

"What do you mean?"

"You've been acting really weird since we left Septimus's office."

"No, I haven't."

"Don't lie to me, Mitchell. I can tell when you aren't telling the truth because your eyes go even pinker."

"I'm just tired, that's all. You seem to forget I was woken up this morning by a maniac assaulting me with a blunt object."

"It was a pillow, Mitchell. This is about the Viciseometer, isn't it?"

"No."

"And there go your pretty pink eyes again."

I stop walking and lower my voice so Alfarin and Elinor can't hear us. "So what if it is? Are you telling me that the thought of leaving Hell and changing your death isn't in your head right now?"

Medusa looks away, but I can see she's biting her bottom lip. When she looks back at me I'm horrified to see tears pooling in her long lashes.

"I don't need a Viciseometer to think about changing parts of my life and death, Mitchell. It's in my head twenty-four seven and has been for forty years."

I've asked the question of a hundred other devils, but have only ever once asked Medusa. Maybe the second time is the charm.

"How did you die?"

She shakes her head and teardrops leak down the end of her nose. I wipe them away with my knuckle; my other arm is around the small of her back. Last night I touched her bare skin and she twisted my fingers until they cracked. But now she lets me hold her. Medusa is so small she fits perfectly against my chest. Both of her skinny little arms are wrapped around my waist. Her wild, snakelike hair tickles my nose, but instead of pushing it away, I bury my face in it and somehow find the top of her head.

I kiss it.

I hate seeing Medusa cry, so I don't ask the question again.

5. The Viciseometer

I'm not a big fan of Hell's library. It's not that I don't like books—I do. I just don't like the thought of touching something that has been previously handled by millions of dead people.

You still get germs in Hell, you know. Our hearts don't beat, and we don't need to breathe, but we still feel pain and we can still become ill. You don't escape anything here, except death.

The library in Hell is gigantic. Colossal. Easily twice the size of Yankee Stadium, with about fifty times the number of people in it at any given time. As I walk in, I'm so intimidated I consider walking right back out again. I may work on level 1 in the most important department in Hell, but right now, as I gaze at the towering rows of dusty books, I don't know where to start. I can't ask for help because Septimus wants discretion. If I start mouthing off about the Viciseometer, devils are going to want to know why. Rumors spread through Hell like the plague. I can guarantee Septimus would hear about his inquisitive intern before I returned to my desk.

So now I have a choice: I can forget the whole thing, or I can stand here looking clueless as I try to work my way through an index of every book that has ever been published in the history of mankind.

I feel a hand on my back. It's probably security. They're going to throw me out for pure stupidity. I turn around and see a vision in white smiling at me. I gulp, trying to dislodge a lump the size of a rock that has suddenly appeared in my throat.

Patty Lloyd—one of the names I originally wrote down on my list for Septimus—is wearing her hair down today. She shouldn't do that. It's long and the ends are colored pink to match her irises. My eyes are drawn to where the tips rest on her tight-fitting tank top.

I'm staring at her chest. Why can't I stop staring at her chest?

"Hi, Mitchell." The melody of her voice goes up and down when she talks to me. She likes to lick her teeth at the end of every sentence, too, which is something a lot of the guys talk about. "I haven't seen you for ages."

"Busy working," I mumble.

"All work and no play makes for a boring devil indeed," she says, giggling, flicking her hair back and then immediately sweeping it forward again.

Why did she do that? What was the point of flicking her hair back, only to bring it forward again?

"Can I help you with something, Mitchell?"

Now Patty's voice is girly and high, and she smells like honey.

She giggles and turns around. She has a Celtic tattoo inked across her lower back. It's on display between her top and her skinny white jeans, which barely cover her bottom.

Now I'm staring at her ass. Why can't I stop staring at her ass?

Suddenly, a missile hits me in the face. I look down and see a bright-blue elastic band lying limply on the ground next to my black Converse All Stars.

I can hear her heavy breathing before she reaches me. Medusa sounds like a sleeping dragon, especially when she's pissed.

"What are you doing?" she seethes through gritted teeth. I get a slap on the arm for good measure.

"I'm looking for a book."

"Doesn't look that way from where I'm standing."

"Oh, hello, Medusa." Now Patty's tone is lower and harsher. Patty squeezes into the small space between Medusa and me. I can see down the front of her shirt because she's pressed up against me.

I stare up at the vaulted ceiling. Black gargoyles leer back at me. One licks its lips.

"I'll catch you later, Mitchell," Medusa mutters. Her pretty pink eyes turn away and I feel ashamed that I've somehow managed to disappoint her.

"Hang on, Medusa. Stay and help me," I call, but she doesn't turn around.

Now I feel sick. I know Medusa hates giggling blond devils like Patty, but I was only talking to her. She works in the library, for Hell's sake. What was I supposed to do? Ignore her? I can't help the fact that Patty is so hot you could fry eggs on that washboard stomach of hers. And I'm not the only one staring at her, either. A quick glance around the library entrance tells me every guy within a ten-yard radius of Patty Lloyd is panting like a dog at the sight of her. A lot of the girls are, too. She has that effect on everyone—and she knows it.

Medusa is being unreasonable. She wants me to think I've done something wrong, when the fact is I'm just being human. Which is something I need to remember. I may be in Hell, but I am not a monster.

I'm about to ask Patty for directions to the time-traveling section when my cell phone starts to vibrate. It's Septimus. He wants me back in the office.

"Gotta go," I say to Patty, but she slips her hand into mine and touches her lips with my finger, which she then transfers back onto my mouth.

"Don't leave it so long next time, Mitchell. I'll give you a private tour of the library when you come back. There are thousands of dark passageways to get lost in."

She winks at me, and I know I could kiss her right now and I'd be a hero to every guy who's ogling in her direction. Her bottom lip is way thicker than her top one. It's plump, like a big purple grape. Patty is the kind of girl who would wear flavored lip gloss. I bet she tastes like a big, juicy purple grape.

Parts of my body start taking over for my brain. Why did I die when I was seventeen? This is so unfair. I'm still pumped with hormones that will always be around to haunt me, and I'll never be rid of them because I'm dead and stuck like this for eternity.

My hand stretches out and wraps around Patty's waist. Her skin isn't as smooth as Medusa's. Her mouth reaches mine as her fingers claw into my short hair. Her uneven lips part and her teeth knock against mine. Then her tongue starts swirling in my mouth.

I pull away. Patty still has her eyes closed, but mine were open the whole time. Mark Roberts—a new dead dude—sticks his thumbs in the air and whistles.

"Call me," whispers Patty before skipping away.

Feeling utterly wretched, as if I've just lied to my grandmother, I leave the library. I don't make eye contact with anyone. I know I'm blushing because my face feels as if it's on fire. My neck, too. It's like having a prickly shaving rash.

Not that I ever get a shaving rash. I can barely grow stubble on my chin. It gets vertigo and dies before hitting my jaw and neck.

Septimus is alone when I get back to the office. He isn't sitting down. He's pacing, which means he's thinking.

"Ah, Mitchell," he says as I walk in. "I know I am being the boss from Hell today, and for that you have my sincerest apologies. I will make it up to you and Miss Pallister, I promise."

"Serve my head on a plate," I reply dully. "Right now that's the only thing that will make Medusa happy."

Septimus stops pacing and cocks his head slightly to the left. His bald black head glows like a marble in the flickering firelight.

"You look unhappy, Mitchell. I would have thought a romp with Miss Patricia Lloyd, however brief, would have the opposite effect on a handsome young man like yourself."

"How did you know about that?"

"There is little in Hell that escapes my attention," replies Septimus with an indulgent smile.

"If you know about Patty, that means Medusa will know, which means my existence is going to be Hell," I groan, cradling my head in my hands. I can still smell Patty's flowery perfume lingering on my clothes. My stomach churns as I think about her tongue inside my mouth.

She didn't taste like grapes.

"Perhaps we should concentrate on work for a moment, then," continues Septimus. "I am most obliged to you and Miss Pallister for the list of names. It is a very impressive collection of the finest devils Hell has at its disposal. Now, I trust you, Mitchell, and you have a sensible head on your shoulders, so I am assuming that you have guessed my plan?"

Taking a deep breath, I raise my head from my hands.

"You plan to send devils back to the land of the living with the Viciseometer. They'll change time and stop evil before it happens. Up There will then have to start taking more of the dead who are processed at the HalfWay House."

"Exactly."

"I have one question, though, Septimus."

"Fire away."

"Most of the dead in Hell aren't evil. Half the time it's just rotten luck that gets a person sent here. Take Elinor, for example. She's the nicest person I've ever met. Why is she in Hell?"

"An excellent question, Mitchell, and one that many a devil, including myself, must have asked a thousand times. One day, when I can do the question justice, I will answer."

Septimus walks to the door of the antechamber and closes it. It locks with a solid thump.

"You've seen the figures, Mitchell. You've worked on the accounting ledgers and answered the phone calls of devils demanding payments for salaries and invoices and expenses. We like to think of ourselves as a celestial superpower, equal to Up There, but the truth is that we are more like Britain, or France, or even Russia these days: small fry trying to keep up with the USA or China, and failing miserably in the process. Up There was created first. It has formulated a myth around itself that has made it virtually untouchable. It is impervious to supervision, and it is the first choice of every single person who dies. Up There has created an elite among the dead. They are the only superpower, and now we have to challenge that."

"But even if Hell stops people from being evil while they're still alive, the Grim Reapers at the HalfWay House can still send people here when they die. I don't understand how—"

"Because we will show intent, Mitchell. When the residents of Hell see that we have first exhausted all diplomatic avenues open to us, we will find it far easier to create a following that will rise up and challenge that power with force."

This is it: Operation H, which The Devil and Septimus were discussing before the Masquerade Ball. Septimus—a former Roman general—is talking about creating an army. I can tell he's excited about it, too. His fiery red eyes are pulsating, as if they're filled with blood, and a glistening sheen of perspiration has now appeared over his entire face. But I don't feel the same way. I don't want to go to war.

Septimus loosens his navy tie.

"It is time for me to show you something, Mitchell."

He walks over to a wardrobe in the corner. It's carved out of dark oak. An archaic language, all symbols and runes, is chipped into the wood. The single door creaks as Septimus opens it. I've always assumed this wardrobe is where Septimus keeps his suits. I've certainly never touched it in the time I've been working in accounting.

Inside, displayed on a single wooden hanger, is a dark-brown leather cuirass with thick, studded strips falling in a fringe at the front. Beneath the cuirass hangs a simple white tunic edged with gold thread. A tarnished sword, bent and dented, lies at the foot of the wardrobe, along with a rectangular shield with curved edges. It's maroon, with a golden eagle imprinted on the face.

"My deathday outfit," whispers Septimus. "My armor and helmet were removed by the healers before I passed on. Shame, really. I would have liked to keep the entire set."

"How did you die, Septimus?"

"Infection," he replies. His long black fingers caress the studs on his cuirass. "Although a sword to the stomach didn't help, of course," he adds with a reminiscent smile. "It was the Second Punic

War, when Hannibal led Carthage into a bloody battle against the Roman Republic."

"Hannibal, wasn't he the one with the elephants?"

Septimus roars with laughter. "The very one, Mitchell. Oh, you have no idea how much that annoys Hannibal. Probably the greatest commander in history, and yet he is best remembered for traveling with elephants."

"I didn't mean to offend," I say quickly. "It's just I read about it in one of the books in Alfarin's collection of warrior tales."

"Offend me?" replies Septimus. "Nothing makes me happier than to see Hannibal brought down a peg or two. Trust me, Mitchell, that man is no friend of mine."

"Do you miss it?" I ask.

"Living?"

I nod.

"I miss...some aspects," he replies thoughtfully, "but death brings with it a certain amount of stability, and after a while, you realize that isn't such a bad thing."

My wallet is in the back pocket of my jeans—it's one of the few belongings I brought with me into death. I pull it out and remove the scrap of paper I keep where a photo would normally be.

Living.

My writing is really messy. My parents used to say it looked as if a drunken spider had fallen into an inkpot and then staggered across the page. At least I don't draw balloon circles over my *I*'s. Medusa does that.

Why did I kiss Patty?

"I have something else to show you, Mitchell."

Septimus walks over to the accounting office's safe. It's taller than both of us, although we're both well over six feet. It has been forged into the black rock, and my first week as an intern was spent practicing and memorizing the combination. We weren't allowed to write it down, for obvious security reasons, although I did have it on a scrap of paper until I could remember it.

A plume of dust belches out of the rock-hewn cavity as the heavy door is released. We keep records of sensitive security breaches in here. The last one was about six months ago. I don't know what happened, but I know it involved the city of Paris. Septimus was very strange that day; he kept looking at me as if I was in some kind of trouble. It wasn't anger—more regret. One day I'll find the time to read all the records in there, including the Paris one, but I'm drowning in paperwork as it is.

Septimus reaches for the third shelf from the top. Underneath a thick sheaf of papers is a small box. It's made of pale wood and is completely plain. No carvings, no etchings. It looks like the box I made in my first woodworking class in school.

Septimus hands it to me. I don't open it. I blow off the thin layer of dusty black crystals that has settled on it. The safe door is pushed shut and locked once more.

"What's this, Septimus?"

"Open it."

The catch on the lid releases with ease. Inside is a purple silk handkerchief. Lying on top of that is a stopwatch unlike any timepiece I have ever seen. It's glowing with tiny particles of red flame.

I don't need to be told that this is the Viciseometer. Medusa would be freaking out right now if she were here.

Septimus remains quiet. He picks up the stopwatch and places it in my open hand.

The Viciseometer is forged from a nugget of gold. It looks substantial, but it feels as light as air. I get an unnerving sensation as I hold it, and the hairs on the back of my neck prickle.

I flip the stopwatch over and see it's double faced. The surface on one side is milky white, with twelve thick golden Roman numerals stamped around the rim. It has three golden hands of differing lengths. For all intents and purposes, it looks like an ordinary watch. I slowly stroke it with my forefinger before turning it over again. The Viciseometer quivers in my hand.

The reverse is very different. It's colored a deep red with three black hands, and it's a lot harder to figure out. In addition to various symbols and runes, there are three rings of writing around the rim. The innermost ring is made up of numbers, one to thirty-one, spaced out evenly in tiny blocks. The middle ring is Latin script denoting the months of the year, starting with Januarius and ending with December. The months are spaced out like the twelve Roman numerals on the other side. As I focus my eyes on the outermost ring, I notice it's not stenciled with a pattern, as I first thought, but stamped with tiny snakes that form the numbers zero to nine. Beneath the twelve and six o'clock positions are a plus and a minus symbol, again carved like snakes.

On the outer rim of the stopwatch are seven buttons. The largest sits above the Roman numeral twelve. It's red and buzzes with an electrical current. Connected to this button, on a delicate golden chain, hangs a thin red needle.

The other six buttons are identical: small, round, and black. Three of them are placed together on the top hemisphere, next to the red button. The others sit diagonally across from these on the bottom hemisphere.

I am mesmerized. I am holding time itself.

"How did you die?" is the question everyone asks one another in Hell.

But what if I had never died in the first place?

6. Blood Oath

It takes me ages to find Alfarin and Elinor. Medusa has disappeared completely and my texts and increasingly lame voice messages go unanswered.

Why did I kiss Patty?

If I had that Viciseometer back, that's the first thing I'd change. I'd go back in time and just walk out of the library before her tongue fell into my mouth.

It wasn't even a very good kiss, so why do I feel strange and hot every time I think about it?

Thomason's Bar is not far from the central business district, but it still takes forever to reach because there are so many devils trying to get somewhere, anywhere. Thomason's serves beer, more beer, and then the dregs left in the keg once the beer is gone. It doesn't have air-conditioning, either—nowhere in Hell does—so when the bar is heaving with Vikings you can literally swim home in the sweat that pours out of the place.

When I explain this to other devils, they usually get an instant look of disgust on their faces. I can't blame them. It does sound gross, but it's *our* gross. Alfarin works here, collecting the dirty glasses. He isn't very good at it and smashes more than he collects, but Thomason is family so Alfarin gets away with it.

Elinor and Alfarin are sitting at our usual table: a rickety hunk of stained wood, situated right by the door so we can get out fast if trouble starts. Self-preservation, even when you're dead, is priority number one when hanging with Vikings.

There's still no sign of Medusa.

A three-legged stool has been left vacant between Elinor and Alfarin, and I squish myself in.

Elinor frowns. "What have ye done, Mitchell?"

I fake innocence. "Nothing."

"Medusa is not pleased with you, my friend," says Alfarin seriously. "If she were armed with a blade, you would be joining the Eunuch Choir tonight."

"I haven't done anything." My voice is a little high. Several bearded Vikings stop their axe-throwing game to stare at me.

"She was crying, Mitchell," whispers Elinor.

Now I feel sick and guilty and annoyed because I really haven't done anything wrong. Medusa and I are friends, best friends. I tease her; she hits me. I buy her hot dogs; she eats mine as well. I complain about being dead; she listens.

"I accidentally kissed Patty Lloyd in the library."

"How can ye accidentally kiss someone, Mitchell?" hisses Elinor.

I choose not to reply; I don't have the energy to argue. Why can't Elinor and Medusa get how hard it is for guys sometimes? It's as if our brains turn to custard and the only thing that matters is that very second in time—thinking about consequences doesn't factor into it. I just wish my friends could see inside my head; that would make everything a lot easier.

I don't understand why Medusa is so upset. She didn't even *see* the kiss. Maybe that's why she's so upset, because I didn't tell her first. Best friends like to be the first people to know, don't they? But then, if I had told Medusa she would have gotten angry with me, because she hates Patty.

My head hurts. I just don't understand girls.

"Where is she?"

"M is near the bar, Mitchell, but I wouldn't disturb her," replies Elinor. "She is a little busy."

"Let me just make it up to her and then we can go get some food," I reply. "I'm starving."

"An excellent plan of attack, my friend," says Alfarin. "Now go claim your woman back."

I push my way through the crowd. The smell of sweat and beer is shocking. And why is that bearded woman setting that table on fire?

Then I see Medusa and an unnatural wave of cold washes over me. It's like having pins and needles in every limb.

Medusa is straddling a guy with long black hair. Her skinny legs are wrapped around his body and his hands are up the back of her T-shirt. Medusa isn't twisting his fingers, even though his fingers are a lot more rabid than mine were at the Masquerade Ball. I can't see what kind of devil he is because I can't see his eyes. I can't even see the dude's face properly because Medusa's wild corkscrew curls are covering most of it.

So is her mouth.

I've never seen Medusa make out with anyone before. She goes on dates sometimes, but Alfarin and I manage to sabotage most of them. I've never seen her open mouth moving against someone else's.

Bloody Hell, I can see her tongue.

The stench in here is overwhelming. I think I'm going to puke. A rage that I haven't felt in years is chomping at my dead heart. I want to pull Medusa off this freak and pummel his head with my fists. I want to chop his tongue out with a Viking axe and then borrow some steel-toed boots and break every rib he possesses.

My fists are clenched so tightly they've gone white. If I push my back teeth together any harder they'll shatter into dust. Two thick, pale arms, the weight of concrete posts, spread around my chest.

"We don't want any trouble, Mitchell. Certainly not from the likes of you."

It's Alfarin's cousin, Thomason. He's a good ten inches shorter than me, but like Alfarin, he's made of iron.

"I'm not going to start trouble."

"Then you won't mind if I kick you and my cousin out. We've been tipped off about a raid tonight."

Medusa finally comes up for the air she doesn't need. She must have heard my voice, because she turns her head away from the jerk with long black hair and stares directly at me.

He has dark pink eyes and his mouth is wet. I can see it glistening in the firelight. I want to place my fist in that great gaping hole. Instead, it's filled with Medusa's skin as he lowers his head and starts sucking on her neck.

It's amazing how hot your eyebrows can get when you want to cry. I feel like a total idiot. I need to get away from Thomason and Medusa and the jerk with dark-pink eyes before I do something I'll regret. I want to forget this day ever happened. I want to turn back time and return to this morning before I kissed Patty, before Medusa let some dickhead suck on her neck.

And now I feel angry and hungry and I swear I'm going to put my fist through a wall because right now only physical pain will do.

Somehow I break free from Thomason's hold. I'm not so arrogant as to think I did it myself; I know he loosened his grip. I push my way back past sweating Vikings. The bearded woman is now setting fire to a set of curtains, beating her chest like a gorilla. Freaks, the damn lot of them.

A glass window shatters, but it's several long seconds before I register the release of pain in my chest. Only when Elinor starts screaming do I notice the pain throbbing in my clenched fist, and that my hand is sliced into ribbons of skin. Thick, slow-moving waves of blood are gathering in the cuts. Because our hearts don't beat anymore, the dead don't pump out blood from injuries the way we did when we were alive, but thanks to the Highers, we can still feel the pain.

Medusa isn't very good around dead blood. She gets queasy and usually needs to put her head between her knees, because it looks like lumpy gravy.

Not today. Medusa takes off the red-and-white-checkered shirt she's wearing over a black vest top and wraps it around my throbbing hand. Her eyes don't meet mine.

"You are an idiot, Mitchell Johnson."

"Go back to your freak, Melissa."

Without a word, she turns away and starts to walk back to him. He obviously heard me, because he's standing there with his hands on his hips like a big girl.

"Medusa, I didn't mean it."

I know I sound pathetic and needy, and I am. Thomason is striding toward me with a scowl on his big round face that could strip wallpaper. He's going to give me a pounding, I just know it. Broken glass anywhere is a sign of trouble. If the HBI is coming, they'll think people have already been fighting. The bearded pyromaniac is coming toward me as well. She's striking matches against her black teeth.

"We need to get ye to sick bay, Mitchell," says Elinor. She turns and smiles at Thomason; her eyes lower and her fair lashes flutter. They're so long they touch her cheekbones.

Not for the first time, Elinor saves me from getting my ass kicked.

I'm lying on starched white sheets that cover a rock-hard bed. My right hand is covered in a gauzy bandage.

Alfarin and Elinor are gone, but Medusa is sitting at the foot of the bed, swinging her skinny little legs over the edge. I still want to slam-dunk her. The thought makes me smile, but my lips are dry and sore so I stop.

"Sorry I ruined your shirt," I mumble. My throat is dry. Someone must have fed me sandpaper at some point.

"You can find me a new one."

"I'll cover a shift for you in the kitchens, too, if you want."

"Apology accepted."

This is why Medusa is my best friend. We argue, we make up.

She won't mention Patty again—I hope—and I'll try not to mention what happened tonight. It's in the past, like everything else.

Blood is oozing through the bandages. They tell me I needed fourteen stitches, but I'll heal quickly because everyone in Hell does. Ironic, right? Septimus sends me a text message and tells me to stop hanging out with Vikings. I know he's only joking. Septimus prefers the in-your-face attitude of the Norsemen to the scheming backstabbing of the Romans in Hell.

I wish I could start this day again.

I *could* start this day again.

Vikings make blood oaths; Alfarin does it all the time. His dinner-plate-sized palms are scarred like a subway map from the number of times he has sworn to do something after taking a knife to his flesh.

I already have the sliced skin, so now I need the oath. It comes in three parts:

I will never go near the library again.

I will pay for the damage to Thomason's window.

I will learn how to use the Viciseometer.

7. **Practice Makes Perfect**

Heating bills remain unpaid and invoices are left to pile up in the office in-box.

A month has ticked by and I have become obsessed with time.

It has taken me weeks to get the operation streamlined, and the stress is beginning to show. I know the others have noticed; girls— and Vikings—are way too intuitive for their own good. Medusa and Elinor are worried about the black shadows under my eyes, and Alfarin almost snapped my spine in half the other day when he rugby-tackled me and I didn't have the energy to even try to put up a fight.

It's the Viciseometer. It has sparked its way into my soul.

I used to go to sleep thinking of girls. Now I dream about changing time. I used to plan my days around meals. Now I plan my entire existence around the Viciseometer.

I have both faces of the timepiece committed to memory. As soon as Septimus heads out for lunch, I send all calls to voice mail and retreat to a corner. Then I practice moving the thin red needle over the roman numerals and symbols, perfecting the same movements again and again.

I was really musical when I was alive. My tutor went so far as to call me a prodigy, which at the time didn't mean anything to me other than the name of a techno band. In no time, my fingers became the fittest and nimblest part of my body. It's the same now.

For the first time in my four years of being dead, I feel awake. I have time in my hands and they feel alive once more.

Since my own attempt at the library failed so miserably, I bite the bullet and ask Elinor to find me a book that will teach me about the Viciseometer. She knows exactly where to go and comes back to me with the perfect book the same day. I know Elinor is going to start asking questions at some point, but right now I need to avoid Patty Lloyd. She's been sending me text messages twenty times a day. She told her best friend, Samantha Clarke, I was playing hard to get. How about impossible to get? The problem is all the guys in my dorm think I'm a hero. They all want to know how far I went with her, and whether she has piercings and tattoos in places that really shouldn't have needles anywhere near them, and it is totally messing with my head.

And Medusa and Elinor wonder why I'm not eating. If I weren't already dead, the stress of my life right now would lead to a heart attack.

Today Septimus's lunch is going to be a long one. It's the annual Roman Empire catchup in the Temple Bar, and those meetings go on for hours. All of the former Caesars like to speak and pass motions and sanctions, and then they feast and apparently have a quick orgy and then it ends with someone getting knifed in the back.

For my purposes, this is perfect.

I open the book Elinor borrowed and start reading. According to the author, two Viciseometers were forged by the Highers and given to Hell and Up There. The function is simple: a Viciseometer enables the bearer to travel through time and realms of the Afterlife.

Powerful is way too understated to describe the feeling I get when I hold this thing. I could do anything, be anyone. Gods and girls would fall at my feet and worship me with champagne and concert tickets. I could steal a Porsche and never get stopped by the police.

I could be that rock star I always wanted to be.

*   *   *

Studying has to be done in sections, like cramming for tests between sleep and food. I learn that the Viciseometer's main milky-white face, with the golden numerals, never changes. The three hands represent the hour, minute, and second of a particular day, as on an ordinary clock. The thin red needle is used to manipulate each golden hand into place beneath one of the numerals. The desired time is then secured by pressing the three black buttons on the lower left of the watch. This part is easy.

The opposite, red face of the Viciseometer took me a lot longer to master, but now I feel confident enough to use it. The three black hands are again manipulated into place by the thin red needle, but once in place, they are secured by pressing one of the three black buttons that now appear on the top left of the timepiece. The lowest button secures the day, the next button secures the month, and the third button secures the year. Only when all six buttons are fixed in place can the larger vibrating button at the top be pressed.

As the tiny numbered snakes slither around the red face, I feel physically connected to the device. It's as if the snakes are tunneling through my intestines. Good luck finding food in there, guys. I haven't eaten anything in days. When I finally get the courage to use this thing, I'm going to binge like a king.

Weeks have passed, and my next problem has presented itself. I've mastered the theory of the Viciseometer, and now I need to test it. But the book says—warns in thick, bold capital letters—that under no circumstances should the Viciseometer be used by a lone time-traveler. If something goes wrong, at least two other devils should be traveling with the user to correct any incidents.

The book doesn't elaborate on what kind of incidents could happen, though. Are they talking about loss of limbs? Time-traveling to another dimension? What if I end up on Mars or the Moon?

This warning has to be why Septimus wanted a team. It's like the marines—no one gets left behind. Septimus has even started interviewing candidates, although it's all very secretive. He holds the interviews here in the office. The poor devils walk out looking very confused. Septimus mentions travel and being away and great responsibility, and I'm sure half of them think they're being sent Up There for a vacation. The Viciseometer is never mentioned.

I hear all of this because Septimus asks me to take minutes. He trusts me completely. I'm such a loser. I should be cleaning the toilets that are being built for when the Kardashians arrive.

Now I have a choice: I can do this alone, and risk ending up somewhere I can't get back from; or I can involve my friends and risk their dead necks as well as my own.

Taped to my computer monitor is a photograph. I like it because the flash gave me red eyes; Medusa, too. It's a picture of the four of us on Alfarin's deathday—although why anyone would want to celebrate that date is beyond me. I certainly don't. Medusa and Elinor are leaning over Alfarin and me from behind; their arms are draped around our necks. The biggest plate of fries you've ever seen in your life is on the table in front of us. Alfarin has two long fries stuck up his nose.

All three of them would risk their necks for me. I know this without asking.

Before I even realize what I'm doing, I reach for my cell phone. The text message is sent in seconds.

thomasons @ 7. something 2 ask u.

8. Friends Like These

My head is pounding. I either have the Underworld's only pulse or there's a battering ram inside my skull.

I grab the fragile box that contains the Viciseometer and open it. One of the hinges has already splintered away from the wood. I wrap the watch in its silk handkerchief and put it into my backpack.

I put the box back on the shelf and cover it with the red security papers, the one marked *Paris* on top. I don't close the safe right away because I need cash and a credit card. Not from the petty cash we use in Hell; I'm talking US dollars.

I'm not greedy. This isn't about the money. I pull open the lower drawer, which contains earthly currency, and take out a wedge of hundred-dollar bills. I don't bother counting it, but I figure there's probably about four thousand bucks in my hand. It won't be missed— not yet. The credit card is for emergencies. It's red, with a long row of sixes. The Devil has a special arrangement with the brokers on Wall Street. Hell is inevitable for them, but they get special privileges once they're dead in return for low-interest lending.

Who did you think finances Hell?

But already I'm regretting sending the text to all three of my friends. I can't risk the girls' necks for this. It's too dangerous.

I'll only ask Alfarin to come with me.

But Medusa will get upset if I don't ask her.

Elinor will balance out the numbers.

But then all four of us could end up floating in another dimension.

I won't ask Elinor.

But then she won't have any friends left in Hell.

So I won't ask Medusa, either.

But I can't go without my best friend, can I?

One thing I know for sure: I *have* to leave tonight. I can't stay in this place anymore. I heard rumors that the cleaners scooped up gallons of congealed blood from the Oval Office this morning after The Devil set the chimeras onto some lawyers. Even Septimus looked pale as he left for the evening. He had a folder marked *Operation H* under his arm, and I know what's in there. When I was filing the notes from the interviews, I read the minutes from one of Septimus's meetings with The Devil. It was impossible to miss because The Devil had drawn black hearts around every word that referred to Operation H. He's nuts, and now Septimus is going to give the Viciseometer away because he's running out of time. Septimus told me late this afternoon that he has a shortlist of five names now. That's a team. The Viciseometer could be gone tomorrow and then I'll be stuck here for the rest of time. I can't let that happen. I *won't* let that happen.

I look at my watch. I'm already thirty minutes late. Medusa, Alfarin, and Elinor are going to be so pissed at me. I know they all think I'm sick or something. They think I don't see them, whispering behind their hands.

My eyes may be pink, but they're not blind.

Picturing the three of them waiting for me, I decide I'll tell Alfarin. I'll give him the choice to come with me. I won't tell the girls. They'll be safer here.

A small weight eases off my shoulders. I've finally made a call. It should feel good, but I just feel sick.

I'm going to miss Medusa so much it hurts. I had good friends— awesome friends—back when I was alive, but nothing like this.

Medusa says it's because everything in Hell is more intense. We're dead and hidden away in the Underworld. It's the biggest secret in history, and we're in on it. It's a bond forged in fire.

I should leave her something to remember me by. My leather jacket. She's always wearing it, even though it swamps her. And my wristbands. Medusa likes to play with those when I wear them.

Her fingertips are burned and callused from working in the kitchens. It was why I was so surprised to feel her soft skin when we danced at the ball; I'd expected her to feel like scales.

I'm not sure why I'm remembering all of this now.

I'll leave Medusa everything. I won't be coming back.

I wonder if I'll ever see Septimus again. I hope so, but not for another eighty years. The next time I die, I'll be an old man. I'll have been president, or, even better, a ten-time Grammy winner. Anything I want.

My wallet goes in my backpack next, but not before I've stolen a few more seconds. The scrap of paper with *living* written on it goes in the wastepaper basket. I don't need to remember; I'm going to be doing it.

My final item is a letter. It has the official seal of The Devil imprinted in the bottom left corner and is signed by Septimus.

It's a forgery. I learned to sign Septimus's squiggle years ago. It was easy because it looks like a treble clef. I never thought for one second that it would be the final link I needed to get out of here.

The contents of the letter are simple: it gives the holder permission to visit the HalfWay House to collect receipts. Not one of the clerks will question it. They're all too dumb. Their stupidity is no match for my cunning.

I'm sure I wasn't this devious when I was alive.

Medusa smells like strawberries; I bet she tastes like them, too.

I snatch the photo of Alfarin's deathday party. I'll have to wait another hundred years for my crack at red eyes.

I'm sorry, Medusa.

I'm sorry, Septimus.

*   *   *

I take no backward glance at the accounting chamber. I head straight for the elevator and then to Thomason's. The bar is on the way to administration, which is where new devils are processed in Hell. You would not believe the amount of paperwork involved in dying. It doesn't end with a death certificate. There are forms of acceptance at the HalfWay House, and then once you're stamped and given a final destination—Hell in my case—there are more forms... it goes on and on and on. Why do you think the rain forests in Brazil are being destroyed? If the environmentalists knew it was all going to make paper for the administration here, they'd *really* start freaking out.

Global warming is nothing compared to the heat of Hell.

Medusa, Alfarin, and Elinor are all standing outside Thomason's. There's a fight going on inside; I can hear the battle before I see it. Bar stools and men dressed in black suits are being flung through the windows. It must be a raid. You have to hand it to the HBI; they're total suckers for punishment. Apparently this is how they train new recruits. Arrest a Viking and you get your badge. Arrest a Viking without slicing an artery and you get your badge and a gun, and your name goes on a special plaque.

Alfarin is watching the scene with a big grin spread over his enormous face. He lives for these sorts of scrapes. If I'd been here on time, he'd probably have been in the thick of it, punching the lights out of some skinny little HBI newbie.

But instead, Alfarin is just standing outside, watching. His arms are spread wide as he shields Medusa and Elinor from flying shards of glass.

The girls have their cell phones out, the ones Septimus scored for us as a reward for all the extra work I do in the office. Alfarin refused one. He likes to read about modern technology among the living, but he doesn't like pants with pockets, so he had nowhere to put a cell phone. At first I think Medusa and Elinor are recording the fight, but then I notice how quickly their fingers are moving. My phone vibrates in my back pocket; I have two messages.

Medusa sees me. She pokes Elinor in the side and points. She's smiling, and from here I can see her dimples. My little raggedy doll.

"Mitchell, my friend," booms Alfarin. "Now that you've graced us with your presence, would you like to tell us why we were summoned?"

Here it is. My moment in time. But I don't know how to say good-bye to Medusa and Elinor.

"I sent you two the text by accident. I need to see Alfarin— alone. Men's talk."

"Well, that is charming," says Medusa. I tense my body, waiting for the inevitable punch on the arm. She kicks me instead.

"Ow."

"Pig."

"Why do girls think they can get away with slapping guys around? If I hit you, the feminist brigade would have me tied to a stake and burned."

"A very good point, my friend," replies Alfarin, nodding, but Elinor's lips are pouting, so he shuts up.

"Ye should count yourself lucky ye have friends like us, Mitchell," says Elinor.

And I know she's right.

"Come on, El," says Medusa, grabbing Elinor's hand. "We'll find our own thing to do."

The girls turn their backs to us and start walking off. Medusa is wearing little denim shorts over black tights. Chunky biker boots make her skinny legs look ten times thicker than they really are.

"Medusa," I call after her. "Wait up."

I definitely hear her tell Elinor to ignore me, but I'm faster than both of them and I catch up before they reach the next flaming torch. Long black shadows creep along the dripping stone walls. They aren't ours.

"I want you to have this," I say, removing my leather jacket. "It's always looked better on you than me."

Medusa doesn't say a word. She just has an abstract look on her face as if she doesn't know how to answer. Which is weird, because Medusa always knows what to say.

"Wow, Mitchell." At least Elinor is impressed.

"Why are you giving me your jacket?" Medusa's pale-pink eyes have narrowed into catlike slits. Her skin looks dark in the shadows and her mad hair is rippling with the warm breeze that whistles down the stone corridors.

"You can have these as well." I pull off the beaded olive-and-black bracelets that I arrived in Hell with. The bands are elastic, and yet they're still a loose fit over Medusa's skinny little wrists.

"What are you doing, Mitchell?"

She's too smart for her own good. Now I'm so worried that Medusa will figure out my plan that I go on the attack. I don't want to say the words that are spilling out of my mouth, but I can't help myself. I have verbal diarrhea.

"Why are you always so suspicious? I just want to give you a present—to make up for the fact that I've been kind of a jerk lately, but I can't even do that right, can I? I don't know why I bother, Medusa. Maybe I should get that jerk with the dark-pink eyes back—he can give you *his* jacket. Payment in kind…"

"Just go away, Mitchell. I don't want your stinking jacket, or your pathetic bracelets."

My farewell gifts are thrown back. Elinor looks at me as if I've just slapped Medusa. Her eyes are wide open and her mouth has dropped to a perfect circle. My best friend turns away, and I see the shudder that convulses her shoulders.

I've made Medusa cry, and I hate myself. It wasn't supposed to be like this.

Alfarin stoops down and picks up the jacket. His stomach gets in the way of his attempt to pick up the bracelets, and they're quickly smashed into bits by the boots of other devils.

"Let us go talk like men," he says seriously, slapping me on the shoulder. "Then you will apologize to Medusa for the slight you made on her character."

"I didn't mean it."

"What happened at the Masquerade Ball, my friend? Medusa has been bringing out the best and worst in you ever since," says

Alfarin, walking past the groaning heap of HBI investigators. Their limbs stick out at strange angles. They look like an enormous pile of spiders that has been run over.

I was hit by a bus. Did I look like that afterward?

"This wasn't how it was supposed to happen," I mutter.

"How what was supposed to happen?"

We turn into a dark corridor. It smells like blocked toilets, and a thin stream is running down one of the walls. I'm not a hundred percent sure it's water.

"I'm leaving, Alfarin. I'm leaving now."

"Leaving what?"

I lower my voice to a whisper. Everything has ears here, including the walls.

"I'm leaving Hell. I can't explain everything here, but I'm going to ask you to trust me, Alfarin. I'm asking you to come with me."

"No one can leave Hell, my friend."

"I've found a way."

Alfarin crosses his trunklike arms and leans back against the damp stone. His blond beard has tiny braids woven into it, fixed with blue and yellow beads. Medusa and Elinor's work. They say the colors remind them of the sun and sky.

"Then when do we leave?" he asks.

I'm forced to hold on to the stinking wall. The relief makes me go light-headed, which is totally embarrassing. I didn't think it would be this easy to persuade Alfarin, but he's the most loyal person I know. Alfarin is like a brother.

"You'll really come with me?"

"The gods would curse me if I allowed you to undertake this on your own, my friend. How much time do I have?"

"I can give you thirty minutes to get what you want from your dorm."

"May I bring my axe?"

"It's a long walk to the HalfWay House."

"I have the strength of ten men," says Alfarin proudly.

"Then bring what you want, but do not, do not, do not tell the girls. I don't want Medusa or Elinor to risk their necks for me."

"May I ask you a question, my friend?"

"Anything."

"Why are you leaving?"

"Because I want to *live*, Alfarin. I don't want to just exist. This is it for me, and it isn't fair. If I told you I'd found a way to control time, wouldn't you want to change the way you died? If you had the chance to fight more wars, or live to grow old and become a Viking king, wouldn't you grab hold of it and never let go?"

"You are my friend, Mitchell, and I will follow you into any battle, but you are playing with fire."

"Here there is nothing for us *but* fire, Alfarin," I reply. "Now go. I'll meet you at the admin center in thirty."

I arrive at the lobby of the admin center on autopilot. This is happening—this is really happening.

There's a devil on duty 24/7. There has to be. Death is too inconvenient to work between the hours of nine and five.

I slink into the shadows and send Alfarin a text.

where r u?

I get nothing back.

The on-duty devil in the admin center is processing someone who has just arrived. I couldn't do that job. All that wailing and crying. The HalfWay House is a lot calmer than Hell's processing center. The newly dead arrive here and think they're going to be encased in fire and flayed with whips and have their teeth pulled out by demons with pliers. Stay on the right side of The Devil, and that won't happen, you hope.

I wonder who will take my job. I hope Medusa goes for it again, because she'd make an awesome intern. She's smart and funny and she doesn't take any crap from anyone. And she gets along with Septimus.

Seriously, if Brian Molewell gets the position, I'll come back to Hell just to spite him. In the end it was between the three of us: me, Medusa, and Brian. He's the same age as me, but he's been dead longer. He died in the Vietnam War. Septimus doesn't need another soldier in the office egging him on; he needs someone peaceful. Someone like Medusa. Except when she's hitting me, of course.

Another glance at my watch. I've been waiting fifty minutes. I'll give Alfarin ten more, and then I'm leaving. The on-duty devil has just called for security. The new devil is refusing to be admitted. Just suck it up, man. Being a pain in the ass won't get you into Up There. Dead people my parents' age are the worst. I know, because I see the insurance quotes for broken furniture and smashed windows. You wouldn't believe the fight they put up when they get here. Troublemakers, all of them, but they soon learn you shouldn't draw attention to yourself in Hell.

I've been banging my head against the wall this whole time, or maybe the shadows were pulling it, I'm not sure. Either way, I have a headache. At some point, I'm going to have to go through the—now broken—administration doors and request passage up to the HalfWay House.

And I'm going to be alone, completely alone, because Alfarin isn't coming.

I'm not scared about using the Viciseometer by myself. I'm pretty capable. I keep my head in a crisis. What was that word Septimus used to describe me?

Stoic.

Stoic, that's me. Mitchell Johnson—four syllables and nothing more.

When I see Medusa again I'll be old and she'll be totally grossed out at the sight of me. She'll have had a hundred boyfriends like the guy with dark-pink eyes. Medusa may even fall in love. And Alfarin will probably get to hold Elinor's hand. They'll all continue to mosh it up at Thomason's, and I won't get to see Alfarin shove fries up his nose.

It's time to leave. I have time in my backpack, but it's starting to run away from me. I try to be angry with Alfarin, but I can't. He's had my back in this place on more occasions than I can remember. This was one request too far. I can hear the three of them in my head, calling my name. Three distinct voices. I'll carry them with me forever: the best friend, the Viking warrior, and the peasant.

I tread over broken glass. The new arrival is gone. He didn't suck it up. He was dragged away by security. They're quick and subtle and they have chloroform. The on-duty devil has gone back to being bored. I can still hear my friends' voices. They're getting louder and louder, and every one of them is shouting my name.

The on-duty devil nods. Her flabby neck wobbles like a turkey. She's gesturing at me. I turn around and see Medusa, Alfarin, and Elinor flying toward me like bats out of Hell.

Alfarin is huffing and puffing and sweating like a pig on a spit. His axe bounces up and down on his shoulder as his braided beard swings like the pendulum of a clock. Alfarin looks as if he's going to drop dead from a heart attack—which clearly he can't. But he's as red as a giant raspberry. Medusa is wearing skintight jeans, a hooded olive-green sweatshirt, and hiking boots. So is Elinor. I've never seen her in anything besides a dress before. She must be wearing Medusa's clothes.

"What—I don't…What are you…" I can't speak. I don't know what to say. Elinor draws level with me first. She grabs my arm and pulls me into a corner.

"Ye can get us all out of here?"

"Yes, but—"

"Then do it now before M takes Alfarin's axe and chops yer boy bits off."

At that moment, an earsplitting buzzer sounds and a red light starts to flash near the check-in desk. My heart leaps into my mouth as Elinor claws my arm. We can't have been discovered already, can we?

The on-duty devil groans, then downs a cup of what I presume is coffee. Maybe it's vodka? It's always the quiet ones who turn out to be raging alcoholics.

"You lot need to clear off. That's the warning siren for a big arrival. I need the space." Her voice is deep, like a man's.

"We just need passage to the HalfWay House!" I cry, grabbing the forged letter from my backpack. It's crumpled and wet. My water bottle must have leaked. "This is permission from General Septimus. He needs some urgent things from the Grim Reapers."

She takes my letter and narrows her crimson eyes. She's obviously squinting as she reads it. I'm guessing her fake eyelashes, which look like hairy black caterpillars, are preventing her from reading it clearly. I start praying that this will work to our advantage.

"Why does it need all four of you?" she asks.

"Because there are many items that require bringing back down to Lord Septimus," replies Alfarin quickly, "and I think you will agree that my friend here is not in great shape."

Alfarin slaps a hand on my shoulder and my knees buckle. Mrs. Flabby Turkey-Neck smiles indulgently at my friends, as if she pities them for having such a pathetic loser as me among them.

"Go on then, quickly, before the guards bring the next lot down," she says with a wobble. She presses a button under her counter and two silver doors open automatically behind her. They're at least ten inches thick. The kind you'd find in a bank vault.

It's that easy. Moments later the four of us enter a claustrophobic corridor that has been hewn through the rock. The silver doors slam shut behind us and particles of rock fall from the narrow roof.

Now Medusa turns on me.

"How could you?" she screams. "How could you leave us like that? Leave *me* like that?" She's punching every single part of me with her balled-up fists. Alfarin and Elinor walk on and leave her to beat me to a pulp.

"Keep your voice down, Medusa!" I cry, trying to grab her hands. "Someone will hear you."

"You don't get to decide our futures, Mitchell," continues Medusa, totally oblivious to the fact that she has probably woken The Devil himself with her screeching. "You don't get to decide what I do with my life or death. You don't tell me this is men's talk, and you don't get to buy me off with a leather jacket, you swine, you pig, you devil."

"Medusa, will you quit hitting me?" I yell back. "Alfarin, will you help me out here?"

"I have already taken my punishment like a man, Mitchell," replies Alfarin seriously. "Now so must you. We owe them that."

"But Elinor isn't the one beating me up."

Elinor walks back and punches me on the jaw. I see black and then stars. I haven't seen stars for four years, but at least Medusa has stopped hitting me.

"Ye will never ditch us again," says Elinor, cradling the hand that just punched me. "We are yer friends and ye will damn well treat us like friends."

"See what you've done?" hisses Medusa. "You've made El swear and get violent, and El never swears or gets violent."

I'm still sprawled out on the ground. I think my jaw is broken in at least seven places.

"Are you all coming with me?"

"Of course we are," reply Medusa and Elinor together.

"But it's going to be really dangerous. Once Septimus knows what we've done..."

"I don't need protecting, Mitchell, and did you really think you could give me your leather jacket and that would make it all right?" asks Medusa quietly as Elinor bends down and helps pull me to my feet.

"No," I mumble, ashamed and relieved beyond measure in equal parts.

"If we are to do this, then we must depart now," says Alfarin.

I'm inches from Medusa. Her mad curls have escaped from her hair clip. I tuck several corkscrew strands behind her little ears. She has really tiny ears.

"Promise me you'll never leave me again," she whispers. I think she's trembling. She's probably cold. It's definitely chillier out here.

"I promise."

My throat tightens. I only make promises when I know I'm going to keep them. I would never lie to Medusa. I wouldn't lie to any of my friends. I'm never going to leave her now—not ever. And now my palms are getting sweaty. Medusa's arms reach out and wrap around my neck. She squeezes me tightly and buries her face in my neck. It feels damp. She smells like strawberries and chocolate. My arms lift her off her feet as I hug her back. A raggedy doll.

"Sure you don't want to change your mind?"

Medusa shakes her head, which is still buried in my neck. I'd be quite happy to carry her like this, and if I were built like Alfarin I definitely would.

Unfortunately, I'm built like me, so I can't. I drop her to the ground, but I can feel her skin against my neck long after she's gone.

It's time to leave Hell once and for all.

9. Skin-Walkers

Why haven't they built express elevators in this part of Hell? We've been walking uphill forever, and every part of me aches as if I've run a cross-country race against the fittest jocks in school.

"Why can't we use the Viciseometer to go a bit farther up?" whines Medusa. "We're going to be totally dead by the time we actually reach the HalfWay House."

Elinor nods; she's panting and clutching at a stitch in her side. Alfarin says nothing. He's lost the power of speech. Every ounce of strength he possesses is now focused on putting one enormous leg in front of the other without falling flat on his face from sheer exhaustion.

"For the eightieth time, Medusa, I don't want to use the Viciseometer in the depths of Hell because Septimus may find out. For all we know, he has some kind of security device fitted on it that would take us straight from here into the furnaces. I'm not using it until we're out in the open, when there's more distance between us and the Oval Office."

I've done my research. There's just the one path from the HalfWay House to Hell, and for the vast majority of devils this is a one-way journey. It's an enclosed route, narrow and slippery, with condensation and oozing pockets of oil. White-eyed rats scurry and scavenge along the ground as we move forward. If either Medusa or Elinor suffers from a fear of enclosed spaces, they don't let on.

My mother—who suffers terribly from claustrophobia—would have already gone back to Hell to beg for forgiveness and a toilet brush by now.

The tunnel has been cleaved out of black rock and is lit at intermittent stages by large flaming torches that cause shadows to rise up menacingly along the dripping walls. I lead the group with a much smaller torch, while Alfarin brings up the rear with a second that we stole on the way. We're constantly fearful of being crushed as tremors from the earth's tectonic plates shake the tunnel, causing fissures and small rock falls that tumble around our feet. My eyes stream and itch, while my arms and legs silently scream in protest as we inch our way ahead.

Occasionally the roof rises from the ground like the ceiling of a cathedral. Bubbling stalactites stretch down from above like the florets of a rancid cauliflower. I notice that the higher we climb, the paler the rock face becomes. The sooty air also becomes clearer. We're getting closer, I'm sure of it.

Then a loud, shrill noise echoes through the tunnel. It's accompanied by a blast of hot, acidic air that blows through Medusa's and Alfarin's hair, singeing the ends.

"Quick!" cries Elinor. "Back the way we came. We need to get into one of the caves. Now!" she yells.

The four of us tear back through the tunnel, leaping over rocks and stalagmites as we go. The ferocious wind remains hot on our heels as the shrill noise continues its terrible, relentless scream.

"What is making that noise?" yells Alfarin.

"Ye don't want to know!" screams Elinor. Alfarin has already torn her backpack away from her in an attempt to help her run faster, but Elinor is slipping over the condensation and bubbling pools of oil.

"Alfarin!" cries Medusa as we run blindly through the dark— the wind is now at tornado strength and has blown out every torch. "Can you carry Elinor?"

"It would be an honor," shouts Alfarin, and he sweeps Elinor over his shoulder without breaking stride.

We run into one of the cathedral caves.

"Behind that rock!" I yell. Alfarin's blazing red eyes are now the only light we have.

Medusa and I hide first; I pull her onto my lap and wrap my arms around her. Alfarin and Elinor are not far behind.

"Shush, quiet, all of ye," hisses Elinor. "They'll be coming through any moment."

I'm desperate to ask exactly *who* is coming, but I do as I'm told and stay quiet. In the four years I've known Elinor, I have never witnessed such a primal descent into panic and fear. I don't think she's ever raised her voice before tonight.

Suddenly the cave illuminates as if a thousand torches have been lit at once. Long stalactites grope down from the roof like grotesquely swollen fingers. The howling wind has reached a crescendo, which rocks the foundations of the stone above. Several smaller formations crash and splinter on the ground.

I throw myself on top of Medusa, while Alfarin throws himself over everyone.

"They're coming," whispers Elinor. "Stay down."

Not a chance in Hell; I want to look. Like a maggot wriggling through an apple, I squirm my way through the mass of bodies and peer around the rock.

Nine forms appear. At first I think they're huge wolves walking on their hind legs; their bodies are covered in gray-and-white fur. Then, as my eyes become accustomed to the sudden light, I realize that eight of the nine figures are wearing pelts and skinned animal heads, all of which are baring ferociously long black teeth. They're fixed on top of human heads.

Human heads with black irises.

I stifle a cry with my knuckles and taste blood. My hands must have been badly scratched as I groped to find a hiding place.

Something other than The Devil resides in Hell that has black irises. Septimus has kept that little fact quiet, and not for the first time I wonder what other secrets my boss is hiding.

The group of eight walks slowly and silently through the cave.

The screaming noise is not being made by the human wolves; it's coming from the air around them, like an aura of pure hatred. I can see it quivering like a heat haze on a hot road. The human wolves don't look in our direction. They are all unaware, or simply uninterested, in anything other than the ninth figure, which is enclosed in the grotesque animal shield.

It's a young man, naked but heavily tattooed. His ankles, wrists, and neck are manacled with inverted spikes that pierce his flesh. A steady stream of blood is flowing down his body. The fluid hisses and steams as it makes contact with the rock, as if the man's blood is toxic.

He must be in agony, I think, but the man makes no sound, despite the fact that his mouth is wide open in a silent scream that exposes dark silver fillings.

Then one of the human wolves suddenly stops. The long nose on the animal pelt rises into the air as if it's sniffing out something. The human wolf smiles, baring blackened teeth. The grin is bone chilling, and the thought that it knows we're here is enough to make me dig my fingers into the rock until they're in danger of breaking.

Then, mercifully, the light in the cathedral cave dims and soon extinguishes completely, leaving the four of us in total darkness. A caustic rotten smell swells over us in an invisible wave, causing everyone to gag.

A small torch flames. Alfarin has relit one of the lights. He hands it to Elinor, who is the first to stand.

"Are you all okay?" I ask, my voice shaking.

"What just happened?" says Medusa. Her hair is all over the place. She looks as if she's been electrocuted.

"We nearly had a run-in with the Skin-Walkers," replies Elinor somberly. "They were taking away an Unspeakable."

"Skin-Walkers?" asks Medusa. "What are they? And what is an Unspeakable?"

We start walking again. Everyone looks back down the tunnel, united in our terror that the Skin-Walkers will suddenly reappear in a blast of painful, hot wind.

"Skin-Walkers have been in Hell longer than The Devil," replies Elinor. "They were the first murderers, the first evil. They are the gatekeepers of a place that most devils fear in silence. It is the final dwelling of the Unspeakables: people who are so heinous in life, they cannot be left to mix with others in the Afterlife. They are the true tortured souls in Hell."

No one says a word as Elinor speaks.

"Rapists, child abusers, those who take another life for pleasure," she continues gravely. "Their tongues are ripped out and their flesh flagellated, and their soundless screams last for eternity."

"I think I'm going to be sick," groans Medusa.

"What part of Hell are the Skin-Walkers in?" I ask. "I've never heard of them before."

"I have," says Alfarin. "My kin have spoken of them before. It is the only time I have ever seen fear in my father's eyes. The Skin-Walkers are not like us, and they do not dwell with our kind of dead."

Elinor nods. "There are huge areas of Hell that are undiscovered by most devils. The Unspeakables are exactly that. No one knows where they are kept, or how the Skin-Walkers are summoned to collect them, but it is said the Skin-Walkers track their victims— future Unspeakables—while they are alive. Their victims can sense the Skin-Walkers' presence, sniffing them out. It is why most repent before they die, because they know what awaits them in Hell."

"Skin-Walkers roam the earth?" asks Medusa in a high, strangled voice. "They're up there with the living?"

"And they can track for years, according to legend," replies Elinor. "They don't just seek out Unspeakables when they are about to die. It is said the Skin-Walkers can track their victims by sniffing out the fear and pain in their nightmares. They like the fear; they exist through it."

"How do you know all this stuff, Elinor?" I ask, amazed, yet again, at her knowledge of…everything.

"I was waiting a long time," she whispers, quickening her pace and moving ahead of us all.

Our journey continues in silence. Is this my fate if I'm discovered with the Viciseometer? Will Septimus set the Skin-Walkers on me, to drag me naked through the bowels of the earth, silently screaming in utter agony? Is that the fate of Medusa, Alfarin, and Elinor?

What danger have I gotten my friends into?

"Mitchell, my friend," calls Alfarin. "Do my eyes deceive me, or is the rock becoming cleaner?"

There's nothing wrong with his eyes. Not only is the rock a pale ash-gray, but the air is filtering a juicy freshness like ripe green apples.

"M!" cries Elinor suddenly. "Yer eyes."

Everyone turns around and stares at Medusa. The pretty pink color is swirling and changing. Her irises go darker and darker until I'm staring at chocolate.

"El, yours are changing, too. Oh, green eyes look so pretty with your red hair."

"Look at Alfarin's. I knew he would have blue eyes."

"What color are my eyes? Can you see?" I ask eagerly.

Medusa stretches up on her tiptoes.

"Still girly pink," she announces.

"No way. Are you telling me...?"

A slim forefinger and thumb push my lips together with a pinch.

"Blue for a boy," says Medusa. "Now I'll race you to the entrance, loser."

10. The HalfWay House

Medusa and I run through the remainder of the tunnel and out into the open air. I win, obviously, because I'm a dude and strong—and also because I pulled Medusa back when it looked as if she was going to beat me. Elinor and Alfarin have already sprinted out. Elinor is spinning around in circles with her arms stretched out; the biggest smile I've ever seen on her face lights up the in-between world that is the HalfWay House.

I stand there, gulping in the fresh air that has been denied to me for four long years. I don't need it, but that doesn't stop the craving. It feels as if I'm inhaling carbonated oxygen that tickles the back of my throat and chills my lungs.

Already I know I've done the right thing.

Medusa and Alfarin have walked a little farther away from Hell's entrance. Both seem keen to observe a little more of our surroundings before celebrating. Alfarin drops to one knee, places his clenched right hand to his forehead, and starts muttering a Norse poem. His axe is gripped tightly in his left hand.

Elinor skips along the ash-colored gravel to where Medusa is standing, and the girls hug.

"It's so pretty, isn't it?" says Elinor wistfully. "I'd forgotten what the HalfWay House looks like. It's been so very long since I died."

A colossal glass-fronted building, at least a hundred floors high and just as wide, takes up most of the horizon. As I stand facing it,

I immediately notice that two different reflections are being cast on its rectangular windows. To the left is an iridescent rainbow sheen that showers the structure in color. To the right are shadow and darkness.

The sky above it is just as mixed: an unnatural juxtaposition of day and night squeezed into one view. From the left, the spectrum of color blends from a golden haze into a deep blue before it settles on dark pink and orange. As my eyes travel east, the sky darkens until it is a dense, starless black mass. The entrance to Hell is positioned directly below this.

"Do ye think we should tell people Hell isn't as bad as they might imagine?" asks Elinor as we watch a group of terrified-looking new devils being rounded up. It's fine for Elinor to say that; she now works in the housing administration area on level 427. Before that she worked for decades in the files of devil resources. She's never heard the screams that rock through the Oval Office, or seen the shadows that slink along the floor like black ghosts. I think Hell is exactly as bad as they might imagine.

A young woman has a baby in her arms, and the Grim Reapers are trying to separate them. Everyone knows that children go Up There to become cherubs, but the mother is refusing to let her baby go. She's screaming and spitting, and then she nearly drops the baby as she continues to fight back.

Medusa and Elinor immediately rush forward, but Alfarin and I hold them back.

"You can't help her," I say quietly. "None of us can. And we can't afford to draw attention to ourselves."

"But it isn't fair!" sobs Medusa. "Why can't they stay together?"

"Death isn't fair."

We don't watch the woman and baby being dragged apart, but we can hear them. It's a sound that pierces the marrow of my bones. Then suddenly the screams of the woman are silenced and we know she has been dragged down into Hell.

She'll be okay, I keep telling myself.

But I don't believe it, and all of a sudden I realize that there are dead people way worse off than me. Why couldn't Up There take the mother, too? Why does death have to be so cruel?

The four of us look pretty frazzled now. We weren't expecting to see that. It's Elinor who tries to lighten the mood.

"We should have a team name," she announces. "If that's okay with ye, Mitchell?" she adds quickly.

"I think that's a great idea." I smile at her, grateful for the distraction. "Any suggestions?"

"What about the Marauding Devils?" she replies.

"I vote for Evil Incorporated," says Medusa.

"What about Dead but not Evil Vanguard in Life? Team DEVIL for short!" I exclaim.

The others laugh. "Well, that beats mine—for once," says Medusa approvingly. "I love it." My stomach feels hot as her pretty chocolate eyes stare directly into mine. I probably need some food. I'd kill for a decent curry right now. Or maybe some Chinese noodles.

"We could get T-shirts," adds Medusa, clapping her hands.

"War paint!" cries Alfarin, pumping his fist.

Now, this is more like it: four friends planning an adventure. I'm their natural leader, and my first decision is met with universal approval. I'm in control of the situation.

Plenty of time for that to change, of course.

"So what's the plan, my friend?" asks Alfarin. He has lent his axe to the girls and they're using the mirrorlike blade to check out their eyes and hair. I nod toward a small copse of leafy trees. I want to tell them how the Viciseometer works before I use it for the first time, but I'm so nervous my feet are shaking in my sneakers. It may take four pairs of hands to hold the Viciseometer steady at this rate.

We head toward a quieter, shady area. There's sand beneath our feet. Both Medusa and Elinor take off their hiking boots and socks and squeal as they bury their toes in the sand. Medusa has sparkly blue polish on her toenails. It makes them look bruised, but I don't tell her that because I don't want to upset her.

"First of all, are you all okay with me leading? It's not that I think I'm better than any of you, because obviously I'm not, but I think one person needs to manage this."

"You're the most organized devil I know, Mitchell, and this was your idea. You should definitely lead, as long as you don't start bossing me around, because if you do…" but Medusa is smiling as she cracks her knuckles.

"A natural dead leader of women and Vikings, my friend," says Alfarin.

"I trust ye completely, Mitchell," replies Elinor.

I take a deep breath. "Great, and thank you. So, um, listen up," I start. Four heads lean in until they're touching. "The Viciseometer not only allows us to travel back and forward in time, but the actual watch face allows us a small glimpse of the future or past as well." Everyone stays silent as they listen intently. "So this is what we'll do. We'll travel back to the present day first. I thought New York City would be a good place to base our operations, because we'll be able to slip in unnoticed. From there, we'll each take turns to travel to our moment of death, and, and…well, if we want to change it, then we can."

It starts off so well and ends up sounding like as lame a plan as I've ever heard. I couldn't even say it without stuttering, but Medusa, Alfarin, and Elinor have gone even paler than normal. I think the enormity of what we're about to do has only just hit them.

We can change time. We are going to change time.

A loud gong starts to sound from the HalfWay House. A ship is leaving for the Pearly Gates. Hundreds of dead people start running to the dock, where a sign reads: DECEASED DOMINION. Some of the dead are waving white tickets in the air. Others less fortunate are trying to steal them. A riot breaks out as punches are thrown; it's all a bit of a mess. I can't remember it being like this when I first arrived, four years ago, but then I was so shell-shocked I can't remember much, to be honest. I don't like it here. I'm dead, so *reliving a memory* is the wrong phrase to use, but I don't know what the right one is. I want to get out of here—now.

"This is our cue to leave," says Medusa. "With everyone distracted by the ship, no one will notice four devils suddenly disappearing."

I pull out the Viciseometer and start to maneuver the red needle around the two faces. Medusa and Elinor shake the sand from their feet and put their socks and boots back on.

"This is so weird," mutters Medusa. The others murmur their agreement.

I close my eyes and let the tingling warmth of the Viciseometer spread through my fingers. It travels up my left arm and eventually through my whole body. I smile as it reaches my stomach. It's like kissing, without the wetness and clashing of front teeth. It helps calm me down.

"Now, according to the book, I need to take the needle and input a time on the white face. Then I press the bottom three buttons, once. That secures the hour, minute, and second of where we want to travel to."

"You can do it, Mitchell." Medusa has rested her hand between my shoulder blades. The smell of strawberries in her hair makes my insides squirm. Jeez, I'm hungry.

I carefully move each hand across the milky dial, connecting the golden arrows. Inhaling deeply, I secure time.

"He is very good," booms Alfarin. "Mitchell has the wisdom of Odin himself."

"Thanks, Alfarin," I croak like a frog about to die. "Elinor, do you know how the Viciseometer can tell whether we want to travel to a time in the morning or evening? I can't see an a.m. or p.m. marker on the face."

"Ye have to wait until both sides are fixed and then ye just will it in yer mind, Mitchell. Now turn the watch over."

I do as I am instructed and the red face glows back at me. I knew Elinor would have read the book cover to cover before she took it back to the library for me. I am so glad she's here. I have a feeling she's going to end up saving my neck if I screw this up.

"Now I need to move the smallest black hand to the month, the next one to the day, and then I press the first two buttons on the top rim."

As quick as my fingers are, and even with all my practice, this is taking way too long. What if we need to escape suddenly? An image of a snarling Skin-Walker with bloody teeth swims to the front of my mind.

"Now, finally, we fix the year," I say, shaking away the image as I carefully manipulate the last hand—the longest—with the thin red needle. I skim it across the four tiny numbered snakes that correspond with the four digits of the year. I'm speaking aloud as if I'm teaching the others, but really it's for my benefit more than anything.

The Viciseometer starts to emit a low-pitched whistle that sounds like a kettle boiling.

"Is it supposed to do that?" asks Medusa.

"This is absolutely normal," I say with a conviction I certainly don't feel. "The next stage is to concentrate my mind on the location we want to travel to."

"New York," say four very different voices. We all burst out laughing. It helps break the bubble of tension that has cocooned us.

The fingers of my right hand curl around the hot skin of Medusa's wrist. The Viciseometer starts to vibrate more urgently.

"Concentrate," says Elinor. "This is when ye decide whether ye want to travel to the morning or evening, Mitchell."

"I'm going to aim for Central Park, and I think we should all be thinking of it, just in case. You guys know what Central Park looks like, don't you?" Alfarin and Elinor nod and smile. "Excellent. I think it's best if we travel under cover of darkness so we don't stand out, but it's going to be early evening, so places will still be open to get food and provisions. When I see our destination appear in the red face, I'll press down hard on the large button. We'll all travel together, so hold on to someone."

"Do not be afraid, Mitchell. Your friends are with you," says Alfarin. He secures one of his arms around Elinor's waist.

"Have the courage of yer convictions and nothing will go

wrong," says Elinor. She wraps both of her arms around Medusa's right elbow, although her head is resting against Alfarin's chest. Her long red hair splays out like a waterfall of orange soda.

Medusa reaches up on her toes and kisses me near my earlobe. "I trust you completely," she whispers.

We hold hands and I stare at her for what seems like an uncomfortable age. If this goes horribly wrong, and we end up floating above Mars or worse, it will be her face I remember last. Those ridiculous little ears and her mad corkscrew hair, and the way her nostrils flare when she's excited or angry, and that really cute dip between her nose and top lip that matches her dimples.

I think it's called a philtrum.

Great. I'm about to get lost in space and I'm thinking of the word *philtrum*.

I screw up my face, willing the red face on the Viciseometer to see into time and space—but not too much space. The snakes, symbols, and runes start to swirl as if trapped in their own tiny circular vortex. They blur into one mass and then, just as the violent vibration continues, the image of a green park suddenly materializes, like a pixelated picture from a small television screen.

"Now!" cry the four of us in unison. I push down hard on the red button at the top center of the timepiece.

The world goes up in flames and the rush forces my eyes into the back of my skull. Then everything goes dark.

11. The Chill of the Big Apple

We materialize out of thin air. For a few terrifying seconds I'm too afraid to open my eyes. I was never this scared of stuff when I was alive. I think death misplaced my balls. Man up, for Hell's sake, Mitchell. This is New York, New York. So awesome they named it twice.

I peek out of one eye. Then the other. I remember I have blue eyes again. Blue for a boy. What I can't remember is New York being this freezing. Has the North Pole migrated while I've been busy being dead?

I chose this spot—behind a row of large bushes—deliberately after seeing it in one of Septimus's travel guides. Central Park: the most iconic patch of green in the world. Our spot is well hidden, beyond the line of sight of any observing living soul. I look up. Beyond the tops of the bare, bending trees is a large wall of illuminated concrete that looms up in front of us like a tsunami. I immediately pull a map from my backpack and we huddle around it.

"Do...y-y-you...know...wh-wh-where...we...are?" asks Medusa through chattering teeth.

"Here...I...th-th-think," I reply, pointing to the edge of a large green rectangle on the map. My finger is shaking so violently that it's difficult for the others to see exactly which spot I mean.

"Wh-wh-where?" asks Elinor. Her lips are rapidly turning blue.

I point again and again to the bottom of the park. I'm now too afraid to speak for fear of biting through my tongue. Clearly, we're acclimated to the intense heat of the Underworld, and not a bitterly cold November evening in North America.

"We...n-n-need...to...find...sh-sh-shelter," stammers Alfarin. Medusa and Elinor wrap their arms around themselves and nod in agreement. At least they have sweatshirts on, which is more than Alfarin and I do. I only have a short-sleeved black T-shirt covering my upper body. I might as well be in a Speedo.

"Follow...m-m-me," I gasp, "and...Alf-f-f-arin...hide...that axe."

"Where?"

Medusa and Elinor stare at Alfarin and then at me. We have no way of disguising the axe. It's too large to fit into one of the backpacks and too bulky to slip under Alfarin's thin blue tunic.

"I...h-h-have...an-n-n...idea," says Medusa. My joints are now starting to ache with a violent shivering that's completely out of control. "El, c-come...w-w-with...me." She motions to me and Alfarin to stay where we are.

"Wh-why...c-c-can't we...c-c-come...with...y-you?" I ask.

"A-a-axe!" is all Medusa can say as she points at Alfarin's weapon.

I let her go. I can't trust myself to speak. My teeth are threatening to chatter out of my gums and onto the grass where we're all standing like vibrating idiots. Medusa dives into my bag, grabs Elinor's hand, and then drags her onto a path, and together they disappear into the darkness.

Thirty minutes later, two arctic explorers appear. To my overwhelming relief, it's Medusa and Elinor, who unzip the fur-lined hoods of their new, thick navy-blue parkas and beam at us. Alfarin's fingers are so cold he's lost the ability to hold on to his axe. It lies at his feet, the silver blade dull in the moonless sky. Any longer and pieces of me would have started dropping off from frostbite.

Elinor is laden with shopping bags, while Medusa has the handle of a hard leather guitar case in her hand. Alfarin and I dive into the bags and start pulling on layer upon layer of clothing. Both Medusa and Elinor have to help with the fastening of buttons and zippers, which is a bit like being dressed by my mother and not at all how I like girls to deal with my clothes. It's another quarter of an hour before we're almost defrosted and able to talk.

"How did you get all this stuff?" I ask. My voice is slightly muffled by the long red scarf I've wound several times around my head. "Did you steal it?"

Medusa slips her hand into her parka pocket and pulls out the cash she took from my bag.

Girls' brains clearly continue to work even when they're frozen like a Popsicle.

"Less than an hour back and I'm already saving your skinny ass." She thumps me, but I don't feel it because I'm padded like a sumo wrestler.

"Surprise, surprise. Ten seconds in New York and the girls go shopping," I counter. "Anyway, I would have thought of that eventually."

"Glad I came now?"

"You'll have your uses, I suppose."

"And what will they be? C'mon. I want a long list of how awesome I am."

I grab Medusa in a headlock, which is easy because now that I'm warm, my strength is back and she's still small and puny.

"You can do the cooking and the washing and the cleaning—"

Her hands grab my calf and she pulls it back, upending me in the process. I take her down onto the grass with me and we roll around, wrestling and laughing.

It feels good to be almost alive again. Not long to go and I actually will be.

"Is the guitar for me, Medusa?" I ask, looking down at the long case half covered by empty shopping bags.

"Don't get excited, Mitchell. It's empty," replies Medusa—she is sitting on my stomach—"but we thought it would be an excellent place to hide Alfarin's axe."

Alfarin flicks open the two silver buckles that secure the guitar case. It falls open, revealing a spotted green silk lining.

"Medusa!" cries Alfarin. "Never before have I been presented with such a magnificent gift. My axe will honor your generosity by gorging on the brains—"

Medusa quickly interrupts Alfarin's well-intentioned albeit bloody rapture. "No thanks necessary, Alfarin, and El was the one who actually chose it."

Elinor lowers her head and does that really cute thing she does, looking up through her eyelashes. Then she staggers back slightly as Alfarin falls at her feet and starts kissing her wrists.

"I think we should get some food before Alfarin starts to eat El," sniggers Medusa. I'm trying my best not to laugh at the expression of panic that's growing on Elinor's red face.

"There's a fast-food restaurant not far from here," says Medusa. My map is open on her lap. I push her off my stomach and snatch it away from her. I'm in charge here.

"There's a fast-food restaurant not far from here," I announce. Medusa slaps me across the head as she climbs to her feet.

"I love this city already," gushes Alfarin, packing away his axe. "It has food that is fast, and has provided a beautiful bed for my axe to sleep in."

The four of us waddle away from the park. I think Elinor and Alfarin are wearing seven layers each, but they've been in Hell a lot longer than Medusa and me, so they need a lot more warmth. The living barely spare us a second look. We all find the vibrant colors hard to take in at first. We're so used to shadows and fire that this rainbow city hurts our adapting eyes. Elinor also find the hundreds of cars too noisy, and after a while she resorts to walking with her fingers in her ears. Alfarin is particularly excited by the crosswalks, having spent many an hour poring over books from the library about anything mechanical. He spends several minutes playing with the walk sign, until an irate Italian man lowers the window of his yellow cab and threatens to do something to Alfarin that would absolutely guarantee the driver would end up in Hell.

The smells of hot dogs and crispy fried chicken lead us down a side street. Alfarin stares in wonder at the colorful menu displayed on a huge window. I swear I'm going to eat everything on it at least twice.

"Never in all of Valhalla have I seen such a wondrous sight!" he cries, turning to me. "May I have the honor of providing tonight's meal?"

I slip Alfarin some cash. "Go for it, big man."

Alfarin slaps his chest and throws open the double doors of the fast-food restaurant. Nothing smashes, which is a novelty. Several diners look up from their cheeseburgers as an enormous, barrel-shaped man with long blond hair strides up to the counter dressed like an Eskimo.

"Why do I think this is going to go badly?" mutters Elinor under her breath. Her fingers are massaging the back of her neck again.

"He'll be fine," Medusa assures her. "Let's go find a seat."

A large woman with an even bigger chest is serving behind the counter. Her red-and-white-striped shirt—which is stretched so tight the seams look as if they're going to explode at any second—bears the logo HAPPY TO SERVE. From the scowl on her round face, she doesn't look it.

Alfarin unzips and throws back his fur-lined hood.

"Wench, give me a bucket of chicken," he demands.

The next sound is Elinor's head hitting the white plastic table where we've just sat.

"What did you just call me?" snarls the fast-food server in a deep southern drawl very similar to Septimus's.

Alfarin slaps some cash down on the counter as Elinor jumps up. She starts rushing across the tiled floor, but before she reaches our Viking friend, she slips on a discarded pickle slice, flies into the air, and comes crashing down on her back.

"Chicken, wench," demands Alfarin again. "My name is Alfarin, son of Hlif, son of Dobin, and this money is my ticket to food. Now, provide for my friends or I will slap your buttocks to prove my displeasure."

"Who are you calling wench, you fat son of a bitch?" yells the woman, shaking her pudgy fist. "Get the hell out of here before I call the cops!"

Medusa is trying to haul a disoriented Elinor to her feet. I'm laughing so hard I don't dare move for fear of peeing my pants.

"Forget me," groans Elinor to Medusa, "just get Alfarin out of here."

It takes several minutes to drag Alfarin's enormous frame out of the fast-food restaurant. He only consents to leave when the woman he has offended starts hitting him with a greasy fish spatula.

"I did nothing wrong!" exclaims Alfarin. "In our halls, all of the serving women are called wenches. It is a compliment."

"I think chocolates, flowers, and calling someone darling are more acceptable here, ye big oaf," says Elinor with exasperation.

"Get out, get out!" screams the woman, who is now brandishing the spatula at all of us.

"You get 'em, Martha," drawls an elderly customer with crinkled black skin and a shock of gray hair. "You show 'em nobody messes with my girl and her buttocks."

Only when the four of us have hurried back into the relative safety of Central Park do I remember the money that Alfarin slapped down on the counter. We can't waste cash. Working in Hell's accounting department has taught me that.

"Did someone pick it up?" I ask in a panic.

"I've got it," replies Elinor. She pats her back pocket. "I grabbed it after the woman started throwing cheeseburgers at us."

"I don't understand!" cries Alfarin. "If I had slapped her rump, a smack across my face would have been expected. In fact, I would have welcomed it. In my day, this was how we attracted the opposite sex."

"You have a lot to learn about women, Alfarin," replies Medusa. "Just don't go asking Mitchell to teach you anything."

"What do you mean by that?" I demand.

"Let's just say your taste in girls needs improvement."

"I have excellent taste in girls, thank you very much."

"Mitchell, I've seen you make out with a girl with an Adam's apple."

"So?"

"Girls don't have an Adam's apple, you fool!" shouts Medusa.

Elinor is making a funny snorting noise like a pig. She's laughing so hard tears are falling down her bright-red cheeks.

I stop walking. Is Medusa saying what I think she's saying? I look to Alfarin for support, but he's too busy trying to get ketchup out of his beard.

"What do we do now, Mitchell?" asks Elinor, trying to be the peacemaker.

"We book a hotel and get room service," I reply. "I'm starving, I'm cold, my eyes hurt, and that girl did not have an Adam's apple. Her neck was just a bit lumpy. I think she died of the plague or something."

"If you say so."

"What hotel would you like to check into, Mitchell?" asks Elinor.

"I vote we check into the first one we come across," says Alfarin. "Mitchell needs to rest before we cause any more trouble today."

Only pregnant women and old people need rest. Even Alfarin thinks I've turned into a girl. Hungry and exhausted, Team DEVIL starts to walk toward the looming bank of stone and light that first welcomed us to New York City. On the way, we pass a large bronze statue of a man on a horse with a winged angel next to it. It looks suspicious, as if it has eyes that are following our every move. A solitary policeman is standing next to it. He looks at Medusa and sniffs the air. Then his mouth widens slowly and he grins; his teeth look twice as long as normal. A rotten smell, probably the city's garbage, fills the night air.

"That looks like a hotel," says Medusa. She points to a château-style building on the corner. "Why don't we stay there, at least for tonight?"

The agreement is unanimous. I look behind us nervously, but

the policeman is gone. All I can see is the outline of a large dog running off into the park.

Arm in arm, we troop up a red carpet and enter the building. I hear music coming from somewhere close by, and it takes all my resolve to not go searching for the piano that's making it. Instead, I clutch my wallet. It holds the cash I stole from the office and my photo ID from when I was alive. I don't know why I kept the ID; I certainly never expected to use it again. Maybe it was too hard to let go. But it'll definitely come in handy today.

When we get to the front desk, I request the two cheapest rooms available: one for Alfarin and me to share and the other for Medusa and Elinor.

The pretty Asian desk clerk smiles at me as I hand her cash and she hands over the door cards. Just like that, we have shelter at one of the most luxurious hotels in the world. "Now, if there is anything we can do to make your visit more pleasant, Mr. Johnson, please do not hesitate to ask the concierge. We hope you enjoy your stay at the Plaza," she says.

Medusa is asleep before her head hits the pillow; Alfarin isn't far behind. It looks as if the four of us will be sharing one room tonight, because there's no way Elinor will go into the other room alone with me, and I wouldn't ask her to. I'm a gentleman.

Elinor tiptoes around the room. It really is impressive, especially considering we're in the cheap seats. The faucets in the white marble bathroom appear to be made of gold. The clothes hangers are all padded like pillows, which I think is ridiculous, but they send Elinor into spasms of joy.

I'm busy counting our remaining cash when Medusa starts screaming and crying in her sleep. Her head thrashes from side to side and her arms fling out in front of her as she struggles to wake up from the terror she has fallen into. I've seen her do this before, and it isn't pretty. Elinor and I both leap onto the bed as Alfarin tumbles out of the seat he was snoozing in. He has his axe in his hand and is about to start swinging. This is just as scary as Medusa's screams, because Alfarin is still only half awake and liable to take someone's head off if he isn't careful.

"Ye were shouting in your sleep," whispers Elinor. She's stroking Medusa's hair away from her sweaty face. I want to do that, because I'm Medusa's best friend, but I let Elinor.

"Another nightmare?" I ask. I put my hand on Medusa's shoulder. She leans into me and I wrap my arms around her bony rib cage. Her chest is rising in short, shallow bursts. If she were alive I'd be able to feel her hammering heart, but she isn't, so I can't.

"Ye relived it again?"

Medusa nods. Large teardrops are leaking from her brown eyes, but she doesn't make a sound. No sobs, no whimpers. Medusa isn't one to make a fuss unless she's really upset.

Like when a friend tries to swap a friendship for a leather jacket.

"How did you die, Medusa?"

I wanted to ask again, but it's Alfarin who speaks. To my surprise, she doesn't tell him to get lost.

"I fell from the Golden Gate Bridge," she says quietly. "I didn't mean to let go, I just lost my grip. I only wanted to scare them into helping me."

"Oh, Medusa." I put my lips against her temple. It isn't a kiss, because my mouth stays there. If I could inhale away her pain, I would in a second.

"And ye regret being there?"

My best friend pulls away. She clambers off the bed and straightens out her clothes, her back to us. She sniffles, wipes her eyes with the back of her hand, and fluffs out her corkscrew hair in the window's reflection.

"I only regret that I didn't take *him* with me."

12. Sleepy Sheep

Checking into two rooms was a total waste of money. Medusa and Elinor are sharing the one bed, but Alfarin wants the four of us to stay together. I have no intention of leaving Medusa to her night terrors, so we remain in the one room and let the other go unused.

Medusa would go nuts if she knew I stayed awake just to watch her sleep, long after everyone else has dozed off. I'm not being a creep or stalker or anything like that. I'm just worried after she's spent an hour locked in the bathroom with the Viciseometer. She was watching something in the watch face, I'm sure of it, though she says she was just cleaning fingerprints off it. She isn't a very good liar. It's another thing we have in common.

Medusa never believed me when I told her I'd died saving kittens. We'd both just had our third interviews for the intern job—that was when we first became friends. She rolled her eyes and walked away; I ended up running after her. The first words she ever said to me were curse words. I liked that. It's a common misconception that boys like girls who fall at their feet. Well, we do like that, but only for that immediate moment. I would never hang out with a girl like Patty Lloyd. She's gorgeous, but way too much work. Medusa is easy most of the time. A round peg in a round hole. She fits into my death effortlessly.

Death is crappy enough without friend drama. The four of us are soul mates, according to the girls. They do this kind of retrospective analysis. Medusa, and especially Elinor, like to get all deep and heavy and say things about fate bringing us all together, or destiny, or some other nonsense. Elinor is constantly going on about how the four of us were meant to be together in death.

I don't believe in fate, or destiny in the stars, or any of that crap, because I think you make your own luck—or bad luck, if you look at my history with large vehicles. Medusa, Alfarin, Elinor, and I are together because we like each other. We each bring something unique to the group: Medusa is the smartest person I know; Alfarin the bravest; and Elinor the most rational.

I am the glue keeping us together—for now.

I stop watching Medusa and walk over to the Viciseometer on the writing desk. I don't know whether to hide it or keep it in full view so we can get to it quickly in case of an emergency. Not a minute goes by when I don't think I'm about to get busted by the Skin-Walkers, but in the city that never sleeps, there is only silence.

And that is just as unnerving.

When I say silence, I mean from outside the room. Inside, the noise is ridiculous. Alfarin and Elinor are clearly having a competition to see who can shatter the windows first with their snoring. Judging by the steam-engine honking coming from Elinor, I'd say she's winning. It's hard to believe someone so fragile can make such a noise.

I'm too wired to sleep. I feel like one of those toys that you wind up by hand and then let go. They're manic for five seconds and then they fall over and just make a whirring noise until the mechanism dies.

It's been too easy. We got out of Hell without a hitch, and as a bonus for my duplicity, I have my three best friends with me. We weren't arrested at the HalfWay House, and the Viciseometer worked on my first try. Apart from the issues with temperature, and Alfarin's run-in at the restaurant, even New York has played nicely.

When the others wake up we're going to have to start making decisions, like whose death we're going to see first. Then it's going to get a lot harder. I'm under no illusion about that.

Tonight's confession from Medusa was horrible. It was the first time she's ever told any of us how she died. She mentioned someone else; someone she regretted not taking with her. If there is a person on this earth who has hurt her, I swear I'll travel back in time and kill him myself.

And if Elinor doesn't stop that incessant noise, I'm going to hold her nose and smother her with a pillow. She doesn't even need to breathe, and that snoring isn't human.

Alfarin died when he was sixteen years old. He was killed in battle. His Viking clan was marauding through some English village and he was cut off from the rest of his family and attacked. A lot of his relatives are now in Hell. The ones who somehow got into Up There are never really talked about, or even mentioned. They're regarded as having brought dishonor to the brethren. Alfarin was the heir of the Viking king. He would have made history if he'd lived long enough to take charge, I'm sure of it. His clan is convinced they saw Alfarin's spirit appear to them after he died, so he's treated like a hero in Hell. He is such a good friend; I'm really excited to see how he'll be revered once he gets another chance at life. I'm sure I'll be reading about him in history books as a legendary warrior.

Everyone should get that second chance, because when you're young you get labeled and written off. When you're alive, some people don't really look for your potential. They only see it once it's too late. The words spoken at funerals should be said when the person is alive to hear them.

Elinor suffered a horrible death. It's really hot in Hell, but I figure burning to death is probably the worst way to go, because some serious pain goes into that. When you die, you want to be old and comfortable, having lived a long and interesting life. You don't want the smell of your own burning flesh to be your last earthly memory. How Elinor has handled that and become the devil she is today—well, I don't think I would have dealt with it anywhere near as well. I would have ended up in Hell's lunatic asylum with all the other banshees. Elinor doesn't talk about her death much because she finds it too traumatic. Medusa thinks Elinor looks at Alfarin in a funny way when we do get around to talking about it—which the four of us try really hard not to. I can't say I've noticed, but then girls see things differently.

If I really can alter time with the Viciseometer, if I can stop myself from running out in front of that bus, I am going to do everything I can to live as long as humanly possible. I think one hundred and one is a good age to die. I'll still have my own teeth and hair—that's really important. I'll be stinking rich and will have sold millions of records on iTunes, and there will be Facebook tribute pages with so many fans that my death will crash the site. I'll definitely be a trending topic on Twitter when I die properly. I'll pass away in my sleep, having eaten steak and mashed potatoes and a huge tub of strawberries for dinner.

I've just had a thought. It was the strawberries that did it. Technically, Medusa is older than me. She was born in 1951. She lived and died decades before I was even a twinkle in my parents' eyes. So if we ever got together, she would be a cougar.

I start laughing. I can't help it. It would be worth asking her out, just to be able to mock her for being a mangy old cat.

She doesn't look like a mangy old cat, though. Medusa is infuriating and opinionated and ridiculously self-sufficient, but she's my best friend and I swear if someone caused her death, they're going to pay. She could have been the first female president or a world-famous chef. I would do anything for Medusa, but sometimes it's just easier to mock her and toss her around and steal her potato chips.

And now I have a stabbing pain in my side. This is why guys don't think about this stuff—it gives us ulcers. Thinking about feelings and trying to work out what goes on in a woman's head is why men die early.

And then it continues in Hell. I'm telling you, there's no escape from it.

"Why were you laughing?"

Crap! When the Hell did Medusa wake up? She was purring like a kitten ten seconds ago. Now she's standing right next to me, running her fingers through her hair like a comb, trying to untangle the curls. It's Alfarin and Elinor's fault. The gruesome twosome is making so much noise I didn't hear Medusa get off the bed.

"Why were you laughing, Mitchell?" she asks again. I can feel the heat radiating off her; she's burning up. Or maybe that's just my face.

"You know there's a forty-year age gap between us," I reply.

"So what?"

"If we ever dated, you'd be a cougar."

I swear I'm my own worst enemy. I could have said I was making plans for our death departures, or plotting an escape route. We're only up the avenue from Tiffany's, for Hell's sake, I could have said I was going to buy her a diamond to make up for the leather jacket.

No. That would be too sane. Instead I have to go and call her a cougar.

"Then thank Hell that unfortunate situation will never happen," she replies, but she sits down on my lap and wraps her arms around my neck. She gently places her head on my shoulder.

I'm so confused. Why do girls do this? She says something mean but then she's cuddling me at the same time. And her ass is really bony and is digging into my thigh. I shift her weight a little and she falls even closer against me. She smells like clean sheets, which is really nice and reminds me of my mom and my old bed and my old life.

"You smell like sleep."

"I smell like sheep?"

"What? That's not what I said."

"You said I smell like sheep."

"*Sleep*, not sheep."

"How can someone smell like sleep? It's a verb. Verbs don't smell."

"I meant you smell like clean sheets."

"Are you saying I usually smell like dirty sheets?"

"Forget I opened my mouth."

"You said I smell like sheep."

"I said you smell like sleep. I was trying to be cute. I thought girls like guys who are cute."

"Why are you trying to be cute? And I already like you."

Why is this so hard? For the love of all things unholy, someone write a manual on girls.

"I'm trying to be cute because you're my best friend and you've followed me out of Hell, breaking about a thousand laws in the process. You're having nightmares already, and for the first time since we met, you've finally told me how you died. I wanted to be nice, so I thought I'd say you smelled like sleep, all warm and cozy. *Not sheep*, okay?"

Alfarin grunts from the chair, but his chin continues to rest on his chest. Elinor now sounds like a jet plane taking off. At some point she'll break the sound barrier and the roof of the Plaza will explode into the sky.

And now Medusa is laughing. I think traveling through time and celestial domains has fried her brain. It has certainly messed with my head. She nestles back into my shoulder, but now I'm too self-conscious to wrap my arms around her. I'm bound to say the wrong thing.

"You're an idiot, Mitchell Johnson."

"And you're a humungous pain in the ass. And speaking of asses, you need to put on some weight. Your butt is as bony as your elbows."

"I thought boys liked skinny girls."

"Nah. Girls should have a bit of meat on them."

"Like Patty Lloyd?"

Don't say the wrong thing, Mitchell.

"I shouldn't have kissed her, and I really regret it, Medusa."

"She isn't good enough for you, Mitchell."

"Do you know anyone who is?"

But Medusa just sits there, tensed like a spring. She doesn't answer my question. Her fluttering eyelashes are the only part of her that's moving.

"Don't ye two look cute?"

Elinor is stretching on the bed. I hadn't even realized the pneumatic drill noise had stopped. Medusa releases herself from my lap and is gone. I feel cold and empty without her sitting on me. All I'm left with are cramps in my right leg. As soon as Elinor speaks, Alfarin starts to stir as well. Her voice is his personal alarm clock.

"You two snore so loud I'm amazed the park police didn't burst in."

"Elinor does not snore," says Alfarin indignantly. "Her dead lungs simply move heavily."

"Thank ye, Alfarin." Elinor beams at him and he gives her a regal nod.

Mitchell Johnson, also known as M.J., also known as total loser when it comes to girls regardless of eye color, 0.

Alfarin, son of Hlif, son of Dobin, Viking warrior, remains manly even when girls braid his beard, 1.

I think it's time to change time.

13. **9 Harpa 970**

Right now neither Alfarin nor I are capable of making a decision on an empty stomach, so our first joint resolution is to order room service. Thirty minutes later, a guy who doesn't look much older than me wheels a silver cart into the room. I want to tell him to get a move on and start living his life because it could be ripped away from him at any second. Instead, I hand him a fifty-buck tip and he thanks me repeatedly before quickly backing out of the room, clearly scared I'm going to take it back. Alfarin has already pulled off the silver-plated covers on the cart and is groaning in a rather indecent way at the piles of scrambled eggs, crispy bacon, and pastries.

"Have ye decided on a plan?" asks Elinor. Alfarin is playing waiter and has taken a plate of food and a cup of hot chocolate over to her.

"We have to decide which of us wants to go back to the moment of our death," I say quietly.

"I think I should be the first to try, my friend," says Alfarin. He opens up the guitar case and takes out his axe. His thick fingers flex around the wooden handle.

"I'm cool with that if the others are," I reply, "but, just out of interest, why do you think you should be first?"

"Isn't it ladies first?" quips Medusa.

"Normally I would adhere to that rule," replies Alfarin, "but this is not as simple as opening a door and being a gentleman. If something goes wrong, you and Elinor need to be able to escape. Mitchell is our leader, the bearer of the Viciseometer, and he must be entrusted with your safety."

"Technically, I am the *stealer* of the Viciseometer," I mutter, "but I get where you're coming from, Alfarin. So are you two okay with this?" I ask Medusa and Elinor. "We'll travel back to Alfarin's time first and help him escape death."

"We're really going to do this, aren't we?" asks Medusa softly. Elinor hugs her. Suddenly my hunger is gone. I want to change my death so badly, and I want my best friends to have the same opportunity to alter theirs, but so many things could go wrong. What if we lose the Viciseometer and get stuck in the time of the Vikings? What happens if we get separated and only half of us can escape? What if the Skin-Walkers find us and take us away to become Unspeakables because of all the laws we've broken? The thought of Medusa, Alfarin, or Elinor being abused or tormented because of my selfishness is hard to stomach.

"You guys shouldn't have come," I mutter. The Viciseometer is still on the writing desk. It looks innocuous enough. The milky-white side is faceup, but when I touch it, I can sense the vibrations humming through it. It's as if it's trying to talk to me, to warn me.

I wonder if it can sense danger. Septimus said it had been used to introduce new inventions on earth, but I'm going to be abusing it. My overactive imagination—fueled by four long, dead years in which I have seen the ultimate in crazy—suddenly considers the Viciseometer a living object. If I don't use it correctly, it could take revenge on me and my friends in ways I haven't even imagined.

"We are not going to have this discussion again," says Medusa, "and you need to stop trying to be our protector, Mitchell. The four of us are here together, and we will see this thing through to the end. Team DEVIL, remember? And what do you think would happen now if we did change our minds and went back to Hell? Do you think Septimus is going to welcome us all back with a party?"

"M is right, Mitchell," says Elinor, casting her deep-green eyes around the room as she rubs her neck. "We know ye are more worried about us than ye are for yerself, but we made the choice to come."

"Then it is in Odin's mighty hands once more," says Alfarin, standing and puffing out his chest.

"Can you remember the exact date you died, Alfarin?" I ask. "We'll need to get the coordinates right. I don't want the girls hanging around fighting Vikings longer than absolutely necessary."

"I'm going to change my clothes," says Elinor. She walks over to Alfarin, who is suddenly very quiet, and strokes his back. "Don't ye leave without me, Alfarin, or I will be very annoyed."

The whole room has gone very still. I sit on the carpet and rest my chin on the edge of the bed so I am looking up at Medusa. She has the clearest complexion of any person I've ever met. There isn't a line or scar or spot on her. She has skin like a vanilla milk shake.

You still get zits in Hell. Brian Molewell—the guy who is almost certainly celebrating my departure from Hell because it will mean he'll get my internship—has acne so bad I bet Up There can see it.

Not Medusa. She has lovely, clear skin that is completely unmarked. In fact, I think the only part of her that isn't perfect is the small chicken pox scar on the right side of her forehead.

She's so beautiful, and she doesn't seem to have a clue.

Medusa and Elinor get changed into some of the new stuff they bought last night. I don't know why they bothered. They're still wearing skinny jeans and sweatshirts. The girls are disgusted when Alfarin and I say we haven't bothered to change our underwear, but I've only had my boxers on for a day. Plenty of death in them yet.

Alfarin hands me a piece of paper. On it he has written 9 *Harpa* 970. The thirty-eighth minute of the sixth evening hour.

"Dude, what's this?" I ask.

"My death moment," he replies.

"Harpa is not a month."

"In your modern language, it is April."

"What was the weather like when you died, Alfarin?" asks Medusa.

"Weather?" I exclaim. "He's about to die and you're asking about the weather?"

"We need to dress appropriately, Mitchell," replies Medusa. "Need I remind you that more than your eyes turned blue when we arrived in New York?"

"It was cold," replies Alfarin quietly. "I remember the snow turning red."

My stomach twists. Medusa swaps a frightened look with Elinor, whose hand has gone to the back of her neck.

"Wear jackets," says Medusa eventually, handing Alfarin his. She pats his arm lovingly.

"Can I say something, Mitchell?" asks Elinor as the four of us stand in a square formation in the center of the room.

"You don't have to ask permission, Elinor."

"We have to see the place of death in order to understand how to change it. But how will ye be able to visualize it in the Viciseometer? Ye haven't seen where Alfarin died. He will have to be the one to hold the Viciseometer, transfer the memory, and then press the button."

Genius Elinor. "She's right, Alfarin," I say. "You're gonna have to do this."

Without a word, but with his large face already displaying tiny beads of sweat, Alfarin takes the Viciseometer from the table.

"Talk me through it," he says. "And hold the Viciseometer with me, my friend. I sense it responds well to you."

"Everyone ready?" I ask, and my friends nod.

I show Alfarin how to input the desired time on the white face. His movements are cumbersome, and he takes much longer on his first attempt than I did. Once the time is secured with the three black buttons, he turns the Viciseometer over and starts to manipulate the date into place.

"Hold on, everyone," I say.

"Don't let me go," whispers Medusa.

"Never," I reply, and I mean it.

Suddenly we hear the sound of several fists pounding on the door. Elinor screams and Alfarin almost drops the Viciseometer. I swear loudly as angry voices echo in the hallway outside.

"They've come for us!" shrieks Elinor, and she lets go of Alfarin and starts pulling at her neck.

"Alfarin, quickly, you need to picture the image. We have to go now!" I shout. "Elinor, hold on with both hands."

"Is it the Skin-Walkers? I can't believe Septimus would actually send them after us!" cries Medusa.

The door handle is shaken violently, and Medusa starts hopping from one foot to the other.

"We have to go now, now, now, now!"

"*I have it!*" shouts Alfarin.

My eyeballs are once again pulled into the back of my skull as a blaze of fire washes over my skin. I swear I can smell the acrid scent of burning, and this time I hear screams in the darkness as the shadows of the dead travel with us.

Our landing in 970 AD is not graceful. Everyone, with the exception of Alfarin, falls into squelching black mud. It is sleeting. Although it's dusk, the sky is alight with fire. Alfarin hauls Medusa and Elinor to their feet and drags them into a small shedlike building: pieces of wood stacked like a one-layer house of cards. Screams and jeers and deep-throated cries fill the air.

I stagger to my feet and stumble into the shed. It has no back and stinks like a toilet. Both Medusa and Elinor have gone green.

"We will be able to see my death from here," says Alfarin matter-of-factly.

"Where are we, Alfarin?"

"An English village. We did not know the name. We came for their stores of crops."

"Are you sure you're up for this?"

"I would not be here if I weren't."

Alfarin and I inch to the back of the shed. From here we have a clear view of a large patch of straw-strewn ground. Several thatched buildings, most of which are on fire, circle it. There is a ring of men and women; I count at least fifteen heads. They're armed with an assortment of weapons, from scythes to long pieces of wood. There are two enormous, snarling wolfhounds with long, stringy-looking legs. They look like engorged rats on stilts rather than dogs, and I'm more scared of them than I am of the men with axes.

The circle of villagers is closing in on something I can't see. They have something trapped.

And then I realize what, or rather, *who*, they are about to attack.

I stagger back. I can't watch this, and Alfarin certainly shouldn't watch this. We can use the Viciseometer again. Go back another hour and get him out of trouble before it really starts. We've arrived too late.

"Mitchell, my friend," whispers Alfarin, beckoning me forward.

"We'll go back again, Alfarin. We messed up."

But Alfarin is shaking his head.

"If you are my friends, you will stand by me in this moment," he says slowly. "It is the moment I have longed to see from the eyes of others for so long now, but I never thought the gods would allow me the honor."

Medusa and Elinor have more stomach than me, and they crawl in the muck toward Alfarin. They are caked in crap, and yet they go to stand by their friend. I am ashamed of myself. Despite every sane ounce of humanity that I possess, I go and join them.

It is beginning.

We are about to watch the death of a Viking prince.

We are about to watch the death of our friend.

14. Death of a Viking

The freezing slush is thickening. I can feel it against my face. It sticks to my mouth and nostrils and starts to layer onto my eyebrows. Thick black smoke has filled the air; the smell of burning wood seems sickly sweet.

A rough hand has gripped mine. I'm assuming it's Medusa's, but I don't look down at it. Right now I feel nothing but terror.

Alfarin is standing just a couple of steps in front of us. The four of us are still hiding in the back of the shed, but even its makeshift walls are shaking under the threat of medieval violence. The entire wooden structure could come down on us at any moment.

I respect Alfarin with every bone in my body, but watching him now...well, I'm speechless. It's as if he isn't human. He looks like a statue on top of a monolith. Not a flicker of movement. He's turned to stone. I can't read his face because it's expressionless. Alfarin stands tall and watches. He's just *watching*, for crying out loud.

But this isn't a television or movie screen playing out a scene. This is real life, albeit a thousand years in the past. This is history in the present, and his placid acceptance of it scares the crap out of me. Our soul is the only thing we have left in Hell, but Alfarin's seems to have disappeared.

We need to go back farther in time. We need to stop whatever it was that caused Alfarin to be separated from his clan. We have to help him. I want to punch those words into his brain. *WE CAN HELP YOU.* That's why we're here in the first place.

I know what's coming next; we all do. Alfarin can probably still feel what happens next. My death was instant. I have no memory of the bus squashing my head like a watermelon, or of what caused me to run out into the road.

Alfarin remembers. He's even joked about it. We were at Thomason's when several Vikings decided to do the Dance of a Thousand Blades. It was just an excuse for them to start throwing knives around, but Alfarin—who was laughing his head off at the time—goes and announces that this was how he died. By the time we had all the gory details, Elinor had almost passed out.

And now Alfarin wants us to watch it for real.

I can hear that mob from here. The surrounding structures may be burning down, but they've trapped the noise as well as the villagers. Everything is magnified tenfold, as if we're in a cave. And now for the first time I can hear Alfarin. Not our Alfarin, the other one—the living version.

He isn't going to be that way for long.

I still have the Viciseometer tightly gripped in my hand. I pick up the red needle and start inputting time onto the white face.

"What are ye doing, Mitchell?"

"I'm taking us farther back in time."

"Now?" sobs Medusa. I look down at her and realize that her filthy face has long wet streaks snaking all the way down into the neck of her sweatshirt. She's been quietly crying this whole time.

"We need to go back another hour. We can't stop this now." My voice is so high it hurts my throat.

"If you leave now, I will not go with you, my friend," says Alfarin. He doesn't look at me; he is watching his living self. He inches closer to the scene. The jeering mob and growling dogs are just feet away from the living Viking prince. A flaming torch has just been jabbed at him. His axe is raised. Alfarin will go down fighting, but he is going down. His death is inevitable. It's already in the history books.

"And ye will have to go without me as well," says Elinor. She inhales a pathetic little sniffle but stands upright. "I am staying with Alfarin."

For the first time since he dragged our asses into this shed, Alfarin takes his blue eyes away from his death moment. He looks at Elinor with pure adoration and then goes back to watching. His two-handed grip tightens on his axe, but I know he won't use it to defend his other self.

"We have to do this, Mitchell," whispers Medusa. "This is Alfarin's moment in time and we can't make the decision for him."

And she is right, because Medusa is always right. So I man up and step forward. Now snow is coming down thick and fast. It settles around our feet, coating the mud like a frothing sea. We're sinking into it. The Viciseometer stays in my hand and I draw courage from its power.

"Then we're all with you, Alfarin."

The living Alfarin doesn't look scared or clueless. He knows he's going to die, but he's going to take as many of the mob down with him as he can. The axe is raised. Thick, freezing rain bounces off the blade, like popcorn. Within moments the slush turns red. The living Alfarin wasn't the first one to attack, he wasn't even the second, but once he starts fighting back, he is lethal.

Watching movie battle scenes doesn't prepare you for the sound or sight of violence. It's the cuts that aren't clean that really test my strength to remain standing. The blood I can cope with, but it's the flash of shattered white bone that turns my legs to jelly.

Six of the baying mob are already down; limbs litter the ground. If it weren't for the screaming, we could be looking at horror shop mannequins. The living Alfarin is so strong he can take on two at a time. His axe is like an extension of his arm, and the blood of his victims is diluted by the slush to make a river of red that flows like a waterfall down his arm.

But a lot of that blood is now his. The living Alfarin has taken blades to the back, shoulders, and legs. A piece of wood is used as a club and is smashed down onto his skull three times in quick suc-

cession before he manages to decapitate the assailant. Thick blood, so dark it's almost black, is running out of the living Alfarin's ears and nose. Leather boots protect his lower legs from the jaws of the dogs, but then one jumps up and clamps its teeth onto the living Alfarin's throat.

Armed men and women could not bring the prince down, but the hound, which is quickly joined by the other snarling monster, does it in seconds.

Elinor's knees give way and she sinks into the mud. Medusa is choking. I have snot running down into my mouth and the tears from my stupid blue eyes are streaming fast and pooling under my chin.

Our Alfarin does not move. His head is held high, his back a straight line. He is dying with honor—a small smile the only flicker of emotion on his round face.

And now comes the worst moment of all, because now we can hear our friend dying. He isn't screaming or crying for help; he is a Viking prince who will not betray his ancestors, but the roars that bellowed from his chest just minutes ago are now feeble and weak. His axe slams into one of the hounds. It yelps with a sound that could shatter glass as it flies through the air, its intestines trailing like the ribbons on a kite. The other hound immediately backs away.

A man, small but heavily built, with a bowl haircut, steps forward. He has a hatchet in his hand. The dull, rusty blade is a quarter of the size of Alfarin's weapon. The man holds it in both hands and raises it above his head.

My chest is rattling; something is trying to force its way out. "No!" bursts out of my mouth and I make to rush forward. Our Alfarin's huge arm is thrust in front of my chest.

"This is my fate, my friend. This is how Odin meant it to be."

"We...can...stop this." I can't breathe. I'm dead, it shouldn't matter, but it does. My hands grab hold of Elinor's shoulders for support, but the force of my weight pushes her deeper into the mud.

It's too late. We were always going to be too late. The hatchet is

thrust down, and what's left of the crowd jeers and cheers as it splits open Alfarin's face.

A hail of thin black sticks rains down. Cheers turn to screams as those still standing collapse like dominoes. There is a roar as a mass of fur-clad men rush into the muddy circular space where the other Alfarin is now lying lifeless on the ground.

Our Alfarin jerks out of the catatonic state he has been in for the last five minutes. He pulls me back farther into the shed.

"My clan, my family" is all he says.

Elinor is trying to get to her feet, but she's like a newborn foal struggling to stand on wobbly legs. Alfarin wraps his arms around her and picks her up. Her eyes are rolling in her head and showing way too much white for my liking. They're eerily reminiscent of the eyes of newbie devils.

"Medusa, Medusa." I try to pull my best friend up, but for someone so little and skinny, she has turned into a dead weight.

"They killed him. They murdered him like an animal." Medusa has gone into shock. Her eyes aren't rolling like Elinor's, but they can't seem to fix on anything, either.

"Mitchell, do you still have the Viciseometer?" asks Alfarin.

"Of course."

"Take us forward one hour, please."

"*What?* Are you insane? We need to go *back* an hour. Alfarin, we need to go back several weeks and stop you from getting in the longboat in the first place."

"This is my death, my friend. Now take us forward one hour. It will be the last request I make of you, you have my word."

Cursing the stubbornness of friends, I chart time on the white face of the Viciseometer. I don't need to change the red face, but I turn it over and pass it to Alfarin.

"You can't visualize what you haven't seen, Alfarin."

"I am taking us into that wooded area, by the water," replies Alfarin, pointing into the smoke-filled distance. "I can visualize that. I need to see how this ends."

I'm confused, but I don't have the energy or willpower to argue

about anything anymore. I feel more drained of life than at any other time in the four years since my death.

"Hold on," orders Alfarin. "Mitchell, take the Viciseometer with me."

I take Medusa in my arms. "I'm so sorry I got you into this" is all I can say.

I make a grab for the Viciseometer, just as the invisible fire crushes me into a black hole.

The screams of the dead are blown away by the howling wind. We have arrived amid dying trees clustered together like rotting bodies.

The sky is black as ink, pitch dark, without moon or stars. The village is still burning, but not as ferociously as when we first arrived. The snow has dampened the fires.

"Why are we here, Alfarin?" I ask. I'm so exhausted I can't stand anymore. Alfarin is the only one on his feet. Both Medusa and Elinor are flat on their backs.

"This was my final journey," replies Alfarin. "I want to see it with my own eyes."

He's standing behind a tree that has split down the middle. I force myself to join him. I don't care anymore if we're seen. I just want this day to end so we can get out of here. We should never have started with Alfarin's violent death. We should have started with one that was more... more... Who am I kidding? Not one of our deaths was easy. We died young, which isn't natural or peaceful. What have I done by bringing them all here?

"Thank you, my friend. I am honored to share this moment in my time with you, my brother."

I rest my arm around Alfarin's broad shoulders. We're from different countries, different cultures, and different times, but we are brothers nonetheless.

A longboat is beached on the shore. Six men make a solemn procession through a torchlit crowd. On their shoulders is a long, lumpy package wrapped in red cloth.

It is Alfarin.

His dead body is lowered into the center of the longboat. Someone I immediately recognize from Hell places Alfarin's axe on top of the cloth. It is Alfarin's father, King Hlif.

There are no tears, no wailing. Just silent respect. The torches are thrown on top of Alfarin's shroud and the longboat begins to blaze. His clan wades into the water and pushes the boat out. It is captured quickly by the choppy water, and it rocks to and fro as it burns.

"This is beautiful, Alfarin," whispers Medusa. She and Elinor have come around, and the four of us stand and watch the longboat burn.

"We can leave now," says Alfarin, and he bows his head. I'll never say a word to anyone, but I'm pretty sure I see a single tear slowly trickle down his face.

Alfarin's soul has returned.

I start to map coordinates into the Viciseometer. I'm taking us back to New York.

But then I realize there is one last thing left to do.

"Alfarin," I call as Medusa and Elinor loop their arms either side of mine.

"Yes, my friend."

"Your clan. They've always claimed they saw you in death, just after your burial."

Medusa immediately gets it and gasps. Elinor and Alfarin are a little slower and look confused.

I point to a gap in the trees. "They saw you, man. This is the moment they saw you. You have to go out there and show them that you're okay."

"Oh, Mitchell!" exclaims Elinor excitedly. "Ye are right. They saw ye time-traveling, Alfarin. It was real."

That faithful axe is swung into the air and Alfarin strides out of the wood and into the open. Medusa, Elinor, and I watch from the shadows. Elinor has her fingers in her mouth; Medusa is muttering, "Ohmygodohmygodohmygod."

We can see Alfarin's clan bathed in the eerie flickering firelight.

At first they don't see our Alfarin, but then suddenly a cry goes up. Fingers start to point and heads start to turn. I recognize Thomason, Alfarin's cousin. Alfarin's uncle Magnus is standing next to his father, and splashing in the icy water is Odd, who is a second cousin twice removed or something, and who lives up to his name in more ways than one. Apparently a hundred years ago he married a banana.

It seems wrong to witness something so private, but I keep watching anyway. Alfarin raises his hand in farewell and steps back into the shadows. Medusa and Elinor are bawling their eyes out now and clutching at each other tightly. The figures on the shoreline do not move.

"Ready?"

Alfarin nods; he has a serene expression on his face. He's at peace. He died with honor and his clan passed him on to the other side with respect.

I know we won't be coming back.

15. There were two in the bed and the little one said...

I take us back to the hotel room, but twelve hours after we left. I want it dark. It's safer in the dark, for us, anyway. Once the screaming of trapped souls has stopped ringing in my ears, I hear rapid knocking on the door again. The handle rattles. Someone is being persistent. Have they seriously been out there half the day?

"Get in the bathroom," I order the others.

"If it is the Skin-Walkers, then we go together," says Alfarin.

"Do ye honestly think the Skin-Walkers are going to knock on the door?" says Elinor, sinking into a chair. I've never heard Elinor use sarcasm before. It suits her.

"If it's the Skin-Walkers, they can damn well wait until I've had a bath," says Medusa. She pulls off her filthy hiking boots and drops them in a leather wastebasket.

The door opens with a crash. A young woman, in a short dress with white cuffs and a starched collar, falls through sideways. She has a white ceramic plate of small chocolates in one hand and a set of jangling key cards in the other; she must be here to turn down the bed.

"Careful, Mitchell," teases Medusa. "Maid service is here to take you away to be beaten with dirty towels for the rest of eternity."

Elinor starts to giggle. I notice she's shaking. It can't be because of the cold—we have the thermostat in the room turned up to its highest level. It's like Hell in here.

The maid takes one look at the four of us, offers a mumbled apology, and runs, taking the chocolates with her. I can't blame her. We're covered in mud and we stink like the cesspit of a hospital dedicated to people with gastric issues. Medusa's hair is now going to need its own passport because, unlike the rest of us, it's alive.

"I need some time alone, my friends," says Alfarin softly. He dries the wet blade of his axe and carefully places it back in its guitar case. I nod and watch him as he leaves the hotel room. He won't go far. We're his family now.

Medusa has already taken ownership of the bathroom, so I take a key card and use the shower in the other room. I lose track of time under the deathly-hot spray.

When I get back to the main room I realize Elinor has also left. I'm hoping she's gone after Alfarin. She may be the oldest member of the team, but Elinor has a naïveté about her. Someone needs to look out for her, and Alfarin won't go far if he knows Elinor has followed him.

Alfarin was amazing today. I just hope he won't regret his decision not to change his death. Then again, maybe he never intended to change it. He seemed to just want to witness it.

I look around the room. It's gotten very dirty since we arrived. A thin layer of pale dust, like fine ash, covers every surface. It wasn't there before we left, and in real time we were only gone half a day.

I curse as I run my finger along a polished mahogany table.

It's us. We're contaminating the room simply by being here.

The bathroom door opens and a blast of swirling steam gushes out. Medusa is wearing short pajama shorts—with sheep, of all things, printed on them. I can see her pink diamond tummy ring glistening in a small pool of water around her belly button, although I probably shouldn't look that closely because I'll get a slap around the head if she realizes.

"I thought you had an aversion to sheep," I tease.

"I have an aversion to someone telling me I smell like one."

"Did you seriously bring your pajamas with you?"

"I was prepared."

"Freak."

"I don't care what you think," she replies, sticking her little button nose in the air. She makes a little *humph* noise and climbs onto the bed and sticks her skinny legs under the white covers.

"I think Elinor went after Alfarin."

"Good," replies Medusa. "He shouldn't be alone."

"I'm getting room service. Want anything?"

"BLT with fries, blueberry cheesecake and ice cream, and see if they can bring up some Diet Coke and coffee, and a basket of dinner rolls, and lots of butter, and maybe some jam…"

Once Medusa has finished listing enough food to feed Hell for a week, I order for both of us. Alfarin and Elinor still haven't returned by the time the cart is wheeled in by three staff members. I only give one tip, which doesn't go over so well. They'll probably spit in my next order.

"Do you think I should go look for them?"

"They'll be fine, Mitchell," says Medusa thickly. She has shoved a handful of fries into her mouth.

"Alfarin and Elinor don't know this city, Medusa. Anything could happen to them."

"Will you stop worrying for one second? Alfarin and Elinor have probably read every book in the library. They'll know more about this time and city than we do, and anyway, what could happen to them here that could possibly be worse than what we witnessed today?"

She has a point. Medusa is amazing in the way she can think ahead and back at the same time. My head aches just thinking about the now.

"Whose death do you think we should see next?"

"I'm not sure I'm quite ready to visit mine yet," says Medusa softly. She's sliding her finger through the topping of the blueberry cheesecake. Previously I would have made a smutty joke, but now all I can think about is her death.

"Who was he, Medusa? The one you wanted to take with you."

She pauses and extracts her finger from the cheesecake. Her face looks pained, as if she has something trapped in her throat. "*He was my stepfather,*" she says eventually.

"Do you want to talk about it?"

Medusa smiles. It isn't her openmouthed, dazzling-teeth, happy smile. It's sad and thoughtful.

"Not right now."

I wish Medusa wouldn't keep secrets from me, but I don't push it. I have the Viciseometer, so I have all the time in this world and the next, and I can put it on hold until she's ready.

Medusa is yawning. Our internal body clocks are all over the place. It's like celestial jet lag, which has got to be worse than living jet lag. Now that she's started, I can barely keep my own eyes open.

"You take the bed, I'll take the sofa," I say, placing the now-empty platters of food back on the cart. I open the door and wheel it out. I jog along the carpeted corridor and have a quick look around, but there's no sign of Alfarin or Elinor. I hope they're all right. They still haven't washed off the thousand-year-old layer of mud we were soaked in, and more worryingly, they don't have any money. They may think they know this time from reading books, but it's not the same as living it.

As I walk back along the corridor, I notice that a huge arrangement of flowers has started to wilt. Pink-and-white petals are falling like a ticker-tape parade. I reach out and touch something that could be a lily, I'm not sure, and it disintegrates into ash between my fingers.

Death has made me poisonous.

Feeling ill, and not because I've eaten so much, I head back toward the room. I'm getting my coat and I'm going to look for Alfarin and Elinor. Team DEVIL is safer together.

But Medusa is on her cell phone talking to Elinor. When she says "El," it sounds like "Hell" and I get strange pangs of what I think is homesickness. I want to talk to Septimus. I want to explain why I did this. He would understand, I'm sure of it.

I hope I didn't get him into trouble.

"El and Alfarin are in the park," says Medusa, disconnecting the call after she has told Elinor she loves her. "They're talking."

"As long as they're okay."

"El also said she wants to go next."

"Do you think that's a good idea?"

"Why wouldn't it be?"

"Because Elinor is more...more delicate than everyone else, and like she said earlier, we have to go to the place of death to see how to change it."

"El is tougher than you think, Mitchell," replies Medusa.

She turns off the main lights in the room but leaves a bedside lamp on. Dark shadows start creeping up the walls. They don't match the shape of anything in the room. The skin on my arms puckers like a chicken leg as the hairs rise. Medusa plumps the bed pillows and flops down. The shadows look as if they're reaching for her, so I turn on another lamp to scare them away.

I grab a pillow from the cupboard and pull out a toffee-colored blanket as well. I'm not looking forward to sleeping on the sofa. I'm at least two feet too tall for it.

"We can share the bed, you know," calls Medusa. Her voice is muffled by the covers. She has buried herself underneath them so that only the top of her head is showing. Curls are splayed over the pillow.

I immediately drop the blanket and pillow on the carpet. "You sure?"

"I think I'll be able to resist jumping you."

I slip in beside her.

"Do you want to put a pillow or something between us?" I ask.

"I'll just use Alfarin's axe to chop off anything that comes wandering in my direction," she says, giggling.

We turn off the lamps and are in darkness.

Outside, New York City continues as normal. The noise of the living is back as sirens wail and car horns blare. We can hear music from somewhere: a heavy thumping bass that vibrates in my back teeth. Raised voices and laughter echo all around. Then there is a long howl, but it doesn't sound right. Not like a normal dog howl. It rises and falls, like howling laughter. Medusa reaches out and grabs my hand, but her fingers grope along my thigh first as she tries to find my fingers in the dark.

I swear I can feel my heart beating. I'm lying on the mattress like a statue in a tomb. I don't know where to put my hands, legs, or head, so I stay straight and completely still, staring up at the black ceiling.

Medusa rolls toward me and hooks her leg over mine; her arm wraps around my waist. She's so warm, it's like having a hot water bottle on top of me. I pull my arm free and move it up toward her head, which is now resting on my chest.

"You were amazing today," she says. My fingers have spread out a bit and are massaging the whole of her neck. She's so warm and soft. Her hand comes to rest against my chest where my dead heart lies useless and shriveled.

"It was pretty full-on, wasn't it?"

"Scary."

"Terrifying."

"Are you glad we came with you now?"

"Yeah, I'm glad you came."

A satisfied sigh escapes her lungs. A devil never breaks the habit of breathing. I feel her body go limp on top of mine, and as I continue to massage her soft neck, contented little purrs sneak out of her mouth.

Medusa has fallen asleep. She doesn't hear the howling laughter coming closer and closer until I swear it's right outside the bedroom window.

We are on the tenth floor.

16. **4 September 1666**

I have time in my hands, yet I have completely lost track of it. Am I in the past, the future, or the now? I just don't know anymore. Alfarin and Elinor come back to us after I doze off with Medusa slumped across my chest. They have another key card with them, and they do try to be quiet, but Alfarin has the build of a baby elephant. It's inevitable that he'll trip over something while trying to tiptoe across the darkened room. As it turns out, it's his axe that betrays him; he left the guitar case lying on the carpet. He goes ass over heels and crashes into the table. Elinor thinks he's being dragged away by some freakish entity of doom and starts shrieking. Medusa flings herself out of the bed but manages to knee me between the legs in the process, and I am now in so much agony I think I must be dying again.

I'm definitely in the present. Pain doesn't stay with a person this long unless it's real.

Elinor goes next door for a shower and Medusa follows her. I think they want to gossip, although what they could possibly have to talk about is beyond my understanding. All Medusa has done is eat and sleep.

Alfarin squeezes himself into our shower, and I find some clean clothes for him out of the stuff the girls bought last night. He isn't self-conscious about showing off his body, and he walks around the room, dripping wet, with a bath towel barely covering him. He has a tattoo of a longboat on his right shoulder. I think it will mean more to him now.

I've been thinking about getting inked, but I can't decide on a design. I like those full-on sleeves. But I'd need to work out a bit more, because they'd look sort of stupid on skinny arms.

Once I've stopped my death, I'll get both arms tattooed.

Medusa comes back to the room, grabs some clothes, and disappears again. Alfarin and I make small talk.

"You all right?"

"Yes, my friend."

Alfarin and I are such good friends, we only need six words.

Medusa and Elinor come back into the room. They're playing twins again. Both are dressed in gray skinny jeans and black T-shirts. They also have their hair tied back, although Medusa's curls are already escaping and falling around her face.

No one mentions the imprints filled with dark gray powder that cover the white sheets where Medusa and I slept.

We are molting death.

The Viciseometer is in my hand. "I need the date, Elinor."

She's sweating and looking as green as I've ever seen her. Both of her hands are on the nape of her neck now. It's almost as if she's checking to be sure her head is still attached to her shoulders. Elinor squeezes Alfarin's arm.

"Promise me ye will do exactly as I ask," she says to him.

Alfarin kisses her hand. "I am your slave."

"Ye know my date of death, Mitchell. It was my birthday: the fourth of September," she says. Her voice is breaking; Elinor is terrified. Yet if anyone deserves a second chance at life, it's Elinor, and if we can stop such a horrible death, that can only be a good thing. Right?

"What time do you want to take us back to, Elinor?"

"It was midafternoon. The boys had come back to tell us that the fire had reached Fleet Street, so try three o'clock."

I don't need reminding of the year: 1666. Devils who died in that year were all given a commemorative pin. It has an enameled image of The Devil with the year imprinted underneath.

The Viciseometer starts to whistle and vibrate long before I've finished inputting the coordinates for time travel. It can sense the expectation of everyone in the room. The snakes on the rim seem to connect with my stomach, which is squirming and writhing with nerves.

"You'll have to imagine it, Elinor," I say, "but don't land us in the fire. We need to be hidden bystanders at first."

"I understand," she says, resting her slim fingers on the Viciseometer as it vibrates in my hand. Elinor gazes at Alfarin with tears in her eyes.

"This is what I was talking about earlier when ye and I were alone in the park," she says strangely. "This is why we were meant to be friends in the Afterlife."

Medusa and I look at each other. She is as confused as I am, which is a relief. I don't want to be the only one out of the loop.

"Ye must hold onto someone now," instructs Elinor. She screws up her face with concentration and the red surface of the Viciseometer face starts to swirl.

"*Now.*"

Screams, much louder than before, echo in the suffocating darkness. Something else is traveling with us. I sense the metallic smell of blood and hot, panting breath. It isn't human. I can feel traces of something fine against my skin, like cobwebs, and then I feel fingers, groping at my body.

We arrive in a blanket of smoke. Everyone falls to their knees.

"There was something there, in the darkness!" cries Medusa. Her eyes are bulging in their sockets.

"What was that noise?" booms Alfarin. "It wasn't human."

"I felt it, something grabbed me."

"I don't want to do that again," says Medusa. She rubs at her arms, as if trying to warm them up.

"Perhaps I didn't do it right," says Elinor, panic-stricken, and she takes her fingers away from the Viciseometer. Tiny reds sparks are spitting around the rim, but it doesn't burn my hand.

"There was nothing wrong with the way you used it, El," says Medusa supportively.

"Listen, everyone. The fire must be near," says Alfarin. "I can hear the crackling from here."

For the first time we take in our new surroundings. We have arrived in yet another rickety wooden tenement. The smell of piss makes my eyes water. Several burlap sacks are stacked up in a corner. Two mice lie dead on the ground.

"Are we in yet another toilet?" I ask.

"This is an old warehouse. Old man Blinkerton used to trade out of here. He's moved to new premises down by the river," replies Elinor. Her past has already become her present.

She walks to a wooden door, which is banging against the frame, and opens it a fraction.

"Do you live near here, El?"

Elinor nods. A glazed, almost drunken expression has spread across her freckled face.

"I haven't seen our John or William in over three hundred years," she sighs. "They're just as I remember them."

"You can see your brothers?" we all cry, rushing to her side.

We peer out of the crack. My eyes don't immediately fall on the two kids fighting in the narrow street. Instead, they're gripped by the blaze of tangerine flame that hovers in the skyline. It may be afternoon, but above the fire, the sky is black. Thick chunks of ash are falling like dirty snow.

"What would you like us to do, Mitchell?" asks Alfarin. "We are in your hands once more."

"I think this one is going to be easy," I reply confidently. "I think we just need to grab Elinor from wherever she is at this moment and get her out of that... that... is that thatched building your house, Elinor?"

"Hold on a second," interrupts Medusa. "We aren't really

117

thinking this through properly. What happens when you rescue the living El? What happens to the version we already have? We can't have two Elinors."

I can't believe I haven't thought of this. I'm kicking myself for not bringing along the reference book on the Viciseometer and I'm mentally thumbing through its pages when a bomblike blast ricochets through the narrow cobbled street. The sound of screaming slices through the air. Medusa and Elinor are thrown off their feet as the wooden door disintegrates into matchsticks, sending lethal splinters flying through the air like daggers.

Alfarin takes the full force of the blast. His head smacks into the wall with a sickening thud.

"Alfarin!" screams Elinor. She crawls along the floorboards to where Alfarin is now lying unconscious. His axe is still in his hand.

Medusa and I rush over to our friend. He's out cold. A pink lump the size of a plum is already forming on the side of his enormous head.

"What now, Mitchell?" screeches Medusa.

"Elinor, you stay with Alfarin. Medusa and I will go into your house and..." But I shut up because Elinor is absolutely freaking out.

"*It has to be Alfarin!*" she screams. "*When the time comes, it has to be him!*"

"What are you talking about?"

"It has to be him. He was the one. It's all gone wrong."

I have no idea what Elinor is screaming about and I don't have time to find out. The fire's crackling has been replaced by a roar. The inferno is coming closer by the second.

Medusa starts pulling at my arm. "We have to go now," she urges me.

I hand Elinor the Viciseometer.

"You know how to use it if you have to get away."

"It isn't mine!" she cries, tears streaming down her soot-covered face.

"Didn't stop me."

We leave Alfarin and Elinor in the cramped warehouse; the sound of Elinor begging Alfarin to wake up disappears in the gusting hot wind. The two little boys have vanished into the thatched building, but we can hear them yelling from inside.

The scene is chaotic. People of all shapes and sizes are running in all directions. No one seems to know the way out of this labyrinth of flame. Just minutes ago the fire was on the horizon. Now it is only doors away. Wood and straw ignite quickly as if soaked in accelerant. The ash falling from the black, heavy sky sticks to my skin. It gets into my nostrils and throat. Medusa's long eyelashes are coated, and her hair is now as gray as her jeans, aging her by fifty years.

We head into the pitiful house Elinor called home. We can hear her living voice, and it sends chills up my spine. If she sees us, she won't know us.

Several adults burst through the entrance. They're covered in black ash, but I get the impression they weren't that clean to begin with. A woman with a dirty white cap on her head lurches forward. Greasy red strands of hair fall from her headpiece, and she tucks them behind her ears. Just the way our Elinor does.

Totally unprovoked, the woman slaps Medusa hard across the face. My best friend falls to the ground.

"Get ye out of my house, ye filthy whore!" screams the woman. "Did ye think ye could steal my belongings whilst the fire burns? Ye stinkin' maggot."

"Touch her again and it'll be the last thing you do!" I yell, pushing the woman away. Medusa is sobbing on the ground and her pale skin is now shining bright pink, seared with the outline of short fingers. I pull her to her feet and shield her behind me.

"Stop yer screechin', ye stupid bitch!" cries an older male with barely any teeth; those that do remain in his sore-covered mouth are stained yellow and brown. "Get the food in the cart before some other stinkin' thief tries to take off with it."

"Get the pigs," grunts another male. He has a deformed arm, which hangs limply at his side. The adults ignore the screaming from upstairs.

"Elinor and two of the boys are up there!" I shout, but the adults ignore me. They're grabbing pots and dirty, cracked plates and are loading up a wooden cart outside. The screams are getting louder by the second. A fat, bearded face pokes through the entrance.

"Bert, Jacob, the fire has reached the McDonalds' house. The firemen pulled it down with old man McDonald and the little 'uns still inside," he croaks. He coughs blood onto his arm. "Get yerselves out of here now. Head eastward, away from the wind."

"What about the kids?" I yell as Bert, Jacob, and the old hag who slapped Medusa join the masses streaming away from the approaching roar.

"Get away from me, boy!" snarls the man with the deformed arm. He has a squealing piglet tucked under his armpit. He smells so bad I'm amazed the piglet hasn't been knocked unconscious.

"Let them go," sobs Medusa, pulling at my arm. "We'll get El and the boys."

The man with rotten teeth suddenly stops. "Boys, ye say? Are my boys up there?"

"And Elinor!" screams Medusa. The pain and humiliation have passed. By the way her back teeth are clenched, I'm sure she's going to punch someone soon.

"Girls are no use to me," snarls the man. "Just another mouth to feed, but I'll take my boys."

Thick black smoke is starting to condense in the room. I can't see the wooden staircase anymore. The living are coughing up the linings of their lungs, while Medusa and I are fighting the reflex to breathe. The screaming upstairs has stopped.

The man with rotten teeth yells out, "John, William, get yer backsides down here!" but no one comes. He hovers by a wooden chair with broken spindles and then runs out of the house.

"He left them!" screams Medusa. "They left their children to die in the fire."

"Yeah, but we're here!" I shout over the roaring and spitting firestorm, which has already reached us. "We need to do this now, Medusa."

I run blindly up the stairs. The wooden boards are uneven and loose. I lose my footing before I'm even halfway up and slip down. Medusa runs past me, skipping up the steps two at a time as if she were weightless.

Terrified that the floor will give way with Medusa up there, I pull myself to my feet and clamber up after her. We can't see our hands in front of our faces. The smoke is as black as coal and the heat's intensity tells me that this building is already on fire.

Parts of the ceiling collapse with a thunderous roar. Flaming wood and thatch crash down to our left. There is a pitiful scream to our right as some of the dense smoke is sucked out of the newly created hole above our heads.

"Elinor!" screams Medusa. "Elinor, it's us, we're here to save you."

"She won't know who we are!" I cry back. "She hasn't met us yet."

A figure in a dirty white dress appears in a doorway.

"I cannot move our John or William," says the living Elinor, choking. "Ye must help me."

I run into the room. The two little boys we saw fighting earlier are huddled together in a corner. Their green eyes are as big as Brussels sprouts. I try to pick one up, but he starts slapping and hitting me. I drop him after he bites me on the shoulder. He gags and spits at the taste of my dead flesh.

"Elinor, can you hold them long enough to drop them out of the window?" I yell as another part of the ceiling falls down. Burning thatch scatters throughout the landing as the embers set fire to the wooden stairs.

"Yes!" she screams back.

"Then drop them to me. I'll catch them and then you."

The living Elinor doesn't know who we are, but she accepts us immediately as people who just want to help. Our Elinor. As trusting in life as she is in death. There are no words of hate against the family that deserted her.

I run back out, pulling Medusa by the hand. We fall down the stairs, landing in a heap at the bottom. The downstairs is ablaze. The fact that we can't die again is cold comfort now that we're back in the land of the living, because Hell is actually safer than this inferno. We dodge the flames and run back out into the street. People are crying and screaming and trying to escape the red monster that is now devouring everything in its path. I secretly hope the fire gets that woman who slapped Medusa. I don't care if she was Elinor's mother.

A face appears at one of the windows. It is Elinor. She has the smaller child in her arms. He has yanked off her cloth cap and is pulling at her hair.

"Drop him now, Elinor!" I cry.

The toddler falls with a scream, but I catch him in my arms before his head hits the cobbled street. A young woman who is heavily pregnant scoops him up and sets him in her cart.

"Hurry, Elinor!" screams the woman. "Throw down young John."

The older boy doesn't fight as much as his brother, but Elinor is struggling. She staggers several times before levering him out of the window. I can see the flames directly behind her. I catch the boy again, although his legs land with a heavy thud on the cobbles. He screams out in pain.

"We'll find Elinor!" I yell at the pregnant woman. "Now get out of here."

With a strength that awes me, the pregnant woman grabs the shafts of the cart and starts to pull it. The boys scream for their sister, but they don't move as they trundle away to safety.

Fire has now taken hold of the houses on either side of Elinor's. Men aren't trying to fight the fire with water; they're just pulling down houses farther up the street. People are still screaming and crying and searching for loved ones. It's absolute pandemonium.

"Elinor, you have to jump now!" screams Medusa, but we can't see Elinor anymore. Smoke belches out of the broken window.

Then there's a sickening crack, like a giant bone being snapped in half, and the entire second floor implodes. The instinct to survive doesn't vanish just because a person is dead, and both Medusa and I jump back as enormous orange-and-blue flames leap into the air.

And then the screaming starts.

I now understand why victims of the Skin-Walkers have their tongues taken out, because the cry of true torture is unbearable. It burrows into every fiber of your being. My stomach heaves as the dying cries of the living Elinor clutch at my soul.

We came to save her, to stop her death and give her a second chance at life, and we have failed.

A huge figure suddenly barges past me. The blade of an axe reflects the hungry flames.

"Alfarin, what are you doing?" screams Medusa.

But he doesn't stop. He runs into the burning shell and disappears.

Before I realize what I'm doing, I run in after him.

17. Blade and Flame

My skin is already blistering in the heat. Two wooden beams, one upright, the other lying across the top of it at a ninety-degree angle, create a tunnel into the remains of the house. If they fall, the entire building is coming down. Trying to see in this blinding mass of smoke is hopeless, but I have one sense that I can use.

My hearing.

The living Elinor is screaming like a trapped animal. We knew she died because her house collapsed on top of her, but I never imagined it took her this long to pass over. The harrowing, gut-churning sound is coming from the kitchen area where Medusa was attacked earlier. Elinor must have fallen straight through the ceiling.

I know that's where Alfarin is now, and a glimmer of hope resurrects itself in the darkness of my mind.

This house is made of wood, and Alfarin has his axe. We can still get the living Elinor out.

With my left arm raised above my head, I push through the burning beams. Alfarin is only a few feet away from me. I tread on his axe, which is lying on the ground, inches from the living Elinor's blackened and bloody face.

She is pinned down on her stomach beneath two thick pieces of wood. One is across her legs; the other is across her back. Blood is filling Elinor's mouth.

"We have to move this one first!" I shout to Alfarin, pointing to the beam across Elinor's back. One end is on fire, and I frantically start stamping on sparking embers that are threatening to set Elinor's long dress alight.

Alfarin and I position ourselves on either side of the beam and try to raise it, but it's jammed fast by other pieces of the walls and ceiling that have come down on top of it. We try again and again. Alfarin is stronger than ten men, but we can't raise it an inch. We get so frustrated we start kicking it, but the beam won't move.

Living Elinor's head is twisted to the side and blood is leaking out of her mouth; she's gagging on it. Her internal organs are being pulped. Soon she'll be drowning in her own blood.

The flames are now all around us. We have no way of extinguishing them. Alfarin's T-shirt catches fire and I jump on him to smother it before the flames take hold. Then Elinor screams out in agony. It's primal, like a woman giving birth.

Her dress is ablaze.

Alfarin picks up his axe and starts chopping at the wood, but the second he does, the beams that are resting above us start to vibrate violently. Everything is about to come crashing down.

I take off my T-shirt and start beating out the flames on Elinor's dress. I swear I can feel my skin bubbling and blistering in the heat.

"I don't want to die like this," sobs Elinor. Pockets of blood are erupting from her mouth and nostrils.

"We can't get her out, Alfarin!" I shout. Panic is spreading through me. How have we managed to screw this up again?

"Please don't let me die like this," begs the living Elinor. She is pleading with Alfarin, who is on his hands and knees by her face.

"I understand," he says quietly, and he bends down and kisses Elinor on the forehead.

"Make it quick," begs Elinor.

"I will see you on the other side, my princess," says Alfarin, and he picks up his axe, grabs hold of the wooden handle with two hands, and raises it above his head.

I realize what he is going to do a split second before the blade slices through the flame.

"*Alfarin, no!*"

I crumple onto the beam that has pinned Elinor's legs. I am now burning in the pits of a living Hell. We came here to save Elinor, not kill her.

Alfarin grabs hold of me and starts to pull me away. I fight back. I don't want him touching me. More beams start to fall. Let them come. Bury me in this inferno. I deserve to burn in Hell for the rest of eternity for what I have started.

"Take us back!" roars Alfarin.

I feel freezing hands on me. Everything is cold now. I'm encased in ice. That was one of Dante's circles of a mythical Hell. The ninth circle, reserved for the treacherous. What greater betrayal could we have committed than this one?

The screaming comes quickly. Burning hands grabbing and pulling in the darkness. Harder and faster than before. And now the howling. The baying wolves of death are coming for us.

"Get them into the shower. The water needs to be ice cold."

Medusa and our Elinor are taking charge. I let them manipulate my body the way a mother would a baby because I am helpless.

Alfarin and I are pushed into the shower; I collapse onto the tiled floor. Elinor turns the dial and freezing water gushes onto our smoking, burned, dead bodies.

"Should we remove their clothes?" asks Elinor.

My eyes lazily trail across the bathroom to where Medusa is standing. Everything is in slow motion. Medusa is in front of the sink with Alfarin's axe in her hands. She is scrubbing the blade. The water runs red.

"Don't look, El," sobs Medusa, but Elinor places a hand softly on Medusa's back.

"It's okay," she says quietly. "I've been waiting four hundred years for this day to come."

And now Medusa is crying violently. She is bent over the sink and her shoulders are heaving. I look up at Alfarin. The water is streaming through his singed beard and hair. His pale skin is red and is blistering. I don't need a mirror to know mine is doing the same, but we stay silent through the pain.

We deserve it.

Alfarin's eyes are closed, and Elinor is comforting Medusa. No one can see me crying. I put my fist into my mouth and bite down hard.

Medusa slumps onto the toilet seat. Elinor hands her several tissues. Then she wipes Alfarin's axe and takes it back into the main bedroom. The rest of us are in pieces, and yet our Elinor is as calm as a summer day.

I don't understand. Why isn't she screaming at us for what we've just done to her? That filthy axe is not something to be revered and handled with care. It is treacherous. Elinor has just watched Medusa wash her own blood from its blade. For centuries Elinor has hung out with Alfarin, waiting patiently for Medusa and me to join them. She said it was fate that we were friends.

Why doesn't she hate us? We're the reason she is dead. And all this time she knew.

Elinor knew.

I pull off my soaking-wet sneakers, socks, and jeans. My T-shirt remains in 1666, incinerated along with everything else in that house, that street, that city. The rubber soles of my Converses have melted. Every inch of my skin is pulsing with pain.

"We'll need some salve for your burns, Mitchell," sniffles Medusa. She wipes her eyes with the tissues, blows her nose, and stands up.

I don't know what to say, so I don't bother. I remove myself from the shower and stand in dripping-wet boxer shorts on the cold tiled floor. Medusa starts to pat me down with a fluffy white towel.

"You were both so incredibly brave," she says quietly. Medusa bites down on her bottom lip, but she can't stop the tears from coming again.

"We killed her."

Medusa shakes her head vehemently. "You saved her."

"I killed her," says Alfarin. He is still smoldering under the water. He looks waxy, like a mannequin. His eyes are red and swollen. The black pupils have completely disappeared.

"*You saved her!*" shouts Medusa. "Don't either of you realize what you've done for her?"

I smash my fist into the door. Screaming, with my burned lungs bleeding into my mouth, I pound the door again and again and again. I need to feel more pain on the outside. The burns are not enough. I have to be consumed by it. It's the only way I can get rid of the agony in my head.

When things get tough, the living will often complain that they wish they were dead. How stupid and naïve can you get? Do you think you can get rid of all the crap in your life by ending it? There is no escape, not ever. The pain and sins in your head will stay with you for all eternity, and now I am cursed with the death of one of my best friends. For the rest of my existence I will carry the burden that my selfishness caused Elinor to die. I didn't strike the blow across her throat, but I was the reason the axe was there in the first place.

I was right all along. I'm a danger to them, and I should have had the balls to do this alone.

Medusa is pulling me into the main bedroom. "Mitchell's lost it," she tells Elinor.

"Ye stay with him in here," says Elinor. "I'll see to Alfarin."

I feel Medusa's rough fingertips against the split skin of my knuckles. Then her fingers stroke my face.

"You promised you wouldn't leave me," she says quietly. "So come back to me. Come back to me, Mitchell."

"I'm evil, Medusa."

"You're anything but, Mitchell. You are the most loyal person I know. You would do anything for your friends—anything."

Her skinny arms wrap around me and I let my head fall onto her shoulder. Another oath is secretly sworn, and I swear it on Elinor's blood because I will not risk any hurt to the one person I love more than anything in this world or the next.

My death is coming, and then this will be over.

18. **Fight, Fight, Fight**

Medusa and Elinor bought clean underwear for Alfarin and me on that first night in New York. The ridiculousness of it makes me want to laugh. Only girls would think like that. We've seen two of our deaths—directly caused one of them—but the world will be okay because I'm wearing new boxer shorts.

They should meet my mother. They'd all get on like a house on fire.

No, I can't ever make that joke again. Houses and fire and death—damn, I can't shake the sound of that axe. It whistled through the smoke. It was singing as it sliced through Elinor's neck.

The girls want to talk about what has happened, so they've called a meeting of Team DEVIL. Elinor feels she has to explain herself, but she doesn't seem to understand that I just want to forget that any of it happened. I certainly don't want to relive it. I'm sorely tempted to use the Viciseometer and just leave for Washington right now.

The only thing stopping me is the thought of leaving the others stranded here in this hotel room, in this city, in this world. I need a plan, but my head is on the verge of exploding with guilt. There's no room for planning, not at the moment.

Medusa is wrong; I'm a coward. I should have done this without them, but I was scared. I thought I needed help. The reality is way different. Medusa, Alfarin, and Elinor needed saving from me and my arrogance and my fears.

Medusa and Elinor are pacing in the bedroom. I'm dressed, sore from the burns, and sitting on the edge of the bed, trying not to move too quickly. You'd think my skin would be used to fire after four years in Hell, but 1666 was an inferno of pain that most devils never have to experience. Alfarin is in the bathroom; he's been in there for hours. When he comes out we all gasp because he's shaved off his beard. From the state of his mutilated face, you'd think he'd used his axe. He has bits of toilet tissue stuck to nicks all over his chin and cheeks.

He looks so ridiculous that the girls start laughing.

I just want to punch him.

I hate myself for thinking it, but I'm so angry with him right now that I want to destroy him. We could have done something differently. We *should* have done something differently. I told Elinor we would go back and drag her out when we first saw her, but she won't have it. She says she'll explain why at the meeting.

Why are Alfarin and Elinor so stubbornly refusing to change their deaths? I just don't get it. Not everyone gets a second chance. This is a huge opportunity to right wrongs—and they're passing it up.

Medusa hands me three white pills and a glass of water. It's medicine for the living, so we both know it won't work, but I appreciate the gesture. Her fingers run through my short hair, but she stops when I flinch.

"When El has said what she needs to say, I'll go out and buy some aloe vera. It's topical, so it might actually help," says Medusa softly.

"Thank you." I have no idea who or what aloe vera is, but I know Medusa is just trying to help.

The girls have their arms around each other and their heads are resting on each other's shoulders.

No chance of Alfarin and me doing that anytime soon. We can't even look at each other.

Elinor is nervous; she's pawing at the back of her neck as she always does; only now I know why.

"I know that ye all hate me right now," she begins, "but now I've seen how it all happened, I just want to thank ye both..." She trails off, her green eyes filling with tears. Now that the crisis is over, Elinor is finally going to lose it. She turns to Medusa and starts to wring her hands; she looks panic-stricken, but I couldn't hate sweet, simple Elinor if my return to life depended on it.

"We don't hate you, Elinor," I say dully. "Do you really think there's anything you can do that would make any of us hate you?"

"You always said it was fate that brought us together," says Medusa, hugging Elinor tightly.

"I knew I would find you all eventually," sobs Elinor. "It took me years to find Alfarin in Hell, but of course he didn't know who I was because he hadn't seen my death yet. And then I had to wait centuries for you two to arrive, but I checked the logs every day. When Medusa arrived, I didn't say hello until Mitchell got there, because it needed to be the four of us... and three seemed... three seemed so uneven...."

So far, Alfarin has said nothing. His eyes are fixed firmly on the carpet. He looks as if he's zoned out.

"We can still change your death, Elinor," I start, but he interrupts me.

"No, we cannot," he says slowly. His deep voice echoes around the room.

"Yes, we can," I argue. "Medusa and I can go back and drag Elinor out when we first see her. I've already said this to her."

"And what of her brothers?"

"I don't know, I'll throw them out of the window myself. Look, you weren't there, Alfarin. You were lying unconscious in some piss-drenched warehouse. You didn't see what happened. I'm telling you we can change this."

"Alfarin is right, Mitchell," says Elinor. "He understands. If ye stop my death, then it will be my brothers who die instead. Ye tried to pick them up, and ye couldn't hold on to them. They were raised in the slums. They could fight before they could talk. Ye would not have been able to get them out."

"Well, guess what, your brothers aren't my best friends!" I shout back. "So if it's a choice between their lives and yours, well, sue me for wanting to save yours."

"But the choice is mine," says Elinor gently.

The bile and heat of pure anger are now swirling inside me. I can't keep on punching windows and doors, but I swear it's the only way I can release my frustration.

"Why won't you let me help you, Elinor?" I cry. "What was the point of coming if you won't let me help you? When we passed through administration, you punched me in the face, you were so pissed, and now that we're here, now that I know how to stop your death, you won't let me."

"I didn't want ye to stop my death, Mitchell!" cries Elinor. Alfarin steps in front of her and glares at me. "I knew this was the moment when I would die, and I needed to make sure Alfarin knew what to do. I didn't want to burn slowly, Mitchell. I didn't want to die in agony. I wanted it to be quick. Ye said yerself in the house that ye couldn't stop it. Alfarin saved me. You saved me."

"*We killed you!*" I roar back.

"Do not raise your voice to her again," warns Alfarin.

"Or what? Are you going to cut my head off, too?"

Alfarin pushes me; I push him back. We start jabbing at each other, but the first punch is mine. His chin is like hot steel, but I don't care. The girls start shrieking as Alfarin and I grapple and fall to the floor. I throw punches and kicks, but I have no idea what I'm connecting with because everything feels like smashing into a solid wall. I take several blows to my stomach, and it feels as if my gut is going to shoot out of my mouth with the force.

The writing table and chair are sent flying across the room. A lamp falls on Alfarin's head. My body feels as if it has been flayed with burning whips, but the pain is a motivator. I want to pummel Alfarin's head into the carpet until he sees stars.

Medusa and Elinor are screaming at us to stop fighting. They both try to pull us apart, and our blows have to be aimed around them. I start swinging at thin air. So does Alfarin. There is wet stuff dripping from my lips. My dead blood tastes really salty, like concentrated seawater. No wonder Elinor's brother spat me out.

I know Elinor is right. If we had saved her, her brothers would have died instead. We wouldn't have been able to get all three of them out. That kid was like a Hell-cat in the way he punched and kicked. Knowing that I'm wrong about saving Elinor just fuels my anger.

I don't know if Alfarin is seeing stars yet, but I'm seeing planets. I fall to my knees as the room starts spinning. Alfarin cuffs me and knocks me over. I fall onto the open guitar case. I grab for the axe and cry from the depths of my soul as I swing it low. The blade connects with the carved leg of one of the armchairs. Elinor has admired it from the beginning of our stay, claiming it's a Queen Anne chair. Well, the only Queen Anne I know was beheaded by Henry "Chopper" VIII, and now that I have this axe in my hands, I feel like doing some chopping of my own. I'll slice through everything in the room if that's what it takes to make sense of all this.

"Stop it, Mitchell, stop it!" screams Medusa.

"Put down my axe!" cries Alfarin, and he grabs the Viciseometer from the one table in the room that hasn't toppled over. He places it on the floor, underneath his boot. "Put down my axe or I will stamp on this and destroy it forever."

It's a face-off. I clamber to my feet with my swollen lip oozing thick blood down my chin. The axe is still clenched in my hands.

Alfarin looks puffy and sweaty, and several of his shaving nicks are also oozing with thick blood. He's trying to balance on one foot, and he's wobbling like a mound of pink jelly.

A snort escapes from my nose, which is very painful; I think the lining of my nostrils is burned as well.

The ends of Alfarin's mouth start to turn up. I try not to catch his eye because I don't want to laugh; I want to cause him extreme pain.

Now his arms are flapping like windmills. If he doesn't watch out, it'll be his enormous stomach that crushes the Viciseometer, not his foot.

"I'll put down your axe if you step away from the Viciseometer." I try to look tough, but now my throat has gone into spasms. It's like trying not to laugh in math class. You can't help it. It's a hidden reflex designed to screw you over.

"I accept your surrender," says Alfarin, and he promptly falls down.

I pass the axe to Medusa and she almost drops it. That treacherous weapon is seriously heavy. Elinor scampers across the room, picks up the Viciseometer, and slips it into her back pocket.

"It wasn't a surrender," I say, walking over to Alfarin. "It's a truce. A cessation in hostilities."

He holds out a plate-sized hand. I take it. I try to pull him up, but I don't have the strength of a forklift.

"You fight well, Mitchell," he says. "You almost connected at one point."

"Dude, I totally got you at least three times."

"Did I hurt you?"

"No," I lie. "Did I hurt you?"

"Yes."

"Seriously?"

"No. I'm trying to rescue your manhood in the sight of the women. In truth, it was like being licked by puppies."

"Murderer."

"Girl."

"Want some food? Room service does an awesome BLT."

"Sounds like a plan, my friend."

The girls are staring openmouthed at the pair of us, but this is how guys do it. We get mad, we fight, and we're friends again. I

instantly feel better for having landed a few punches on Alfarin's body, even if I've shattered every bone in my right hand doing so.

Two deaths down and nothing has changed. I'm still angry at my own failures and worried sick about what's to come. I'm sitting on the floor with Medusa's back to my chest, the remote control in her hand. She wasn't too impressed by my suggestion that she feed me. In fact, she told me where I should shove my BLT and fries, which would be totally gross and unhygienic. A vibrating ringtone shrills from the pile of muddy clothes we threw in a corner after coming back from the year 970.

"What's that noise?" asks Elinor.

"Sounds like a cell phone," replies Alfarin. He burps twice in quick succession, having just demolished two main courses and half a chocolate cake.

"I think that's my cell phone," I say.

"Who on earth is calling you?" asks Medusa. She crawls across the carpet and starts rummaging. Her jeans have crept down so I can see the top of her black underwear, and I wonder if she's the type of girl who wears a matching bra. I don't know why I think of dumbass things like that when I'm stressing out, but I do.

Medusa finds the cell phone in the back pocket of my jeans. It's glowing red.

"Since when has your phone been able to do that?" she asks warily.

I don't answer, because as far as I can recall, it's never done that before.

The glowing stops. Just like the light filament in a bulb, the red fades away and the casing returns to its normal black.

"Oh, mother in Hell," gasps Medusa. She's thumbing through the directory. I know without seeing the screen that she's looking at the missed calls.

"Who was it, M?"

Medusa's face is white. Even her curls seem to have gone limp.

She looks at me with panic in her eyes and hands me the phone. As soon as it's in my hand it starts to ping and vibrate. The glow returns, and the snakes in my stomach contract as if electrocuted.

I have a message from Septimus.

He knows.

19. **Paradox**

i know

The message is just two words, but it's enough to send me into a blind panic. We have to get away. Septimus is the number one civil servant in Hell; he has no alternative but to inform the HBI if there has been a security breach. The safe in our office is full of files on them. I had to dig past several red files to get to the Viciseometer so I know, firsthand, just how much trouble we're in.

Stealing money and The Devil's credit card was bad enough, but I stole the Viciseometer: an item so fabled that even those who hear about its existence don't truly believe the reality.

"We have to leave," says Alfarin. "Immediately."

I wipe my mouth with my hand. My split lip is throbbing. In my head I can already hear the screams and howls of time travel. I agree with Alfarin, but I'm in no rush to feel the hands of the dead again. Every journey is worse. I'm terrified that next time, I'll be able to open my eyes in the darkness and actually see what is reaching for me and making the noise.

"What do ye think, Mitchell? You're the leader."

"Would it have killed Septimus to write a longer message?" I wonder aloud. The black casing of the cell phone is cold and heavy. I'm so used to the delicacy of the Viciseometer that anything else in my hands seems crude.

"A longer message about what?" asks Alfarin impatiently. "My friend, do you honestly think that Lord Septimus is basking in the glory of our escape from Hell? I would wager with the god Loki himself that our treachery has already been reported."

But I shake my head as the sensible part of my brain starts to overtake the panic. "I don't know, Alfarin. A few months before I died, I borrowed my father's car without asking. There was a party, and this girl, and . . . well, that doesn't matter. When my father found out, he didn't send me a text message saying 'I know.' He sent me a message saying he had called the cops and he had no intention of posting bail. I damn near crapped my pants. I got in that car and went straight home before the cops got me."

"Did he call the police?" asks Elinor.

"No," I reply, "but that's not the point I'm trying to make. What I'm saying is if Septimus had reported us, I figure we'd already be under arrest by now."

Everyone shudders as if a dark cloud has passed over the room. We don't have to mention the Skin-Walkers anymore to be scared of them.

"Look," I continue, "Septimus tried to call me before he sent the message. I think he wants to talk to me."

"You aren't seriously considering calling him back?" cries Medusa. "Are you insane?"

"Who has the Viciseometer?" I ask. Elinor raises her hand. Her other is already on the nape of her reconnected neck.

"Right, get your things together. We're checking out," I decide. "Everything you want to take, put in your backpack. Everything else, like dirty clothes, gets left behind. Okay?"

Alfarin and Elinor nod and start getting busy in the room. Elinor folds everything neatly, but Alfarin just starts piling clothes into his backpack like he's stuffing a turkey. Elinor slaps his hands away and takes over the organizing.

Medusa hasn't moved from my side.

"You cannot call Septimus."

"I haven't decided yet what I'm going to do."

"Yes, you have. I can see it in your eyes."

"Medusa," I say wearily, "you put way too much faith in people's eyes."

"It's the only way I can see if they're telling the truth. I lived for seventeen years among liars. I know the signs."

"Go pack, Medusa. We're leaving in two minutes."

"Where are we going?" she asks.

"I haven't decided."

"Why are you lying to me? You, of all people."

I move to hold her hands, but she jerks them away. She's biting her bottom lip and her little nostrils are flaring.

"Please don't be mad at me."

"You never had a real plan, did you, Mitchell? You've just crashed from one situation to another, making it up as you go along."

I can feel the red mist of anger descending again. I never asked Medusa to come along, or Elinor, for that matter. According to my memory, the girls gate-crashed despite my best efforts to keep them away. I only ever wanted to protect them, and now Medusa has the nerve to take a shot at me. I've been covered in crap and burned to a cinder, one of my best friends has used me for boxing practice, and I'm still no closer to stopping my death.

"If you don't like the way I'm managing this, go back to Hell, Medusa," I snap. "No one is forcing you to stay."

"Is that what you want?"

"Of course it isn't. What I want is for you to get off my back for ten seconds."

"Well, why don't you try ditching us again?" Medusa taunts with her hands on her hips. "You have the Viciseometer. You could leave us anytime you wanted."

"For the last time, I wasn't ditching you. I was trying to protect you."

"No one has ever protected me!" she screams back, arms thrown wide open.

"Why do you say things like that? Why are you blaming me for something that clearly happened when you were alive? Do you seriously think I wouldn't have tried to stop it if I had been there? I'd stop it now if you just told me the truth, but no, it's easier to have secrets, isn't it, Medusa? Maybe if you trusted *me* a bit more—"

I notice Alfarin and Elinor backing away toward the door. "Stay where you are and finish packing!" I yell at them.

Medusa opens her mouth to say something again but mercifully closes it. Instead, she grabs Elinor and drags her into the bathroom.

Loud muttering comes from within. I don't think the girls are arguing, but Medusa is getting pissed about something else now, judging by the rapid stream of words gushing from her mouth. Alfarin is just shutting the lid on the guitar case when the girls reappear. I've punched in Septimus's number and my thumb is hovering above the green key.

I miss him. I hope he knows I never wanted to let him down. If I talk to him, explain everything, maybe we can work this out. I don't want to be dead anymore, and he of all people will understand that.

Medusa and Elinor grab their bags and sling them onto their backs. Common sense has prevailed. We shouldn't fight with one another, and the girls have to understand that I'm only trying to look out for them. They're my best friends.

Elinor wraps her arm around Alfarin's biceps and hugs him tightly. "Don't forget yer axe," she whispers.

Medusa slips her hand into mine. "Can we please stop fighting, Medusa?" I ask. I see that she's also linked arms with Elinor, who has turned her back to me so I get a faceful of her backpack. Which reminds me, where is mine?

"*Now, Elinor!*" cries Medusa.

My neck jerks back as the floor falls away beneath my feet. I'm spinning in the darkness with the tortured screams of the dead passing through my head. Groping hands are replaced by teeth. I can feel them biting at me, tearing at my skin as snarling wolves circle me in the blinding black.

It's wet. We've landed face-first in shallow water. My hands and feet find the bottom of the pool and I lever my aching body up. The sun is setting, and flaming pink streaks are shooting across the indigo sky. A towering steel obelisk stands in front of us, pointing skyward to the first stars.

"What have you done, Elinor?" I choke out. "What day is this? What time?"

"Elinor took us back in time six months, which is what you should have done in the first place, Mitchell," replies Medusa. "If you hadn't kept us in the present, Septimus wouldn't have tracked us down already."

There are people staring at us, pointing. Four teenagers have just materialized out of thin air into one of the fountains next to the Eiffel Tower.

It's early evening in Paris.

In the summer.

We couldn't have asked for more witnesses if we had landed on the stage during the Super Bowl halftime show.

I am seething.

"You can't just imagine a scene from a book and take us there! Now give me the Viciseometer," I say through gritted teeth.

"No," replies Medusa. "Not until you've given me your cell phone and promised me you won't call Hell."

"I won't need to call Hell, Medusa!" I shout, splashing through the water toward Elinor. "You've just announced our existence to half of Europe. I need to fix this now before it's too late."

Alfarin leans forward, snatches the Viciseometer from Elinor's hand, and throws it to me.

"Take us back."

Medusa jumps onto my back as I start to manipulate the red needle across the dials. Her hands are around my neck as she claws for the Viciseometer. Alfarin tries to remove her and promptly trips over Elinor's long legs. The four of us splash back down into the fountain. We can hear the laughter of those watching.

I fix my thoughts on the hotel, but the dying flowers in the hall are what I see.

"Grab someone, now."

I feel as if my head has disconnected from the rest of my body. Flaming wind whips at my skin as images of the screaming dead finally emerge in the darkness. Their open mouths swirl in a cloudy gray vortex. Then the images change and blood-soaked teeth on top of human heads lunge forward for the kill.

I land on top of Elinor; Medusa is on top of me. For one panicked moment I think we've lost Alfarin, but then I see his boot sticking out from underneath Elinor. He's bearing the weight of all of us.

We're in the hallway outside our hotel room. Steam is rising from our bodies and the walls around us are streaked with a thick black coating that looks like tar. As I glance up, a black shadow shaped like an enormous dog creeps along the wall toward us. It opens its huge jaws near the girls' heads....

"I can still hear the screaming," sobs Elinor, shrinking into the doorframe opposite. "I saw the Skin-Walkers, and they saw me."

"I saw them, too," gasps Medusa. She's shivering, and her hands and lips have turned blue.

"We need to get inside the room!" I shout. The shadow disappears. "Who has the key cards?"

"I don't."

"Don't you have them?"

"I don't even have my bag, why would I have the key cards?"

"They were on the table."

"Why didn't anyone pick them up?"

Alfarin starts slamming his fist on the door. Then he rattles the handle.

"What are you doing?"

"I'm trying to get in."

"Alfarin, you need to calm down, dude." I think the big guy is starting to get spooked out by what happens when we time-travel, and if there's one person we need to keep calm, it's the one with the lethal weapon.

"Mitchell, why didn't you have the key card?" asks Medusa.

"Because I had no idea you and Elinor were planning a mutiny."

"Sssssh," says Elinor. Alfarin is still banging on the door. "Listen."

We listen at the door. We can hear voices inside our room, "Now, now, now, now," and then "*I have it!*" booms out through the door, vibrating against our ears, which are pressed up against the wood. A huge roar of wind blasts out from inside the room, and a plume of gray dust erupts from the gap beneath the door.

Silence.

"That was Alfarin's voice," says Elinor, her jaw dropping in astonishment, "and Medusa's."

"We're in a paradox," I reply, slumping to the floor. I rub my temples; I have a headache from Hell. How did we—I—make such a mess of this?

"Explain, my friend."

"A paradox is a true happening but one that defies logic," I reply, thinking back to the days when I was an avid reader of sci-fi comics, instead of *Rolling Stone* and other magazines with images that I'm sure Medusa wouldn't be happy to know about. "Remember when we were about to travel to Alfarin's death? Well, we heard people at the door, didn't we? They were trying to get in. You all started to panic that it was the Skin-Walkers. Well, it wasn't. It was us. Here. Now."

"So we were dead in there and dead out here at the same time?" asks Alfarin, scratching his face. Stubble is already starting to break through his skin, even though he shaved a few minutes ago.

"Yes."

"Is this going to mess everything up?"

I hardly have the energy to speak. I can still see the bared teeth snapping at my face. The Viciseometer is in my hand, where it belongs for now. I know I have a decision to make, but I need the courage to make it. I thought there would be safety in numbers and strength in our friendship to make this work, but I was wrong.

I'm taking the others back to Hell. To the exact moment when those heavy, vaultlike doors closed on us. It will be as if they never left in the first place, but I need to go on before everything falls apart.

I *will* go on and finish what I started.

Alone.

20. **Evil Among Us**

I need to get into the hotel room. In their rush to stage a coup d'etat, Medusa and Elinor forgot that the room card, credit card, and cash were still in my bag. They reminded Alfarin to get the guitar case with his axe but forgot about my stuff. The important stuff.

"I'm so sorry, Mitchell!" cries Elinor.

"We're losing control of time, aren't we?" says Alfarin.

"I'm not sure we ever had much control in the first place," I reply. "Look, I've got to get my stuff. I want you three to stay here, and I'll travel alone this time. As a group we're creating too much toxic waste."

"Why don't we just break the door down?" suggests Alfarin. "That lock is no rival to the blade of my axe."

"I think we've caused enough trouble today, don't you?" I reply with a sideways glance at the girls. Elinor's freckled cheeks immediately flame with embarrassment, and Medusa looks at the floor. "We can't risk drawing more attention to ourselves, and smashing in a door at the Plaza will do exactly that. I'll be a few seconds at the most."

"Ye will come back to us?"

"Yes, of course. I promise."

The Viciseometer is spitting deep-crimson sparks into my hand. It reminds me of a firework about to explode. There's something comforting about being in control of it. I'm not handling the others very well now, I'm all too aware of that, yet this little stopwatch I can manipulate. It responds to me, even down to the way it fits perfectly in the palm of my hand. It could have been made to measure.

I leave the date as it is and check my own watch for the current time. I need to start recording things the way I would on an accounting ledger. I have a good head for numbers, and I need to start paying better attention.

The room materializes on the pixelated red face of the Viciseometer. I don't look at the others as I press the large button. I tense in anticipation of the screaming, the bared, bloody teeth of the wolves.

But there is only silence.

I land in the hotel room, and for the first time, I remain on my feet. Everything unclenches. My stomach is spinning, but that's it. Death didn't reach for me. The Skin-Walkers weren't there to scare the crap out of me. Even my scorched skin is feeling cooler and more comfortable.

I open the bedroom door and the relief on all three faces is obvious. Medusa and Elinor fall on top of me and I'm smothered with hair.

"Those were the longest five seconds of my death," says Alfarin, slapping me on the shoulder.

"What was it like, traveling on your own?" asks Medusa. She hasn't let go of me, and her skinny little arms are wrapped around my waist.

"Nothing happened." I drape my arm over her shoulder and walk with her to the bed. We sit down together. I like the way this feels.

"Ye mean it wasn't any worse?"

I shake my head. "I mean nothing happened. I didn't hear any screaming or see any faces at all. Even the darkness was different. Before, it's always felt as if there were a blanket over my face, but this time there was a reddish glow trying to push through the black. It was like a candle flame."

"Maybe it was because you weren't traveling very far," suggests Medusa. She's now resting her head on my shoulder.

"You are very wise, Medusa," says Alfarin. "I think you must be correct."

I don't voice my opinion, but I think they're wrong, and from the way Elinor is massaging her neck and refusing to look anyone in the eye, I think she suspects another reason as well. After all, she was the one who read the whole book on the Viciseometer. Elinor is probably more learned in the theory than I am.

That thick black streak in the hallway is worrying me. This is the Plaza in New York, one of the most expensive hotels in the world, according to the in-room magazines. There's no way in a million years that anything other than Team DEVIL caused that black streak to appear. Gray dust is one thing, but that tarlike smear is something else. It's a toxic mark of death. A shadow that has become permanent.

But nothing happened in the room when I appeared. There was no plume of ash, no streak of contamination. I didn't hear the screams of the dead, or the hot, panting bloodlust of the Skin-Walkers.

The question is bubbling away in my brain. I try not to form the words in my head, because if I see them, it makes the question real.

Which one of us is the Skin-Walkers tracking? Which one of us is evil?

No, I can't think like that. I'm confused. This all started with Septimus's message, and now I'm being sidetracked. I had one goal on this mission, and I intend to see it through.

"Everyone has gone very quiet," Medusa observes. Her big chocolate eyes gaze up at me.

"I'm thinking," I reply.

"Mitchell, are ye feeling all right? Ye have gone very red."

I wipe my face with my hand; I'm burning up. Sweat is pouring off me.

"I've made a decision. I want to take you all back to Hell," I announce. "I'm going on alone."

I wait for the protests and the arguments from the three best friends I've ever had, but not a word is uttered. Perhaps my intentions didn't come out clearly?

"Do you all understand?" I say. "I'm taking everyone back to the exact moment we left. No one will know any different. You won't get into any trouble."

They ignore me the way I would ignore a teacher at school when I didn't want to do a homework assignment. Why aren't they arguing with me? Do they think I don't mean this? I'm not looking to be center of attention here. I'm going on alone. I've done it once, and the journey through time was easier solo than with a team. The book was wrong; solo time travel is easy. I can do this after all.

"We need to give both rooms a final check before we leave for good," says Elinor. "Alfarin, could ye have a quick scan of the other room? I'll make sure Mitchell's bag is packed and ready this time. M, can ye look in the bathroom? I don't think there is anything left in it, but we should pack the lotion for the boys' burns. Ye never know, there might be an ingredient that actually works on the dead."

"Will do, El," replies Medusa genially.

"Your wish is my command," says Alfarin with a bow.

I'm not stupid; I know what they're doing. They think if they just carry on as normal, I won't go through with it.

"I'm taking you all back, Elinor."

She continues to fold clean underwear into my backpack. "Of course ye are, Mitchell."

I raise my voice to a shout. "I'm serious!"

"I don't doubt yer intentions for a second."

"Then what are you all doing? Why are you all being so...so... indifferent?"

Medusa's voice calls out from the bathroom. It echoes and bounces off the marble interior, making it sound much deeper than normal.

"Would you rather we had a fight about this, Mitchell? Is that what's bothering you? I don't know if Alfarin wants to give you another pounding, but El and I could tag-team up against you if you would prefer."

Sweat continues to drip down my face and pool around my neck. I feel as if I'm on a roller coaster. Only it's hurtling into space and darkness and I'm not strapped in properly and I'm going to fall.

I don't know what's happening to me.

Alfarin bounds back into the room. "All clear, my princess."

"Okay," says Elinor, "so we have the money—check; the credit card—check; Mitchell has the Viciseometer—check; cell phones—check."

"Clean underwear for the boys," calls Medusa, "check."

I haul myself to my feet and make it into the bathroom just in time to vomit into the sink. What hurtles out of my stomach is just plain nasty and looks like dark-green mud.

"That's disgusting, Mitchell," says Medusa, screwing up her face.

"I think I'm dying again," I groan.

"Well, there is a first for everything," says Elinor. She is now standing by the door, twirling her long red hair around her fingers.

"You're acting like you expected this to happen," I reply, slumping to the floor.

Medusa soaks a white towel in the shower and places it over my face.

"There is a reason the dead shouldn't time-travel alone," she says, stroking my hair. "Elinor told us back in Hell when we were trying to catch up with you. There are side effects, horrible ones, apparently."

I look up at Elinor. Alfarin has joined her by the door; he has all four backpacks slung over his shoulders and his axe in his hand. He looks much younger without his beard. Being hair free doesn't suit him.

"I took another book out of the library," says Elinor. "It was said to be written by someone who had used the Viciseometer thousands of years ago, but it was in the fiction section because no one believed him."

I don't need to know what happens when someone travels alone; I can feel it. My internal organs are dissolving into soup. I didn't think it was possible to be dead and feel so wretched at the same time.

"You let me travel alone, even though you knew it would do this to me?" I cry.

"It isn't permanent, Mitchell," says Medusa. "It's called Osmosis of the Dead."

"I hated biology," I groan, before puking up something that looks like brown baby food. "So is there anything else I need to know about the Viciseometer before I combust into moldy custard?" I throw up again.

"Every time someone uses the Viciseometer, it becomes a fixed point in time," replies Elinor. "We can time-travel all we like, but once a person has pressed that button, ye can never go back in time and stop them from doing so. Ye also need to know that the dead leave traces of death when they travel, and I think we have been seeing that. The more of ye there are, the less likely ye are to notice, because the Viciseometer spreads the toxic load."

"But nothing came out when I traveled alone," I say slowly. "I've seen the dust and the streaks of tar when we traveled together, but with me there was no dust, no nothing."

"There must have been something," says Elinor.

"I'm telling you, there wasn't. The Skin-Walkers weren't there, and there was nothing when I arrived. Not this time."

Elinor's eyes flicker over to Alfarin. He has moved away from the door and is back in the open room, staring at his newly shaved reflection in the blade of his axe. He doesn't appear too impressed.

"Are you thinking what I'm thinking?" I whisper.

But Elinor shakes her head vehemently. "No, never."

"What are you thinking?" asks Medusa quietly. She's bending down and mopping my face with the towel. The heat from my skin has already parched it bone dry.

"It doesn't matter."

But despite her protestations to the contrary, I can tell Elinor is thinking the same thing I am, because she can't stop looking at Alfarin. Elinor never has been able to stop looking at him.

The toxicity of death still left me alone when I traveled solo. When I finished traveling, it hurled itself out of my mouth in solid chunks. So the gray dust plumes and tarlike streaks aren't coming from me, and I'm betting they aren't coming from Medusa or Elinor, either.

And if the Skin-Walkers aren't reaching for me in the void, they must be tracking someone else in our group.

Alfarin is a killer. He always has been. The son of a Viking king would have been taught to handle a blade before he could walk. We saw it with our own eyes, the way he took down several of the armed villagers before death stopped him.

And then there is the small matter of Elinor's death.

Death made me duplicitous, but there are some times when even though every bone in your body is screaming for a different answer, you have no choice but to be honest.

The dead are coming for Alfarin.

21. Secrets and Lies

The sickness is easing off and the sweating and shaking have calmed down. My skin starts to prickle again as the burns sustained in 1666 affect my nerve endings once more.

It is getting easier, though. When you're dead, you heal pretty quickly, which is the definition of ironic as far as I'm concerned. I burned my hand on a gas stove when I was five—and alive. It took three months to get better. The fact that my grandmother insisted on slapping butter on the raw skin didn't help—she said it aided the healing, but all it managed to do was roast me like a chicken. But when you're dead you can even reattach a head, as Louis XVI—and Elinor—can attest.

Medusa has soaked the towel once more and is still mopping at my face. I don't need it anymore, but I let her because I like having her near me. I gesture to Elinor to move a little closer.

"You know what I'm thinking, right?"

Elinor purses her lips and narrows her green eyes.

"It isn't Alfarin."

"We don't have time to argue, Elinor," I reply. "So can you at least agree to go along with what I suggest?"

"Can someone please include me in this conversation?" asks Medusa. She has stopped dabbing at my face with the towel, and I can hear short, reflexive snorts coming through her nostrils. It means she's getting annoyed.

I shuffle across the bathroom floor on my ass so we're as far away from the door as we can be. I don't want Alfarin to think we're talking about him—which of course we are.

"I think the visions we hear and see when we time-travel are the Skin-Walkers and their victims," I whisper, casting my eyes furtively to the connecting bedroom, where Alfarin appears to be tugging at his five o'clock shadow, as if willing it to grow back.

"I think we've all guessed that now," replies Medusa.

"The point is, they weren't there at all when I traveled alone," I add.

"So why don't they affect you?"

"Because they aren't tracking me, they're following someone else in our group. I think they're coming for Alfarin."

"No."

Medusa gasps. "Why?"

"Elinor said the Skin-Walkers were the first evil. They come after the child abusers and the killers. I think I'm in a whole world of pain for stealing the Viciseometer, but I bet the Skin-Walkers are coming after us for a different reason now. Theft isn't too big a deal in the grand scheme of things."

"Alfarin is not evil," snaps Elinor.

"Of course he isn't," I hiss back, "but do you think the Skin-Walkers are going to make that distinction? You said yourself that the Skin-Walkers stalk their victims when they're alive, but what's to stop them stalking the dead, too? I've seen them, Elinor. They're here, watching us. They're in the crowds and they're in the shadows. Now there's that disgusting black streak outside in the corridor. As the four of us have been time-traveling, the trace we've been leaving has been getting worse. It's almost as if the Skin-Walkers are playing with us. Alfarin killed you and I'm pretty sure he took down several of those villagers back in 970 as well, and those are just the deaths we know about."

"But that was different," she argues. "Alfarin was acting in self-defense back then, and as for me..." She trails off as tears bubble up to the surface of her pretty green eyes.

"I understand what you're saying, Mitchell," whispers Medusa, "but I don't think you're right about this. El makes a good point. Back in 970 Alfarin was acting in self-defense, plus he would have been taken by the Skin-Walkers as soon as he died if they had considered him a murderer who killed for pleasure. Remember what El said back in the tunnel: the Skin-Walkers track their victims while they're alive, and a killer will sense their presence. Alfarin has never said anything about sensing them when he was a living Viking. And for the record, he didn't murder El, either; he put her out of her misery. It was like euthanasia. He can't be branded evil for doing that. It was merciful, not evil."

Part of me wants to argue, but I'm hoping beyond hope that the girls are right. Alfarin is like my brother, and I would defend him with everything I had—until there was nothing left.

But their passionate reasoning has now opened up another door that I don't want to go through.

If the Skin-Walkers aren't screaming for me, and they aren't coming for Alfarin, what if they're after one of the girls?

We have to leave now. My legs wobble as I try to stand, but Medusa and Elinor instinctively grab hold of each arm and hold me steady. As I stumble, I think back to the early days of our friendship. Elinor was waiting for us all that time. Somehow we were bonded in life as well as death. Could fate exist after all?

"Alfarin, you ready to leave?" I call. My voice doesn't sound as if it belongs to me. It's detached, like an echo.

"I want my facial hair back," says Alfarin, pouting. "My chin looks like a baby's bottom."

"Ye are still a real man without it," says Elinor soothingly. She slips her hand into Alfarin's, and his smile threatens to split his face open. He looks almost angelic.

"It could be worse, Alfarin," adds Medusa. "You could be like Mitchell and take a century to grow a beard."

"I would have to hide in the deepest cave for eternity if that fate ever befell me," says Alfarin, wrapping a trunklike arm around my shoulders.

"Watch the burns, dude."

Medusa clenches her fist and coughs into her hand. "Baby."

I know how to shut her up, and seeing as Osmosis of the Dead has canceled my plans to go on alone... "Well, let's see how brave you are, Melissa Pallister." I hand Medusa the Viciseometer as her jaw drops. "You're next."

I give the hotel room one last glance. The white sheets on the enormous bed are crumpled and have been stained with what looks like dark-gray chalk. A big pile of dirty, wet clothes is heaped in a corner. The smell in here is ripe with mold and filth.

"Have you put the date in?" I ask Medusa.

"Yes," she whispers. Her pale face has gone the color of sour cream.

I turn to Alfarin. "We need to keep hold of the girls even tighter than before."

"I'm scared, Mitchell."

The Viciseometer is spitting tiny red sparks in Medusa's hand. It's lying flat against her palm. She's too afraid to clasp it tightly.

"Hang on," I say. I twist around to pull my backpack from Alfarin's shoulder. I unzip it and rummage among the clean underwear. As I reach my arm down into the depths, my fingers skim the edge of a glossy piece of paper and I grab it.

"Look at this," I say to Medusa. I show her the photo of the four of us, gleaming rosily—eyes and all. My raggedy doll reappears as Medusa smiles and the dimples indent her perfect skin.

"I love that photo!" exclaims Elinor, laughing. "Didn't Medusa fart or something just as it was being taken?"

Alfarin chuckles as Medusa makes an indignant *humph* noise through her nose.

"I burped, I did not fart. Ladies don't fart."

"You should tell my mother that," says Alfarin, taking the photo between his sausage-sized fingers. "She has been known to flatten trees with her trumpeting."

"Why are you showing me this?" asks Medusa.

"Because we're a team," I reply. "We're best friends, and regardless of what may happen now, we can't ever forget that."

"Team DEVIL," sings Elinor.

"Yeah," says Medusa, but her voice is low and sad.

"Don't let go of me, whatever happens," I say to Medusa, tightening my grip around her waist.

"We're going to see the Skin-Walkers again, aren't we?"

"Only for a second," I reply.

The four of us make a tight circle. I can't see the date Medusa has put into the Viciseometer, but I know we'll arrive in 1967: the so-called Summer of Love.

"Are you ready for this?" I ask.

"Reality can't be any worse than the nightmares," replies Medusa.

The Viciseometer appears to be hovering above Medusa's hand. I gently close her fingers around the rim and I don't let go.

"Close your eyes and don't look."

Elinor has done the same. Alfarin nods to me and tightens his grip on the axe. We don't say it, but a kind of telepathy is bouncing between us. Alfarin and I have enough eyes for everyone. We'll both keep ours open, and woe to anything that attempts to break the circle.

"In three...two...one..."

The tight group is immediately thrown apart as the Viciseometer hurls us into the past. My eyes stream as heat and flame tear at my face. The Skin-Walkers surround us; the wolf pelts on their heads come alive in the darkness. Blackened, razor-sharp teeth snap at my neck as cries of pain echo in the vortex.

But this time I recognize one voice in the darkness. A continuous cry of terror that is beyond my reach. It calls to me, begging me not to let go.

The sun-parched grass shatters beneath my hands. I've landed on all fours like a dog. It takes me a second to realize I'm panting like one, too. A pernicious, bright sun hovers high in the sky; its rays are cooking everything in sight.

Medusa and Elinor are lying on their backs, their faces still scrunched up. Elinor has her hands over her ears.

Alfarin is gagging where he stands.

I crawl over to Medusa and take her face in my hands. My thumbs trace uneven lines across her skin.

"Wake up, we're here," I whisper. "It's over."

The lids of her eyes are threaded with tiny veins that spread across the thin skin like ink on tissue paper. Medusa's dry mouth parts just a little; her lips look as if they're glued shut. I pull myself away and look at Alfarin and Elinor.

"What was it like that time for you two?"

"Worse than before," says Alfarin, "and I heard one particular scream more clearly than the others."

"Me too," says Elinor.

Medusa stays quiet. She has propped herself up on her elbows, but her eyes are open. They're as bloodshot as her lids.

"Did either of you recognize it?" I ask.

Alfarin and Elinor shake their heads. "Did you?"

My eyes drift away from the three of them and toward the red steel bridge that stretches into the distance. I don't care for the sight-seeing; I just don't want them to realize I'm about to lie.

"No," I reply.

There's a smell of smoke in the air. In Hell, you get pretty good at deciphering the different stenches of burning. Wood, for example, will make your eyes water if you inhale it for too long. Cigarette smoke is unique because of the chemicals; it's almost sweet. Burning fatty flesh will instinctively make you gag, and paper leaves just a discreet trace in the air. San Francisco is a melting pot of all those flavors, minus the burning flesh. That has been replaced with the pungent smells of barbecued food and sweat.

Medusa has taken us to a large park next to the Golden Gate Bridge. There are people all around; most are lazing on the scorched earth, but no one appears to be paying us any attention. Music fills the air: singing and lamenting guitars. I love music from the sixties, but I'm guessing the living here are all too stoned to care right now how important this moment in time is. Several bonfires dot the brittle yellow grass, and groups of hippies circle most of them. One couple, oblivious to the world, are making out while balancing on a low-hanging branch that looks like an elephant's tusk.

"Is this the day ye died, Medusa?" asks Elinor.

"Yes," Medusa replies softly. Her eyes are fixed on the bridge.

I turn to Alfarin and Elinor. "Can you two wait here while I walk with Medusa for a bit?"

They nod in unison and walk over to a blackened tree. Names have been scored in the rotting bark. Most have hearts carved around them. Alfarin starts to scratch away at the tree with the edge of his blade as Elinor watches. He manages an *E* and then an *L* before a loud crack splinters the air and part of the tree falls beside them. Dying leaves explode into the air like confetti and then gently float back down to the dusty earth. Elinor starts giggling as Alfarin picks up the branch and attempts to reattach it to the tree with spit.

"They make such a cute couple," says Medusa. Her voice is still really sad.

"I don't know how Elinor managed to keep her secret all that time," I reply. "Especially from Alfarin."

Medusa slips her hand into mine. "We all have secrets, Mitchell."

We start to walk farther into the park, beyond the couple in the tree and past three girls who are dancing in long dresses that skim the dirt. They're all barefoot. Medusa is wearing skintight jeans and a red-and-black-plaid shirt, which she takes off and ties around her waist, revealing a tight gray tank top. I like casual clothes on girls, especially pretty girls like Medusa. They don't needs sparkles or bows or makeup to look attractive. Just beyond the dancing girls is a man with flared brown trousers and no shirt. His hairless chest has writing scrawled all over it in black marker. He's selling paper packets filled with small strawberries. I hand him all my loose change, hoping he won't notice the difference in the coins from 1967 and the New York of the future we just left.

"If you aren't ready for this, we could jump straight ahead to my death," I say, popping a ripe red berry into Medusa's mouth.

Medusa leans into me and tightens her hold on my hand. "I think I'm ready now."

"Are we going to see your stepfather?"

"No," replies Medusa. She pauses, as if she wants to say something more, but she doesn't.

"If you want me to do something, anything, to him for hurting you, you know I will in a heartbeat."

"You don't have a heartbeat anymore."

"But I will soon."

We pause by the trunk of an enormous tree. Medusa pulls me around to the other side so we're partially hidden from Alfarin and Elinor. Not that I think they're looking anymore. Alfarin could be in a crowd of thousands, but he would only ever see Elinor. He can be romantic without trying.

I'm just trying.

"Tell me a secret, Mitchell," whispers Medusa, pressing her hands against my chest. "Tell me something no one else in Hell knows."

"Why?"

"Because I want something from you that's mine forever, just mine."

"Hey, I tried to give you my jacket, remember?"

"I could have gotten one of those anytime I liked," she replies. "I want something from in here," and she spreads her hand across my dead heart.

I don't know what to do with my hands. It's harder to touch her when she's so self-assured and confident around me.

"If you tell anyone this, even Alfarin or Elinor, I will never speak to you again," I say.

"I promise."

"I want something from you, though." The bark digs into my back as I slide down the trunk of the tree. The ground is dusty and my jeans quickly become layered in dirty red chalk. Medusa straddles my lap. It gives her several extra inches in height, but my mouth still hovers in front of her button nose instead of her mouth.

"You can have anything," she whispers, running her fingers through my hair.

"When I was alive, my mom didn't call me Mitchell."

"She called you M.J., didn't she?" says Medusa. She's smirking and showing off one dimple.

"How did you know that?"

"Septimus told me."

"How did Septimus know?"

"Septimus knows everything."

I puff my cheeks out and blow upward. My hair is too short to ripple, but Medusa's hair dances like cobras under a spell.

"I think it's cute," she adds. "My M.J." Her thumb traces a line across my chin.

For the first time, I don't mind Medusa sharing the nickname with my mom. It's kind of a shock, how natural it sounds. And it's suddenly crystal clear how much I want to hear it again, from Medusa, the one person who gets me—all of me. The good and the bad. She instinctively knows what to say and when to say it. It may not be what I want to hear, but it's usually what I need to hear.

"My M.J."

It's definitely what I need to hear. In this moment, for one sweet second, the anger I feel about being dead is diluted. The pain doesn't go away, but Medusa covers it like a Band-Aid.

Her mouth is inches from mine. I feed her another strawberry and she does the same to me. Her juice-stained fingers sweep through my hair again and then down my neck and across my chest. A look of concentration is carved onto her face, as if she's committing my body to memory. Every internal organ I possess is wriggling and squirming out of place. It's a good thing I don't need to breathe, because I think I've been holding my breath longer than is humanly possible.

"I know I'm not as pretty as other girls."

"You're prettier than any girl I've ever known, Medusa."

"Prettier than Patty Lloyd?"

"You're a level one compared to her six hundred sixty-six." That brings a smile to Medusa's face—the big, toothy kind of smile that people give when they're really happy. I can see Medusa's tongue resting behind the gap between her two front teeth.

"Close your eyes," she says, and I do as I'm told. I know she's moved her head closer to mine because I can feel her mad hair on my face.

"Keep them closed," she instructs, and I do, even though I can feel something wet against my face now. It's like a trickle of water from a dripping tap.

"I love you, Mitchell," sobs Medusa. "I always have."

Her mouth is on mine, and it is way better than kissing Patty Lloyd, because this means something. The heat of Medusa's skin scorches mine, but it feels like home.

Medusa was under my nose all this time and I never realized. I take my hands off the ground and move to touch her.

Suddenly her weight is gone. I open my eyes with a start as a blast of hot wind sucks at my clothes like a vacuum cleaner.

Medusa is nowhere to be seen.

I peer around the tree and see Alfarin and Elinor running toward me. Elinor is screaming.

"Where's Medusa?" I yell.

"She's gone, she's gone!" cries Elinor.

I can't move. My legs feel like dead weights. There's an ache in my chest as if my dead heart has been replaced with concrete. I fall to the ground and my fingers grope at the Viciseometer, flickering feebly between two exposed tree roots.

Medusa has left us, left me, ripped away like a Band-Aid, and I have nothing but the taste of strawberries on my lips and the stain of my best friend's tears on my cheeks.

22. Bridge to Nowhere

"What did ye say to her?" screams a distraught Elinor.

"I didn't say anything!" I yell back. The Viciseometer is in my hand once more. I clasp it to my chest.

"Did Medusa tell you she was going to use it, my friend?" asks Alfarin. His eyes are darting in all directions, even upward into the trees, as if Medusa is a bird that has tricked us all by flying away.

"She told me…to close my eyes…and then…and then…" I can't finish. My throat has gone into spasms. I look at the date on the Viciseometer. It reads: 18 June 1967. The time: eight o'clock.

Elinor snatches it from my hand. "It's okay!" she cries. "We have the date and the time. We'll just follow her and bring her back."

"We don't know *where* Medusa traveled to, though," says Alfarin. His deep voice reverberates like the chime of a grandfather clock.

"Then we go back in time a few minutes and stop her from having the Viciseometer in the first place," sobs Elinor.

"But we can't!" I cry. "Once that button is pressed, it becomes a fixed point in time, you said so yourself. We can't stop her—and she must have known that."

I wipe my mouth and then my tongue on the back of my hand, trying to remove the taste of strawberries. The paper packet I bought just moments ago lies discarded in the dirt. Red juice, like diluted blood, seeps through it. I stand up and stamp it into the ground with my feet until there's nothing left but a smeared crimson pulp.

And in that instant I know who the Skin-Walkers have been coming after all this time.

"Do ye think she has gone to stop her death without us?" Elinor's question jolts me from my thoughts.

I snatch the Viciseometer back from her and look again at the date Medusa entered into it as I sat like a love-struck fool with my eyes wide shut.

"But this isn't the date of her death," I say, completely confused. Either San Francisco is spinning or I'm swaying where I stand.

"How do you know?" asks Alfarin.

"Because I looked up Medusa's records once on the computer. I wanted to know how she died, but the details were classified."

"But ye definitely know the date of her death?"

"She died on the twenty-fifth of June in 1967, which, if she was telling the truth, is today's date. We're a week forward from the date she just set in the Viciseometer."

"So why has she gone back a week?" asks Alfarin.

I squat down and put my head between my legs. *Think, Mitchell*, I say to myself. *Think.*

Medusa has rarely talked about her life—her living life, that is. I know she wanted to be a ballerina when she was four, and then a doctor. She told me she had lived in Texas for a while when she was thirteen, but that was only because her parents had split up and her mother was staying with relatives until she got back on her feet. They moved back to San Francisco when Medusa was fourteen and her mother had remarried again...

The answer suddenly hits me.

"It's her stepfather."

"What about him?" say the other two together.

"Do you remember what she said the first night we were in New York?" I shout. "When she woke up from the nightmare. She said she wished she had taken *him* with her."

165

"And *he* was her stepfather?" asks Elinor.

I nod furiously. "She told me it was her stepfather. Medusa has gone back to do something connected to him."

"But where?" demands Alfarin. "Where has Medusa gone? Time is nothing without the destination. We have to see the place she has traveled to in the red—"

"I know, Alfarin!" I interrupt. "I know we have to see it in order to travel to it."

"Has she ever said anything about her mother, or where she used to live?" pleads Elinor; she is clawing at my arm.

But I can't remember. My mind is like a blanket of pale-gray fog. I try to think back to past conversations with Medusa, but I can't even remember what her voice sounds like. I try to grasp it in my head, but it has turned to bloodred sand. It's slipping through the cracks in time we've opened.

"Let's try the bridge first," I say, wiping away the beads of sweat that have gathered around my top lip.

"But this date in the Viciseometer isn't the date of her death!" cries Elinor.

"*I know!*" I yell. I immediately regret shouting as Elinor blanches and Alfarin's face turns to thunder. "I'm sorry, Elinor, I'm sorry." I hold her trembling hands in mine. "But we have to start somewhere. We will find her. I promise you, we will get Medusa back."

Tears cascade down Elinor's freckled cheeks. I feel more responsible for her than ever. How could I have let Medusa go?

Why did she let me go?

I do not touch the red needle. It hangs on its chain like a delicate pendulum as I imagine standing on the Golden Gate Bridge. The red face begins to glow and spark.

"Hold on to someone," I say, but I don't need to. Alfarin, Elinor, and I have been holding each other since Medusa left us.

Our flight through time is hot but quiet. No screaming or wailing of the dead accompanies us. Just a haze of pink in the darkness, like the seconds before a sunrise. The Skin-Walkers have gone.

We arrive on the bridge next to one of the colossal towers. Up close, it looks more orange than red. A steady stream of traffic thunders past: Buicks; Pontiacs; and my all-time favorite, the Chevrolet Camaro. Classic muscle cars.

But I only want Medusa.

"Can you see her anywhere?" I yell, pulling out of Alfarin's and Elinor's grip. I run to the edge and look along it and then down into the water. The futility of our presence is laid bare by the sheer scale of this bridge. It's so long, it's impossible to see the full length. Medusa could be here right now and we wouldn't see her unless we used the Viciseometer to travel along every inch of it.

I look along the strait to the Pacific Ocean. Fingers of fog are already starting to grope inward as the sun sets. The fog is coming to claim the bridge, and us with it.

Elinor is running up and down, screaming Medusa's name. I try a different tack and start yelling for Melissa Pallister.

But my raggedy doll isn't here. This wasn't her time.

"Should we try the other side, or the middle of the bridge?" asks Alfarin. His voice is steady and calm. His blue eyes are narrowed with intense concentration.

"I don't think she's here, Alfarin," I reply as Elinor continues to scream. "We could scan every inch and we wouldn't find her."

"There's something in the water!" cries Elinor, and Alfarin and I rush to where Elinor is pointing down into the murky depths. Something bobs in the froth, hundreds of feet below.

"It's just a seal," says Alfarin, and he wraps his arms around Elinor, who collapses sobbing into his arms.

I always considered Medusa my best friend, and myself hers. I never really gave much thought to anyone else's relationship with her, even though the four of us are inseparable. But Elinor was like the sister Medusa never had, and Alfarin was like a brother. We *were* a family.

Medusa has been gone just minutes and already I'm referring to her in the past tense. Is this how those who are alive move on without those who've died, I wonder? Is it that easy? One minute you're there, the next you're gone. A memory. A photo. A ghostly imprint.

Medusa is already dead. The living won't mourn her passing again. Will the bustling kitchens in Hell notice one departure among the steam and noise?

Well, screw them all, because I will. If I have to travel along every inch of this bridge, this city, this world, I will find Medusa. I will stop her from doing whatever it is she couldn't tell us she was planning to do. I will not let the Skin-Walkers find her. She isn't theirs to take.

My cell phone vibrates and beeps. It's Alfarin who hears the incoming text. I'm too busy trying to find Medusa's voice. I pull out the cell phone—it's glowing red.

"Do ye think that's her?" asks Elinor.

I don't have to look to know who it is, because I can hear his voice in my head instead of the one I really want. I just don't understand how. We're forty years in the past and I won't be born for decades. My life and death are still to come.

So how does Septimus know we're in trouble?

23. The Other Thief

go back

Another two-word text. I show the message to Alfarin and Elinor. They guessed it was from Septimus as soon as they saw me pull the glowing cell phone out of my backpack.

"Go back," repeats Alfarin. "Lord Septimus is asking us to go back to Hell?"

"We can't…leave without…Medusa," says Elinor. She has finished sobbing, but her words are punctuated by hiccups.

"Try holding your breath," suggests Alfarin rather unhelpfully. I make a WTF face at him.

Alfarin gets it. "Sorry," he mumbles. "I forgot."

I grip the cell phone in my hand. I came close to calling Septimus once before, and our situation has become even more hopeless. Yet I hold back once more. I don't even scan my directory for his number.

"Why do you think Septimus said *go back* instead of *come back*?" I ask Alfarin.

"It has fewer letters?" he replies without a hint of irony.

I laugh. It's completely inappropriate, but in normal circumstances that's exactly why Septimus would have done it.

"Go back…go back," I mutter to myself. I'm searching for clues in the six characters. Septimus enjoys being cunning in a way that's almost Machiavellian.

My eyes follow a fine-looking 1965 Chevy Nova. The driver stares at me glassy-eyed as he takes a drag on a long cigarette. He finishes crossing the bridge and heads toward the park we just exited, in a cloud of black exhaust.

I slap my forehead. The park. That's it.

"Go back, Septimus wants us to go back!" I yell.

"We knew that, Mitchell," says Elinor. The whites of her eyes are as red as her hair.

"Hold on, quickly, we're going back to the park."

"Do ye think Medusa has come back?"

I shake my head. "No, but I bet you anything Septimus is there."

Elinor suddenly lets go and both hands grasp her neck.

"Ye cannot take us back, Mitchell. Septimus may have the HBI with him. We'll be arrested and locked up and then we will never find Medusa."

"Elinor." I try to keep my voice as calm as possible, even though I'm tempted to just grab her in a headlock and take her by force. "Please, Elinor. I am asking you to trust me. I know Septimus. He wouldn't betray us."

"How can ye say that? Ye have only been dead for four years, Mitchell. You forget we are in Hell and there are different rules for us."

"What if Lord Septimus can help us find Medusa?" asks Alfarin.

"Exactly."

Elinor transfers her gaze to Alfarin. "Do ye think we should go back to the park?"

He nods. "I trust Mitchell."

It doesn't bother me that Elinor believes in Alfarin more than in me—not much, anyway. They have an impenetrable bond now. I just want to keep us together. I need to see the park in the red face of the Viciseometer. I fix my mind on the tree with the tusklike boughs because that seems as good a place as any to go back to. I slap Alfarin on the back in a show of thanks, and he reciprocates and almost sends me tumbling to another doom over the edge of the bridge.

Elinor is muttering under her breath. I only catch every third or fourth word, but it sounds as if she's praying.

"*Now.*"

A reddish-black mist swallows us whole. As before, there are no screams in the darkness. I can feel flames tickling at my flesh, but they aren't hot. They're light and wispy, like feathers. For the first time, I want the gnashing of teeth, because it would mean the Skin-Walkers were back and not tearing at my Medusa in another time.

The three of us land on our feet. Just above our heads is the couple from before. They're so busy getting it on that they don't notice us materializing out of nowhere. I doubt they would have noticed even if we'd landed on top of them.

"No Skin-Walkers again," says Alfarin quietly, with a sideways glance at Elinor.

"Do ye think that means they already have her?"

Alfarin says nothing; he's looking beyond me with his eyes wide open like blue-and-white china saucers.

"Lord Septimus!" he cries, and he immediately goes down on bended knee with his axe clasped between his hands.

I spin around and see my boss striding across the patchy yellow grass. Septimus appears a foot taller than I remember, long and thin and achingly cool in a black pinstriped suit and red shirt.

I start walking backward. I can feel my duplicitous tongue swelling in my mouth. I want to hug him and run from him at the same time. Has he always looked this fierce? His black skin is glistening, and the sun is reflecting off the golden hoops that hang from his ears.

I wait for the crooked white teeth to appear as characters in his enormous grin, but they stay hidden. Panic forces every swear word I know to come tumbling out of my mouth as I continue to stumble backward, away from the most important civil servant in Hell—a former Roman general who intends to incite a million tortured, tired souls in Hell to rise up and create an army.

What was I thinking by coming back here?

Septimus is now just feet away from me. His eyes are boring into mine. I cower in front of him as I wait for the roar, the condemnation, the absolute disappointment as time finally catches up with me and my betrayal.

"I don't think I have ever seen any devil go to quite this amount of effort to change the color of his eyes."

"What?"

"Although I have to say your particular brand of blush quite suited someone with your skin coloring," continues Septimus, gazing around the park. "Not as good as mine, of course. Black is far superior. Everything goes with black."

"What?"

"Come now, Mitchell, is that the best you can do? You disappoint me. Earth has made you monosyllabic."

"What?"

Septimus turns to Alfarin. In my haste to move backward, I trip over a tree root and sprawl on the ground. Elinor appears to have passed out.

"So, son of Hlif, son of Dobin, I take it the manner of your death pleased you? I say that because you are still standing here with The Devil's intern."

"Lord Septimus, I could not have chosen a more honorable way to cease and pass over."

Septimus finally smiles as he turns to Elinor. His outstretched hand pulls her to her feet. I swear I hear a sizzle, like frying bacon, as their skin connects. The sun is setting behind Septimus's head, which gives him the appearance of being on fire.

"Your discretion and faith in others, Miss Powell, is an inspiration to us all. I trust it was not too traumatic to finally see the end come to pass?"

"No, sir," replies Elinor faintly. "I think it was more upsetting for Mitchell than anyone."

My boss turns to me. At this point I'm waiting for the ground to split open and swallow me whole.

"And what of your death, Mitchell? Is your demise the next path in time to be challenged?"

"Medusa has gone missing. We all came back here, but then she took the Viciseometer and traveled on somewhere alone."

"And yet she left you with Hell's timepiece?" asks Septimus in his deep southern drawl.

"Medusa couldn't have been holding it when she pressed the red button. She didn't want to leave us stranded without it."

"So Miss Pallister intended not to return?"

"Can you help us find her?" I'm back on my feet, face to face with Septimus. His forehead wrinkles into a frown. His dark-brown eyes have a thin red ring around the irises. I guess the heat takes longer to leave when you've been dead for two thousand years.

"No, I cannot," replies Septimus, and he doesn't flinch, even when Elinor starts to sob once more.

"You can't or you won't?"

"This is your doing, Mitchell," replies Septimus slowly, "and you must fix it."

"Do you know where Medusa is?"

"It would not matter if I did, Mitchell."

"Is this my punishment for stealing the Viciseometer?" I shout. "Is this how it works? Instead of punishing me, you retaliate against Medusa?"

"Medusa made her choice to leave, Mitchell."

"She wasn't thinking straight," I cry, "and I was the one who forced her to come here. I told her it was her turn. I forced her to take the Viciseometer; she even told me she wasn't ready."

"Please, Mr. Septimus, sir," begs Elinor. "Please help us find Medusa. The Skin-Walkers stopped chasing us once Medusa was gone. We think they have gone after her."

Septimus places his hands in his pockets, throws his head back, and starts to stroll around. The panic I felt before is turning into anger and loathing with every nonchalant step he takes. How can he be so calm when Medusa is in so much danger? I thought he liked her.

"Let me ask you a question, Miss Powell," says Septimus. "At what point do you believe a person—either living or passed on—becomes liable for their actions?"

"We are all liable for our actions, sir," replies Elinor, "but that does not mean we don't go to the aid of a loved one when they need it."

"But your paths are now destined for another direction," says Septimus softly.

"You guessed I was going to take the Viciseometer, didn't you?"

Septimus laughs, but his laughter is cold. "I did not guess, Mitchell. I knew. I have known for six months."

"How?" asks Alfarin.

I answer for him. "Paris."

"Indeed."

Elinor looks confused, so I explain further. "Six months ago, Septimus had to deal with a security breach. It was in one of the red files we keep in the safe. It was me—us. When you and Medusa took us back to Paris, we were seen."

Alfarin is massaging his temples. "Is this the paradox you were explaining, my friend? We were in two places at once?"

I nod. "Six months ago, the four of us were hanging out at your cousin Thomason's—and we were also splashing around in a fountain next to the Eiffel Tower."

"So this is my fault?" gasps Elinor. "Mine and Medusa's?"

"Miss Powell," says Septimus, "almost everything that your Team DEVIL has done to date since you all—rather cleverly, I might add—tricked your way out of Hell has been determined by time. Your pasts, presents, and futures are inextricably linked in ways you haven't even seen yet."

"You said *almost* everything."

Septimus sighs. "Miss Pallister's actions today were... unexpected."

"Is that why you won't help us?" I ask. "Because you don't know Medusa's future anymore?"

"That is one reason."

"How did you find us, Lord Septimus?" asks Alfarin. "Are there other ways to travel through time?"

Septimus reaches into his breast pocket and pulls out a white silk handkerchief. A round object is hidden in its folds.

"Let's just say my intern is not the only thief in Hell."

Carefully, Septimus peels back the corners of the silk. It ripples like a quick-moving cloud. Elinor gasps.

"That's another Viciseometer."

I look down at the timepiece Septimus is now holding in his outstretched palm. Unlike my version, which is made of burnished gold, this new one is forged from the brightest silver. It's almost white. The face displayed in Septimus's hand is the same as our red one; it shows the days and months of the year in Latin script. The exception is that it's colored like the densest sapphire, and instead of slithering snakes forming the numbers for the year, Septimus's Viciseometer is edged with glittering thread that marks the numbers zero to nine.

"Where did you get that?" I ask.

"Where do you think, Mitchell?"

"Up There," reply Alfarin and Elinor together.

"Why? How?"

Ignoring me, Septimus carefully starts inputting time with a thin blue needle. I'm sure I can hear the tinkling of tiny bells as the watch starts to vibrate. The Viciseometer in my pocket is bouncing around as if it's on a spring, as if it's trying to get to the one in Septimus's hand.

"Did you honestly believe you were the only person in history who has desired to change his death, Mitchell?" asks Septimus kindly. "Did you really think you were the first to actually try it?"

"You've known all this time." I'm not asking a question; it's a statement of fact.

"And now, speaking of time, this is the moment when I must leave you all. Sir will be wondering where I have gone off to."

"Help us find Medusa," I beg.

"I believe Washington, DC, is your next stop," replies Septimus. He nods to Alfarin and Elinor. "Miss Powell, Prince Alfarin, be wise with your counsel until we see each other again." Septimus turns to me and smiles. "Life isn't easy or fair, Mitchell, and neither is death. Remember that when it is time to choose."

"Don't go!" I shout, but with a blinding, air-sucking flash, Septimus is gone. The patch of grass where he was standing is charred black.

I start swearing. I get louder and louder, and eventually even the couple making out in the tree stop what they're doing and yell at me to peace out.

"At least the great Lord Septimus hasn't informed the HBI," says Alfarin.

"What are we going to do, Mitchell?" asks Elinor.

I gaze into the red face of my Viciseometer, willing it to help me in some way. Yet it sits benignly between my clenched fingers.

A million thoughts are racing through my head like a fast-moving film. I see Medusa in all of them.

"We have to go back to Hell," I announce. Alfarin and Elinor immediately start remonstrating, but I shout at them to let me finish.

"We're going back to Hell for Medusa's record. We'll break into devil resources, get her file, and come straight back here again. Even if we can't find anything on the eighteenth of June, 1967, we'll still have addresses, names of people she was associated with..."

"Including the stepfather," adds Alfarin knowingly.

"Exactly."

"Give me the Viciseometer, Mitchell," demands Elinor. "I'll take us back to devil resources. I worked there for decades as a filing clerk after the Spanish influenza pandemic of 1918."

"Remember, we're looking for Melissa Pallister, born in 1951, died on the twenty-fifth of June, 1967," I say urgently. "As soon as we have the file, we come back here."

As Elinor moves the red needle around both faces of the Viciseometer, Alfarin takes me aside.

"Do you think we will find her?" he asks.

I can see the oozing pulp of mashed strawberries on my sneakers. The metaphor is not lost on me.

"I won't rest until we do."

24. Resourceful Devils

It feels as if we've landed in a furnace. And we have. The biggest oven most of the living will ever know—once they're dead, that is.

We are back in Hell.

Elinor has taken us deep into the heart of the devil resources department. It is spread over levels 211 to 278 and contains the devil resources details of every dead person now residing in the overpopulated Underworld.

Bright-red, sticky-looking letters displaying the number 267 are stamped on the glistening rock walls. Brilliant, resourceful Elinor has taken us straight to the section containing all the surnames beginning with the letter *P*.

The files are in towering black cabinets. All have a smiling picture of The Devil on them.

"Should we spread out?" asks Alfarin.

"Yeah," I reply, blinking as my eyes stream from the hot air blowing through the labyrinth of dark corridors. "We'll stay close to each other, though. We'll take one row each, side by side. Holler if you find the last name Pallister."

We spread out and start searching. You'd think someone whose surname begins with *Pa* would be quick to find, but we walk for what seems like hours up and down the rows. It takes me ten minutes to get beyond all the dead Paddocks.

Four have become three, and Team DEVIL feels unstable with

one of its members missing. I keep expecting a puny little fist to punch me, or mad corkscrew curls to brush against my face. I want to hear her voice mocking me.

I miss my friend. I miss her so much it's like a constant stabbing pain in my chest.

As I search the names written on the dusty black cabinets, images of Medusa being tortured by the Skin-Walkers start to flicker into my head. I can't help it. The more I try not to think about them, the more images arrive to spite me. I see her silent scream because her tongue is missing; I see her blood bubbling on the ground; I see the inverted spikes on chains piercing her skin...

Stop. No more.

We'll find her. *I* will find her. I still have ownership of time.

Elinor yells to Alfarin and me. I run to the end of the row and turn left. I can't see her, but Alfarin is hurtling toward me with his axe bobbing up and down on his shoulder. He's like a freight train and can't stop easily once he builds momentum. He runs straight into me and we collapse on the floor. His blade nearly scalps me in the process.

"*Elinor!*" cries Alfarin, and my eardrum shatters. "Where are you?"

"Down here!" she yells.

"Down where?" I choke. Alfarin is still lying on top of me.

"I'm here."

This is not helpful.

"Get off me, Alfarin," I grunt.

"I am sorry, my friend. I thought Elinor was in danger."

Alfarin hauls himself up and offers me a hand. Together we go in search of Elinor. We find her standing a third of the way down a dark corridor of files. She's bathed in the light from a single torch, lit high above her head. Her shadow stretches behind her. It's moving, although she is not. Alfarin and I jog toward her, but something doesn't feel right. Of all the drawers in all the rows, why is there a single flame in the exact place we need to look?

"I've found the surname Pallister, Mitchell," says Elinor proudly.

Her pale hand is splayed out across the front of a cabinet. She still has the Viciseometer in her other hand.

Scores of drawers have that surname written on them. Without a word, the three of us stand side by side and Alfarin and Elinor start opening them. The drawers squeal and rattle, and plumes of black dust belch out as my friends rifle through files that haven't felt the touch of a devil in centuries.

"This is full of first names beginning with S," says Alfarin, slamming the drawer shut. The towering cabinet rocks precariously.

"I have the Cs," says Elinor.

I haven't started opening any drawers. My eyes are trained on the single torch burning brightly above us.

"Don't you think this is too much of a coincidence?" I ask as they each open another drawer. "We're looking for a Melissa Pallister, and there just happens to be a lit torch directly above the section we need."

"Ye are just being paranoid," replies Elinor; she sneezes as an explosion of dust showers her. "It just means someone has been filing down here recently."

But I'm not so sure.

"I have the Ms!" cries Alfarin. "Curse the gods, there are so many Melissas in Hell. Does our Medusa have a middle name?"

"It's Olivia," I reply.

"Melissa Olivia Pallister," mumbles Alfarin; his thick fingers are searching through the files. Elinor is bouncing from one foot to the other in anticipation, but my eyes are now shooting from one end of the corridor to the other.

Something is going on. I'm developing a sense for trouble, and I can hear the whispers of the shadows. They're laughing at us as they continue to dance in the darkness.

"Melissa Oliphant...Melissa Olive...who in Odin's name would give their daughter the name of Oliphant?" mutters Alfarin. "Melissa...oh, no, this can't be correct. Why in Odin's name is this file in here?"

"Alfarin," I say through gritted teeth. "Now is not the time to question freak names or filing errors. Just find Medusa's file and then we can go."

But Alfarin has turned white. He has a file clasped in his hand, and his mouth is open.

"What's wrong, Alfarin?"

"Is that Medusa's file?" asks Elinor.

Our Viking friend shakes his head. "No. It is Mitchell's."

I snatch the file from him. Someone is messing with us. Why is my devil resources file in place of Medusa's?

"Is her file in there?" asks Elinor, but she doesn't wait for an answer. She peers into the drawer herself and starts pulling out thick, dusty files. She throws them on the floor. She doesn't seem to comprehend the fact that my file was sitting where Medusa's should be.

For someone who only lived seventeen years and who died just four years ago, my devil resources file is surprisingly thick. I open the beige cardboard cover and am immediately faced with a passport-sized photograph of myself. It was taken at the HalfWay House. My eyes are white, and I don't look human.

It's horrible.

There are other photos in the file as well. Large color prints of my moment of death. Pathetic and crumpled, my body is lying on the road in front of the Greyhound bus that slammed into me. There isn't any blood that I can see, but what turns my stomach is the reaction of the people on the bus itself. Several have their hands over their mouths, but two passengers have their cameras out.

Morbid sons of bitches are taking photos of my body as if they were sightseers and I was the main attraction.

"That is sickening!" exclaims Alfarin.

It gets worse. The next photograph is of my gravestone. It's made of gray marble. It has a sculpted angel on top with outstretched arms that are holding a harp. How revolting can you get? According to the file, my parents buried me in DC, instead of Rhode Island, where I lived with my mom.

Then I read the inscription on the gravestone and I want to scream.

My mom inscribed my grave with M.J., the nickname that was my one link to being alive. But now it's forever linked with my death.

No, no, no, no, no. Mitchell Johnson, that's me. Four syllables and nothing more.

"Medusa's file isn't in here!" screams Elinor, and she slams the drawer shut and then kicks the cabinet in frustration. She runs to the end of the row, turns left, and then, after an absence of a few seconds, reappears. She's like a headless chicken. She runs back to us and, seeing the look on my face, immediately apologizes.

"I'm so sorry, Mitchell. I wasn't thinking. Are ye all right? Is yer death coming back to ye now?"

Then Elinor doubles over and pukes her guts up. Alfarin immediately goes to her aid, and I am left with my file and my memories.

But nothing new is coming back to me. Any repressed thought I may have had about why I ran out into the road fails to materialize. I am as clueless as before.

In fact, my devil resources file poses more questions than answers.

On the cover, in neatly typed, bloodred lettering, is a form. It shows the file subject's current status. Most of it is self-explanatory. I live in the H1N1 accommodation block—The Devil had all the blocks named after dreaded diseases—and I am employed as his intern in the accounting office on level 1. I am noted as a musical prodigy unsuitable for manual labor. It evens lists my hobby as eating. Medusa, Alfarin, and Elinor are mentioned as known associates.

But at the bottom of the page is a box that reads *Earthly Status*. In block capitals, it reads *REPLACED*.

"What does it mean by 'replaced'?" I ask Alfarin. He shakes his head. Elinor is groaning and sweating on the floor.

Now I'm really starting to freak out. Does this mean there's another Mitchell Johnson? Did the Fates take my soul to live in this Underworld, only to replace my broken body with someone else? Are my parents in danger?

Is someone living my life?

My head is going to explode. I sink to the floor and put my head between my knees. I clamp my temples tightly.

I can hear Alfarin whispering to Elinor. They're talking about Medusa. I'm filled with self-loathing because now I want to forsake my best friend and travel to Washington.

"It's your call, Mitchell," says Alfarin gently. He places a huge hand on my shoulder. "Elinor and I will follow you into fire itself. You know that."

I gaze into Elinor's freckled face. She looks pale and clammy and is biting her bottom lip. Her eyes are welling with tears, and already her irises are turning pink. I guess that means my girly-pink eyes are coming back as well.

Medusa has a tummy ring that matches her eyes.

"I don't know how to find her," I whisper.

"We have time," says Alfarin.

I slowly rise from the floor. My entire body clicks and twinges and aches. Elinor passes me the Viciseometer, and I start moving the red needle around the dial.

I look up to the rock-hewn roof of level 267. The flaming torch is licking at the black ceiling. If I were a superhero, I would use my X-ray vision to see all the way through to level 1.

This was Septimus's doing. I'm sure of it.

Why is he so desperate for me to go back to the time of my death? Does he want me to change it? Is he so sick to death of working with me that he would sacrifice Medusa to get me to go back? Why doesn't he just fire me?

I don't understand any of this.

"Are ye ready, Mitchell?"

"I'm forgetting what Medusa looks like. What she sounds like."

Alfarin opens my backpack and takes out the photo of Team DEVIL. I take it from him.

It's still in my hand when we arrive in modern-day Washington, DC.

25. The Replacement

We arrive in daylight. Most of me is past caring whether we're suddenly seen popping out of thin air. The rest of me is just sick of the darkness.

Although I saw my gravestone in the file, I took a guess at the location of the cemetery. I didn't know Washington very well when I was alive—it was just the place my dad lived and the place I happened to die. I wonder why my mom agreed to my being buried here. Then again, my parents were never the traditional kind, even when they divorced. They were nice to each other, for a start.

So I take Alfarin and Elinor to the only cemetery I know in this city besides Arlington: Glenwood. It's a pretty place, and I can understand why the living choose it, even if the site does reek of death. I can certainly smell it. It isn't the stench of rotting corpses, six feet under the ground. It's the smell of fire and salty tears and earth all mixed together.

Like all cemeteries, it's a little piece of Hell on earth.

The chapel is a funny-looking building; it looks as if a child built it out of enormous bricks: a rectangular base and a wide-bottomed triangle on top. There are trees everywhere. This isn't like Arlington cemetery with its regimented rows of white tablets. Glenwood is a smorgasbord of monoliths and angels and crosses.

And there are thousands of them.

"Where do we start?" cries Elinor, clearly horrified at the size of the cemetery.

"I'm guessing there must be an office or something," I suggest.

"Cremation on a longboat is easier, my friend," says Alfarin, looking around.

"Yeah, but longboat cremations aren't really done nowadays," I reply. "There are probably health and safety regulations and a million bylaws against it. Plus, I hate to break it to you, Alfarin, but I wasn't a Viking."

Elinor jogs over to an office building that is partially hidden by towering green firs that look like stretched broccoli florets. A narrow rainbow arches above it, stretching as far as the eye can see. The sky above us is as blue as Alfarin's normal eyes, but to our right the sky is bruised purple. The grass beneath our feet is wet and bouncy.

Where am I?

Where is Medusa?

"We will find her, my friend," says Alfarin, guessing my thoughts.

I apologize for the millionth time. "I'm sorry I got you all messed up in this, Alfarin."

"We are immortal friends," replies Alfarin, gazing across the grass and a bank of gravestones. "If I were not dead already, I would die for all of you."

"Do you think Medusa is being hurt?" The words haunting me somehow make it out of my mouth.

Alfarin snorts. "I have been trying to understand this thing you call a paradox. And so now I believe in one thing. We have the power to corrupt time. We can stop her from doing whatever it was that alerted the Skin-Walkers to her presence."

"We'll save her?"

"You would follow Medusa's trail until the end of time, my friend. We all know that." Alfarin fixes me with a solemn stare. "We *will* save her."

I like talking to Alfarin. He's so calm. It doesn't matter whether we're traveling through time or deciding what to eat next. His voice alone is enough to stop my idiotic panic attacks.

Elinor skips back out of the office building. She looks like a little girl, with her red hair flying in the breeze. There's a large piece of paper in her hand.

"You aren't far from here, Mitchell," she calls, coming to a sudden halt next to Alfarin.

"Lead the way," says Alfarin, and he heaves his axe onto his shoulder. Should we have brought the guitar case with us? Too late now. We left it behind, along with traces of ash, a stinking pile of clothes, and pulped strawberries.

And yet the living will never really know we were there.

It isn't as cold in Washington as it was in New York, although we've arrived on the same day, month, and year. As Elinor leads us along the dewy grass, I can't help looking at the gravestones. I wonder if I know any of these dead bodies in Hell. Chances are I work with some of them.

Many of the older graves are weathered, but nothing seems neglected. Glenwood looks after its dead as if they were still alive.

We pass a creamy-white sculpted angel blowing a trumpet. I get the feeling it's mocking us. A man is standing next to the sculpture. He doesn't look much older than me, but he's dressed in a worn brown uniform that looks like old-school army. He can't seem to take his eyes away from the angel, but he looks weary.

A girl with light-brown skin and long, wavy black hair calls to him, and she sounds really pissed off. She's standing about a hundred feet away from us, next to a glistening white cross. She's the most gorgeous girl I've ever set eyes on. She doesn't look real. She's wearing a short orange sundress under a pale-pink cardigan. A golden haze surrounds her, like a full-body halo. You'd think the sun was setting behind her, but it isn't. If the girl is cold in this November weather, she doesn't look it.

"Owen," she calls with an accent that I think is French, and then she catches sight of me staring at her. For some reason, her demeanor quickly changes to one of absolute loathing. Her eyes narrow and her top lip curls into a snarl.

Elinor and Alfarin don't notice any of this, as they're carefully following the map that's supposed to take us to my grave.

The guy called Owen looks at the gorgeous girl and then follows her gaze directly to me. I stop walking. Owen's eyes are twinkling like stars, and the same delicate halo surrounds him. I get goose bumps on my arms as I realize what these two are.

Unlike his beautiful friend, Owen nods to me, and I nod back. I look for Alfarin and Elinor because I want them to see this, but when I look back, the soldier and the gorgeous French girl have disappeared.

I've just seen two angels from Up There for the first time.

"Mitchell, will ye keep up?" calls Elinor.

I stumble forward, and my sneakers immediately catch on the edge of a stone border, half hidden in the grass. My hands break my fall, but I still sprawl across tiny red pebbles and onto someone's grave.

"Are you okay?" asks Alfarin as he pulls me up by the neck of my shirt. "You have gone very pale, my friend."

"I haven't seen the sun in four years, Alfarin," I mumble. "I'm always pale."

But as we continue to walk toward my final resting place, I keep my eyes peeled for the two angels.

Either Elinor was lying when she said I wasn't far from the office, or she has no concept of distance. We've been walking for hours and have doubled back at least three times. It's time to admit we're hopelessly lost.

I need to see my headstone. If it's real, I can't understand how I could have been replaced. Perhaps someone has just stolen my identity, not my life. If that's the case, I should still be able to change time and stop my death. I can still reclaim what's really mine. As we continue to walk, more morbid and fantastical theories about my replacement start seeping into my brain. Most involve zombies and body snatchers.

A cute little kid with a thick mop of blond hair runs past us.

He can't be more than three years old, and his chubby little face, with round red cheeks, is half hidden by a navy beanie that's too big for him. He's giggling as he tries to outrun a harassed-looking man with round wire-framed glasses. I assume the man is the father. He's talking into a cell phone as he chases the little boy, and his glasses keep slipping down his long nose. The man ignores us, but the little boy sees me and an enormous grin spreads across his face.

The dad scoops him up under one arm and continues talking on his cell. The little boy waves madly at me with both hands, and I smile and wave back.

Suddenly the little boy starts wriggling and struggling under his father's arm as they walk farther away from us. "Mitchell!" he cries.

Alfarin, Elinor, and I freeze in our tracks. Elinor grabs my hand.

"Did that little boy just say yer name?" she cries.

"Coincidence," says Alfarin quickly.

But the little boy is now putting up a fight as his father continues to walk away from us.

"I see Mitchell!" he screams. "I see Mitchell!"

Then he yells something that sends my stomach shooting into my mouth.

"I want M.J.!"

The little boy has burst into tears. The dad abruptly ends his call and sets his son on the ground. The boy continues to wail at a decibel level that sets my teeth on edge.

"Michael James, you will stop this right now," says the father, wagging his finger an inch from the boy's streaming button nose. "You can see the photos of M.J. when you get home. Now be quiet, Mommy is coming."

And then I see *her.*

A strange rasping, gurgling choke lodges in my throat. I actually clasp my dead heart.

"Oh, no!" squeals Elinor, and she drags me behind a white marble plinth.

"What is happening?" whispers Alfarin as he crouches down beside us.

"I have to see her."

"Alfarin, sit on Mitchell—now."

Alfarin, being Alfarin, does exactly what Elinor says. At least he has the decency to roll me onto my stomach before he obliges her and crushes every vertebra in my spine.

"I'm so, so sorry, Mitchell," whispers Elinor, stroking my cheek with her hand.

"I won't run to her, Elinor, I promise, but please, let me see her."

But Elinor is shaking her head; already silent tears are streaming down her cheeks.

"What if she were to see ye, Mitchell?" sobs Elinor. "We aren't in the past, this is the present. Just imagine what it would do to her if she saw ye."

Suddenly I feel Alfarin's weight leaving me. He isn't my jailer anymore, because now he understands what's going on.

"Is that woman your mother?" he asks.

I nod because I can't speak. Elinor scowls at Alfarin, but he just shakes his head at her.

Crawling on all fours, I peek around the hard stone edge of the plinth. Walking across the wet grass is my mom. Her skin is darker than I remember and her thick blond hair is shorter. I don't recognize her clothes: a red trench coat and tall black boots that reach her knees. She must have bought them after I died.

I guess my mom carried on living.

She's holding some stringy-looking weeds in her gloved hand. They're dead flowers. Her eyes look black and tired, but then I realize she's just wearing a lot of makeup. I can't remember my mom wearing that much makeup when I was alive. It doesn't really suit her; it makes her look older.

She is older.

Mom is smiling to herself, though, and I wonder what she's thinking. Is it me? Is she remembering me? She must be. She's been here to see my grave, to lay fresh flowers—probably something bright and sweet-smelling, knowing my mom.

The urge to run and hug her nearly overwhelms me. It's as if an invisible hand is pushing me from inside. It's a little embarrassing, to be perfectly honest.

She waves at the man holding the little boy. She must know them.

I'm inching like a caterpillar around the corner of the mono-lith so I don't lose sight of her. Alfarin and Elinor quietly creep around with me, although Elinor is now holding on to the back of my T-shirt. Her hands feel hot against my skin.

I wish Medusa were here to see this.

"Mommy."

The little boy squeals and runs to my mom.

My mom.

It hits me with the force of ten Alfarins. Elinor—who is more intuitive than anyone gives her credit for, especially when it comes to family—is now the devil sitting on my back. She's pinning me to the wet grass to stop me from running to the woman who carried on living.

Because this is what my devil resources file meant by *replaced*. No one stole my identity or even my soul.

That little boy—my brother—is my living, breathing replacement.

26. M.J.

The screaming voices are back as we are sucked through the flames of time once more. Only this time the rage is coming from me.

She replaced me. I couldn't have been dead for more than a few months before my mom got herself knocked up.

It's beyond gross. It's vile, disgusting. I don't even know who that man is. Probably just some sperm donor she picked up off the street. I'm amazed she let him hang around long enough to see the end result, but then, maybe he's the jerk who's buying her new clothes.

My mom probably has a nice new house and car to go with her brand-new life. The life she continued to live once I was worm bait.

Alfarin, Elinor, and I slam into an alley lined with brick buildings. We've gone back four years to July eighteenth. I can't even remember flicking the red needle over the dial, but here we are, and the Viciseometer is spitting feebly in my hand. I grip it between my fingers.

She even gave my replacement my nickname. I heard the man call that little kid Michael James. He's another M.J.

"Mitchell," whispers Elinor. Her long fingers stroke my hand, but I shrug her away. I can't see properly. The brick walls around us are a blur of crumbling red stone. It's Alfarin who stops me from punching the ground in despair.

"It is just a word in a file, my friend," he says. His arms, thick like branches, are wrapped around my chest. "Your mother would not have replaced you in her heart."

"Bullshit," I spit. "You saw her, Alfarin, you both saw her. She replaced me with a new version. Dammit, she even gave that brat my name: M.J. That was what she called me when I was alive—she even had it put on my gravestone. It was mine. My one link to being alive, and she just gave it away, gave everything that was mine away like I was something to be recycled. It isn't just a word in a file, Alfarin. It's the truth—my mom replaced me the second I was dead."

"That isn't true, Mitchell, and ye know it!" cries Elinor. "Yer mom loved ye, she still loves ye. Ye heard that man—they have photos of ye. They kept yer memory alive. Yer little brother knew who ye were."

But the anger is redwashing away any sensibility I have left. The fire of rejection and humiliation is surging through my veins. It's so toxic I expect it to kick-start my shriveled heart.

And Septimus knew.

I shrug Alfarin off as if he were made of paper. I slam my hand against the brick wall, again, again, again. I hate her, I hate her, I hate her.

I slump onto the ground between two big recycling containers. We're in an alley near an Italian restaurant Dad and I used to go to once he'd finished work on Capitol Hill. I wonder if my dad has also replaced me with another blond kid with blue eyes. How many more M.J.s are there in this world?

Elinor steps closer to me, but I can't stomach the thought of looking her in the face, so I continue to gaze at her kneecaps. Skinny jeans make her legs look like sticks.

"This is the day of yer death, isn't it?"

I nod, which is embarrassing because the sudden movement of my head dislodges the tears I've been trying to will away with my hate. I quickly wipe my face with my knuckles and then realize that was a stupid idea, because now I've smeared thick blood onto my face.

I can't even cry without making a mess of it.

In a few minutes, seventeen-year-old Mitchell Johnson will be walking down the opposite street. He is living. He'll be wearing a pair of brand-new black Nikes and a Juilliard sweatshirt, which is a little pretentious because he doesn't go to Juilliard—yet. He'll be chewing a stick of gum that he's had in his mouth for over an hour, and Radiohead will be slamming into his ears.

And then he will die.

I can remember I was chewing gum, and I can remember the line Thom Yorke was singing before I ran out into the road.

So why the Hell can't I remember *why?*

But now everything is going to change.

I'm not going to die. I'm going to reclaim my old life. My mom and my dad and my friends who all carried on living their lives are going to find out they can't replace me if I never left in the first place.

And then I will make them suffer for thinking they could.

Alfarin and Elinor are talking. Their voices blend in with the noise in my head. I'm trapped in a vacuum of space that is rushing through my eardrums. It's as if I'm cruising through a wind tunnel at two hundred miles an hour and nothing is making any sense.

I hear Elinor say she's scared.

Alfarin replies, but the words are muffled.

And then I hear Medusa's name.

But Medusa left me. She went somewhere I can't find her.

A wailing police siren shrieks through the sultry summer air. I like this oppressive heat. The sweat starting to pool around the back of my neck feels comforting because I'm used to it. I gaze up at Elinor through half-opened eyes and wonder if she can feel the same sensation. Maybe her nerve endings were damaged beyond repair once Alfarin's axe sliced through her throat and that's why she's constantly grabbing at her neck.

"Did you close your eyes before Alfarin killed you?"

Elinor shudders. "Let's not talk about that now," she says softly.

"Alfarin didn't close his eyes," I add, looking down the alleyway and into the open, busy avenue beyond. "He looked that villager right in the eyes before he died."

"Where are you going with this, my friend?" asks Alfarin warily.

"I can't remember what I was looking at when I died," I reply, jumping to my feet. "So let's find out, shall we?"

Elinor screams and pulls me back. "Ye can't just run out like that."

"Why the Hell not?"

"Ye are hurting, Mitchell. The three of us should leave this time and go back to searching for Medusa."

"Why?" I yell. "Medusa doesn't care about us. If she thought anything of you, or Alfarin, or me, she would have told us what she was doing—but she didn't. She deserted us as if we were things that could be thrown away. Medusa is no better than my mother."

"Don't say that, Mitchell," sobs Elinor.

I thrust the Viciseometer at Elinor, but she backs away with fear in her eyes. She won't take it, so I offer it to Alfarin. The thick folds of skin on his pale brow are creased like the crust on a pie. He leans his axe up against the wall and crosses his arms.

"Dammit. Will one of you just take this away from me?" I cry. "This ends for me now. I'm finished screwing with time."

"You cannot stop your death, Mitchell," says Alfarin slowly. "Not now."

"Watch me."

I make to run out of the alleyway, but Alfarin tackles me.

"*Get off me!*" I shout as we wrestle on the ground. Another police siren screams past our alleyway.

"It is too late for you, Mitchell," says Alfarin.

My anger at Alfarin is not the same sickening rage I felt toward him when we returned to the Plaza after Elinor's death, but it is more impassioned because this is personal. It is *my* death now. This is *my* turn.

"You and Elinor and Medusa made your choices!" I yell. "Don't you dare try to stop me from making mine."

I stagger to my feet, Alfarin grabs an ankle, and I trip, banging my forehead on the sun-parched tarmac. The ground is sticky.

"You cannot change your death, Mitchell," says Alfarin. "Your death is what links us all together. If you aren't in Hell to steal the Viciseometer in the first place, none of us will ever travel back. I won't be there to appear after death to my clan—to give them the peace of knowing I am in a better place. If we don't go back to the Great Fire, Elinor will burn to death in agony. Is that what you want?"

As Alfarin speaks, the rushing noise in my head slows enough for me to register the whimpering and sniffling that are coming from Elinor.

My back is toward the open street. I don't have much time for good-byes. When I run out and grab the other Mitchell, I know that this dead form will disappear. Everything that has happened to me in the last four years will be wiped clean. I won't be starting again, I'll just be continuing where I left off. I'll get to hear the rest of the Radiohead song, spit out the gum, and go eat lasagna with my dad.

Life will be normal. *My* life will be normal.

And Medusa, Alfarin, and Elinor won't be memories, because I'll never know they existed.

"Don't do it, Mitchell," begs Elinor.

"Medusa will become The Devil's intern if I'm not there," I whisper. "She could still find out about the Viciseometer. The three of you can still change time without me. You don't need me—you've never needed me. You're all smarter than me."

My feet are slowly taking me away from Alfarin and Elinor. Neither is making a move to stop me, although Elinor is so upset, I'm surprised she's still standing.

"Medusa would take the Viciseometer and go straight to where she is now, Mitchell," calls Alfarin, "and we would never be able to find her or bring her back because she would do it alone. With you, we still have a chance to save Medusa."

I swear I can hear the lyrics of "Creep" in my head. They're eating into my dead soul.

"And what about yer brother, Mitchell?" adds Elinor. "If ye do this, ye end his life as well. He won't exist anymore. He'll never have existed."

"That's low, Elinor!" I cry. "My mother's choices are not my problem."

"You're angry, my friend," says Alfarin. "Do you think for one moment that Elinor and I don't understand the rage you feel? Death isn't fair—and perhaps you were unlucky to be sent to Hell—but I will give thanks for the rest of my existence that I found you, and Elinor, and Medusa in the fire and heat."

"Do ye regret finding us?" Elinor asks.

"Of course I don't!" I shout.

"Medusa needs you," says Alfarin. "She left because she was trying to protect you; she was trying to protect all of us."

"Alfarin is right!" cries Elinor. "Medusa must have known the Skin-Walkers were coming after her, but we can still save her, Mitchell."

"Think back to the cathedral caves," pleads Alfarin as I continue to back away. "We saw that man being led by the wolves. Do you want Medusa to suffer that fate?"

The pain I feel at my mother's betrayal is nothing to the loss I feel, the gaping chasm that fills my chest, at the disappearance of Medusa. I can still taste her mouth on mine. Her hot tears against my skin.

"I was too young to die! *It isn't fair!*"

"We were all too young," shouts Elinor, "and it isn't fair, Mitchell, but if ye leave us now, everything changes."

She collapses against Alfarin's broad chest, and everyone's guilt and pain threatens to crush me into the ground.

A fire engine wails in the distance. The sound of an emergency is the sound track of this city, of this country. They'll be coming for the real me in seconds if I don't act now.

But *I* am the real me, and now that other Mitchell, the one who is still alive, feels like the impostor.

I reach the edge of the alleyway. A young busboy strolls out of the Italian restaurant carrying several cardboard boxes. He stops, takes one look at me, looks back up the alley, sees Alfarin and his glinting axe, and runs yelling back through the kitchen door.

I'm out of time. I have to do this now.

Alfarin and Elinor are rooted to the spot, and the big man has his arms around his princess. My arms feel so empty without Medusa. My mom won't feel this way; she has little M.J. in hers.

I was perfectly happy being the only child when I was alive. Mom and Dad were so busy with their careers that I was glad to have their undivided attention once they had time. But now I have a little brother, and regardless of how this ends, I'll never get to take him to Little League, or the movies, or out for ice cream, or do the other things that big brothers do with their little hero-worshipping shadows.

And I wouldn't call him M.J., because I wouldn't want his life to end up in death like mine. My brother would be Mickey, like the mouse, and then, once he was older, I would just call him Mike, and he would be allowed to call me Mitch—the only person who could do that.

Mitchell Johnson, that's me. Four syllables and nothing more—to all except my little brother.

But that will never happen, regardless of the choice I make now.

The long avenue stretches out on either side of me, and the heat from the sun distorts everything in the distance. White buildings are offset by rows of bulbous green trees.

And lumbering toward me is a big gray beetle on wheels, shimmering like a wet stone.

The Greyhound bus is right on time.

Medusa would know what to do. She wouldn't be wasting time, dithering one way and then the other. Even if the choice is almost impossible, Medusa has the guts to see anything through to the end.

Medusa and M.J. and my mom and Alfarin and Elinor aren't here anymore. I am standing on this street, being pushed by sightseers desperate to get to that big white-domed building on the hill, but I feel completely alone. At this exact moment in time, my three friends are already in Hell. Elinor has been waiting hundreds of years for the final piece of the puzzle to arrive. My little brother hasn't even been born yet.

If I do this, Alfarin and Elinor are right. Everything changes.

And then on the opposite side of the road, I finally see the living me.

The hairs on my arms stand to attention as a sensation of intense cold washes over me. My stomach drops into my sneakers as I watch myself walking down the street.

I'm just walking. Two girls in very short skirts skip past me and turn their heads to look at my back. They giggle and flick their long blond hair, but I don't even notice them. How lame was I? Instead, my living eyes are fixed on the ground as my head nods up and down; the white wires from my headphones disappear into the front pocket of my sweatshirt. Mitchell Johnson is completely oblivious to the world he is about to leave.

It's now or never. I have to run across the street and push myself to safety. This form I now have will disappear into smoke and ash. A toxic streak that has existed for four years in Hell will have been erased forever.

But instead of Radiohead singing in my ears, I hear something else. I want to turn the sound up, but it's muffled, as if a pillow has been placed over the speakers.

Don't let me go.

It's the voice I heard the last time I time-traveled with Medusa. I knew it was her in the darkness.

And yet I let her go.

The bus is picking up speed. I see the lights changing to red, but the bus carries on, moving right through them. The driver has a schedule to keep.

Don't let me go.

And then the moment of truth arrives. I lock eyes with my other self and I remember, after all this time, what made me run out into the road to my death four years ago.

Who made me run out into the road to my death four years ago.

It was me.

The other Mitchell, the living, breathing impostor, pulls the headphones from his ears and runs out into the road. His blue eyes still gaze in disbelief at his dead mirror image, standing across the street from him.

And I don't disappear in a plume of ash and smoke, because I don't stop my death. I am the last thing I see before the Greyhound bus collides with my body and sends me somersaulting fifteen feet into the air. The sound of compressing brakes isn't enough to mute the sound of snapping bones as my lifeless body lands in the road.

M.J. is dead.

Long live M.J.

27. **Fault Line**

Death has a symphony. It isn't violins and crashing cymbals and beating drums; it consists of screaming and yelling and, in my case, the screeching of brakes.

There's something oddly comforting about the strangers who are now rushing to my dead body. They must know they can't do anything, but it doesn't stop them from trying. My faith in humanity is restored, even if I don't have any in myself anymore.

One guy in a pink T-shirt is giving me the kiss of life. His friend is pummeling my chest. They're both yelling at me to stay with them. That fact that my legs are twisted underneath my broken back doesn't stop them.

In the devil resources file, I saw the morbid spectators taking photos, but in reality there are a lot more bystanders on their cell phones, calling 911. Then I see the bus driver, and for a second, just for a second, I want to run across the road and punch his fat, sobbing face in.

He's yelling that it wasn't his fault.

There's no need to rub it in. I'm standing right here, after all.

It was my fault I died. It was *always* my fault.

"I think you should come back into the alley, my friend," says a deep voice just behind me.

"I want to watch, just for a bit longer."

"Then view it from the shadows. Ye don't want people to look up and realize ye look exactly like the boy who just died."

The three of us fall back. A red-and-white-striped awning above the Italian restaurant provides enough shadow to shield us from view.

"It was me all along," I whisper as an ambulance screams up the avenue, effortlessly weaving in and out of the stationary traffic. "I saw the dead me and ran out into the road. I caused my own death in a paradox."

"Do you think Lord Septimus knew?" asks Alfarin.

"Of course he knew. It was why he wanted me to come back here in the first place."

"Why didn't ye stop yer death, Mitchell?" Elinor is holding my hand; her head is resting on my shoulder. I lean into her.

"Because of everything that was left," I reply. "I wouldn't be able to exist with myself, knowing your deaths were worse because of me. Or that my little brother might never be born if I lived. And—and I have to find Medusa."

"But if you had lived, you would never feel the guilt, because you would not know everything you know now," says Alfarin. "We would cease to exist in your world."

"Do you want me to go back and try again, Alfarin?" I ask. "I have the Viciseometer. I can go back and watch this moment another hundred times if I want to. I can still change my death."

"That isn't what Alfarin meant," says Elinor.

"Then spell it out for me," I snap. "One minute you're telling me I can't change my death because it's too late, and the next minute you're saying I could have done it anyway because I would never feel the guilt in the first place."

"You have a choice, Mitchell," replies Alfarin calmly, "and we cannot move from this moment in time until you have made it."

"I've made the choice. I'm still dead, aren't I?"

"Your head made the choice—now your heart must agree. You have to let this moment in time go. Now and forever, my friend."

I watch the paramedics in their blue uniforms. One is covering my broken body with a white blanket. The cops have arrived, and they're instructing the paramedics to set up some screens. Others are directing the traffic for the living. The fat, sobbing bus driver is still declaring his innocence, but he's being Breathalyzed just in case, because the main witness is dead.

I could stand here and watch how this unfolds for hours. Questions I've never really given much thought to are now rushing through my head: Who identified my body? How many people came to my funeral? Am I missed?

Then a despairing, pained voice drags me away from my self-obsessed thoughts.

"Not my son...not my M.J."

My dad towers above the policemen who hold him back; I get my height from him and the blond hair from my mom. Elinor instinctively steps out onto the pavement, as if she intends to rush to comfort him, but this time I'm the one holding her back. He called me M.J., too.

My dead feet are protruding from the bottom of the blanket. I wait for someone to straighten me out. One leg lies at ninety degrees to the other. Only one has a black Nike sneaker still on it. I can't see the other sneaker. I hope someone finds it. They were expensive.

Bizarre, the things you think of when you're watching your death.

But now the picture in front of me is getting smaller, as if it's being replayed on a television set. Reality is slipping away from me and I'm back in a paradox. Mitchell Johnson is lying dead in the middle of the road, and yet his soul, or whatever I am now, is watching from the shadows.

But there is also another me. I've just arrived at the HalfWay House. I'm looking for the way out, because seventeen-year-olds shouldn't die.

Over the next four years I will meet Alfarin, Elinor, and Medusa. They will welcome me as if they've been waiting forever. Medusa and I will battle it out to become The Devil's intern, and when I get the job, instead of hating me, Medusa will become my best friend.

From the moment I learned about the Viciseometer and its power, I've been obsessed with stopping my death. All I wanted was to go on living. To live those dreams that haunt the dead. I wanted to be a rock star, I wanted to party with my friends, I wanted to live. My heart stopped beating before the wheels on the Greyhound bus had stopped turning, but that doesn't mean it can't feel. Alfarin is right. I have to let this moment go, now and forever. My life is over, and I am immortal now. I'm in on the biggest secret the world will never know until it is *their* time.

This isn't fair. This will *never* be fair.

"Ye can draw comfort from knowing they have yer photos, Mitchell," says Elinor softly. "Yer little brother adores ye."

"You are not forgotten, my friend."

Seventeen-year-olds shouldn't have to make this kind of decision. *No one* should be forced to make this decision.

In my head I tell my dad I love him and I'm sorry. Then I turn away from my dead body.

"Hold on to me."

The Viciseometer sparks to life in my hand. The red needle dances around both faces as if it's skating on ice.

It is time to say good-bye to my life.

It is time to find my best friend.

We arrive back at the park in San Francisco. The same scent of smoke lingers in the air; the same guitar laments; the same couple are still making out in the tree that looks like the wooden skeleton of a mammoth.

Nothing here has changed.

"Are we likely to see ourselves?" asks Alfarin, hastily looking around for any other Alfarins that may be lurking in a paradox. Elinor pushes his axe away from her head; she doesn't need another extreme close-up.

I shake my head. "Ever since New York, I've been keeping track of where we are in time. We left here about a minute ago."

"What about Septimus?" asks Elinor.

"I think it's pretty obvious that no one can control Septimus," I reply.

"You say that with pride, my friend."

We sit down on the sun-parched grass. Most of it has died, or at least looks as if it has withered away.

"We have to think," I say. "Every little detail, every conversation you've ever had with Medusa about her home, her family. Where she liked to hang out—places she hated. We need to be able to visualize everything."

"You think she is here in San Francisco, then?" asks Alfarin.

"Absolutely."

And I am sure of it. I imagine closing my eyes and opening them again to see her standing before me. Medusa could be so near we just have to reach out and grab her. Take her back before the Skin-Walkers find her.

"Let's narrow it down to what we do know," I say, drawing circles in the dusty ground with my finger. "We know Medusa left us with the Viciseometer showing eight o'clock on the eighteenth of June, 1967, and we know she hated her stepfather. She dies on the twenty-fifth, and we know where." I jerk my thumb to the towering red bridge behind me without bothering to look at it.

"Are ye sure Septimus isn't coming?" asks Elinor. Her voice is rather high-pitched, like a child's.

"Elinor, I have no idea what Septimus is going to do anymore," I reply. "For all I know, we could get back to Hell and find that while we were time-traveling, a celestial war has broken out between the Vikings and those two humping in the tree."

Elinor takes her backpack off and opens it. Her long fingers fumble with the straps as her green eyes dart in all directions.

"I took this from devil resources," she says, pulling out a slightly bent red folder. "I thought it could help Alfarin and me find Medusa if ye left us."

I take the file from Elinor's trembling hands and swear. It's Medusa's devil resources record.

"How did you get this? It wasn't in the drawer."

"I had an idea," replies Elinor nervously. "I thought if yer record was in Medusa's place, then the same person might have just done a straight swap and put this one in yer place. So when ye were looking through yer papers, I used the Viciseometer and traveled up a few floors. Medusa's file was sticking right out of an open drawer."

"You're a genius!" I exclaim, recalling the moment I thought Elinor was running around like a headless chicken in the files, when in reality she was the only one who had actually kept her head.

"A princess among peasants," sighs Alfarin.

"This is why you were throwing up, wasn't it? You traveled alone?"

Elinor nods. "Osmosis of the Dead is not very nice."

"Elinor, you are an absolute genius," I repeat.

"A rival to better the goddess Frigga," says Alfarin.

"Oh, behave, the pair of ye," replies Elinor, but she is beaming with pride.

I start tearing pieces of paper from the file and handing them to Alfarin and Elinor.

"We'll start with addresses," I say.

A color photo slips out. It's Medusa's deathday picture. Her brown eyes are already swirling with white; they look like miniature pools of milky hot chocolate. Her head is leaning back slightly in the photo. My raggedy doll doesn't look scared or confused the way I was, but she does look shocked. The wild curls are wet against her face, making them look longer, and leaves and other river debris are caught up in several ringlets. She made a mistake, she never meant to let go.

My stomach feels hot and flustered as I gaze at her. I haven't eaten in days, or at least it feels that way. I don't understand why Medusa makes me feel hungry all the time. When I see her I think of chocolate and strawberries.

"I have Medusa's home address and a photo!" cries Alfarin.

"She worked weekends in a shoe store; the address is here," says Elinor.

"And I have her stepfather's name and place of work," I say darkly. "He's a mechanic—"

A howl interrupts me. The three of us turn around in a panic, but we can't see anything that could have made that noise. It seems to be coming from above us, as if it's being carried through the wind.

"Where do you want to start, Mitchell?" asks Alfarin. He's shivering. "We are down one, but you are still our leader."

"We'll go back ten minutes before the time Medusa put into the Viciseometer and try to intercept. We can't stop her time-traveling because of the fixed-point-in-time rule, but we can get her as soon as she arrives somewhere. Plus she'll be suffering from Osmosis of the Dead, so she'll be easy to get to. We'll go to her family's house first, but we'll have to be careful. Elinor arrived in Hell already knowing us—but Medusa didn't. We'll have to make sure we intercept the right one: the dead Medusa, not the living Melissa."

Alfarin is rubbing his temples with the flat side of his axe. He probably finds it comforting, but it makes me really nervous. One slip and he'll take off half his face.

"Is this going to work?" he asks.

"It has to. I won't let the Skin-Walkers take her."

The three remaining members of Team DEVIL stand and link arms. The air feels heavy around us. Even the laughter and music seem to have stopped. I move the minute hand on the white dial back by ten minutes. I hope it will be enough.

Warm fire wraps around us as we rush through the wind. Alfarin and I are on either side of Elinor, and I swear I feel someone holding my other hand, but when we land outside Medusa's run-down house, it's only the sparking Viciseometer that I see when I look down.

* * *

Medusa's house is old and wooden and sits on a small lot on a quiet street. The outside is painted white, but even from our position in a small park across the road, I can see the thick curls of peeling paint. A metal screen covers the front door. There are large windows on either side, and the upstairs floor looks cramped, with two dormer windows settled into the roof like watching eyes. There's a white Dodge Polara parked on the street right outside the house. The hood is up and the windows are wound down, but I can't see anyone around.

It's ten minutes to eight in the evening. The sun is still setting and the sky is splashed with pink. The color reminds me of Medusa's pretty dead eyes.

It's my fault she's here, hidden somewhere from me and her other best friends, who would do anything to protect her. I want to shout her name until my throat bleeds.

I won't let her go again.

28. **Mom's Loaded**

"Should we knock on the door?" asks Elinor.

"Absolutely not."

"But we need to find her," she protests.

"And we will," I say, "but we've blundered from one time to another since we left, Elinor. My leaving Hell caused me to die in the first place, and now it's something I'll never be able to fix without screwing up a bunch of other lives and deaths in the process. I won't mess this one up."

"Mitchell is right," says Alfarin, looking up and down the quiet row of shabby detached houses. "So do you think they serve buckets of chicken in this time?"

Elinor huffs. "Medusa is missing and moments away from being snatched by Skin-Walkers and all ye can think about is yer big ol' stomach?"

"Your point, my princess?"

"I'll stay here," I say. "Leave your axe with me, Alfarin, and you two see if you can get us some food from somewhere." Elinor is now scowling at me. "Elinor, don't look at us like that. We have to eat. Our brains work better when they're fed, and I haven't eaten anything but a few strawberries since we got back from 1666."

She starts walking away. I can hear her muttering under her breath about boys having one-track minds.

"How will we pay?" asks Alfarin seriously.

I shrug. "Our money is useless here because it's future currency, and I'm not even sure they had credit cards back in the 1960s. You'll just have to improvise."

"How?"

"You're in Hell for a reason, Alfarin—steal something! And hurry up. Our Medusa arrives in just over seven minutes."

My attention turns back to Medusa's former home. I can hear raised voices coming from inside, but the conversation is followed by the echoing laughter of a crowd. I think it may be a television turned up really loud.

The screen door suddenly flies open, but it isn't Medusa who steps onto the wooden porch and down the front steps. It's a man.

He isn't as tall as me, but then again, few guys are. He has long, sun-streaked blond hair and sideburns all the way down to his chin. He looks as if he could be in his late thirties, but he dresses as if he wishes he were younger. For a few moments, I wonder if he's Medusa's brother, but he looks nothing like her, and as far as I know, Medusa was an only child like me—well, before M.J. 2.0, anyway.

The guy slaps his hands together and heads toward the open hood of the Dodge Polara.

And right away, with a sudden surge of hatred, I realize who he is.

This is Medusa's stepfather.

Alfarin's axe is lying by my feet. My first raging thought is to charge at the mechanic and slice his head off. My hands are reaching for the handle when the screen door clatters open again and another figure comes running out of the house. The guy immediately looks up, and the figure freezes in her tracks.

It's Medusa.

Only, right away I know it isn't *my* Medusa. It's the living Melissa from this time. She looks the same: mad corkscrew hair, skinny little arms and legs dressed in denim shorts, and a peach-colored top that ties around the back of her neck.

But something is missing.

The living Melissa looks back at the house and runs down the path. She opens the gate and makes to sprint across the road, but the mechanic, her stepfather, slams down the hood and catches her, holding her tightly by the wrist. She doesn't see me standing opposite, peering out from behind a bush like a child, debating whether to run across to the car and punch his teeth in.

Shadows of the living and inanimate are stretched along the road as the sun sets lower in the sky. I can hear Medusa pleading with her stepfather. I reach down and pick up Alfarin's axe.

A woman calls from the house.

"Melissa..."

It's the reason I need to stay where I am. This isn't Medusa—*my* Medusa. That girl is Melissa Pallister, and she doesn't know it yet, but her life will end in one week, on the twenty-fifth of June, 1967. I can't change this because it isn't mine to change. I need to wait for Medusa to appear; she'll know what to do.

But I don't let go of the axe.

I think back to that first night in New York. Medusa awoke from yet another nightmare and told us for the first time how she died.

I only regret that I didn't take him with me.

What does he do to her? Has it already happened? Where is Medusa? Why *this* moment in time?

The voice calls again. It quivers, as if worried. The living Melissa breaks free from her stepfather's grasp and runs back into the house. He turns, kicks his car, and wipes his top lip with the back of his hand. Then he leans in through an open window and reappears seconds later with a bottle, which he swigs from before going back into the house, stumbling over the steps in his haste.

Alfarin and Elinor reappear; both are looking flushed and sheepish. Elinor dips in behind the bush and gesticulates to the house; she has a glass bottle of milk in one hand and a loaf of white bread in the other.

"We were watching from back there," she says quietly.

"Not ours?" whispers Alfarin.

I shake my head. I don't take the bread or milk from Elinor, or the cookies that Alfarin has stuffed into his pockets. It looks as though they've raided a 1967 fridge.

"Any sign of our M yet?"

"Who do you think that man is?" asks Alfarin thickly. Cookie crumbs spray into his blond stubble as he speaks.

"Her stepfather," I reply.

"Why are ye holding Alfarin's axe?"

"I was looking after it," I mumble.

Alfarin takes it from me. "Whatever that man has done, we cannot take his life with intent, Mitchell," he says solemnly. "If there is one thing I have learned on this journey, it is the honor of living that we take for granted. I fear now that some of my clan, those we believed had been taken by Up There, have become victims of the Skin-Walkers. Too many killed in cold blood, for enjoyment, for the thrill. I will not allow that fate to befall you, my friend."

There's a sudden change in the air: a quick blast of intense heat.

"What are you doing here?" gasps a voice I feared I would start to forget.

I turn around and my hand connects with burning-hot skin. My Medusa is standing right next to us. Instinctively, I fling my arms around her and crush her tightly. Alfarin and Elinor join in the group hug. And now I know why the living Melissa didn't appear real to me when I first saw her, because what I have clasped against my chest is pure soul and nothing else. In the same way I recognized those angels in the cemetery, I know a devil when I see one.

"Why did you leave us—leave me?" I growl into the mass of curls that is invading my mouth and nostrils.

"How did you get here before me?" she replies in a muffled voice that's smothered by my T-shirt. "I left you just seconds ago."

"A lot has happened since then—we can time-travel, remember? So we went back to Hell and Elinor stole your devil resources file. Did you seriously think we wouldn't follow you?"

"You've let him corrupt you, El."

"She's been worried sick the Skin-Walkers were going to get you. We all were."

I can feel Medusa's hot little body trembling under my grip. I hate her and love her at the same time.

"The Skin-Walkers were there, in the fire, as I traveled. They were snapping and screaming at me. I could see every soul the Skin-Walkers have taken, begging in the flames. They were reaching for me, touching me; they wouldn't let me go."

"If you kill your stepfather, the Skin-Walkers will take you," says Alfarin gravely, releasing us all from his grasp.

Medusa gasps. "I was never going to kill him; I just wanted to frighten him."

And now I pull away from Medusa. I can hear her voice crying in the background, and yet her mouth in front of me isn't moving— this is weird and confusing.

"Why did you leave us?"

"Because I guessed the Skin-Walkers were after me and I wanted to get them away from you...and...and because I need to protect my mom," replies Medusa, and for the first time, her eyes take in the house she hasn't seen in forty years. "Mom goes to pieces after I die, and he takes everything from her—her money, her dignity, everything. He gets worse, Mitchell. Rory does horrible things, sick things, to girls even younger than me. And people blame her—for not stopping him sooner."

"He abused ye?" whispers Elinor, asking the question neither Alfarin nor I want to ask.

Medusa nods and says softly, "He hurt me, El."

It's a good thing Alfarin has taken that axe back, because right now I'm prepared to risk the wrath of the Skin-Walkers. But judging by the look of boiling hatred on Alfarin's face, so is he.

"Yer mother was not to blame for what happened, M."

"That doesn't stop people, though," she replies. "People go after her, El. Some of the moms and dads of the other girls he hurt. They burn the house down."

"But how do you know this?" I ask.

"Because I've seen her future, Mitchell. I looked into the Viciseometer back in Hell. You weren't the only one who was stealing it out of the safe, you know."

"Ye have been watching yer mom?"

"I don't understand how you got the Viciseometer, Medusa," I say. "How did you get into the safe?"

"You wrote the combination down on a piece of paper to memorize, Mitchell. I saw the numbers and put them into my cell phone because I thought they belonged to another girl's cell phone. I was going to crank-call—but they never connected anywhere. Then I overheard you and Septimus talking about the safe combination and I put two and two together. The second Septimus mentioned the Viciseometer, I knew that was where he would put it."

"Why didn't you tell me? Why didn't you trust me?"

"Because we all have secrets, Mitchell. I used the Viciseometer again in the bathroom of the Plaza after I had that nightmare. Just seeing how her life is ruined by what he does in the future...She did nothing wrong, but she gets blamed anyway. It was breaking my heart. I want to change *her* life, not *my* death. I owe it to her."

"It wasn't your fault, Medusa. You don't owe anyone anything."

"But you don't understand the guilt I've been carrying, Mitchell. She lives on thinking I killed myself, but I only wanted to scare her into believing me about the abuse. That's what haunts me in my sleep. I feel myself slipping...falling..."

Medusa breaks off. I try to hug her but she pushes me away.

"We only want to help ye," sniffles Elinor. She's trying really hard not to cry, and seeing her so upset just makes me angrier.

"Please try to understand," begs Medusa. "I thought if I came back now, like this—dead—then maybe I could scare him into stopping before he hurts those other girls. But I had to come back to a time when I'm still living, since I need to appear to my mom, too. I need to warn her, I need to make her listen to me, and I can't do that after my death because I don't want to frighten her or make her think she's going crazy. I can't change Rory if I live, but I think

I stand a chance of stopping him and saving my mom now that I'm dead."

Medusa pulls me farther behind the bush. Tiny thorns scratch the bare skin of my arms, leaving faint white lines. She's trembling and sweating as the effects of lone time travel catch up with her.

"Are you all okay?" she groans.

"Do you care?"

I think Medusa's sharp intake of air is real, as is the hurt look on her face, but I don't trust her, and I hate myself for thinking it. I don't want to be an asshole to Medusa. She's everything to me. But she left us—she left me. I promised her I wouldn't do that to her for any reason. Why couldn't she have just trusted us to help her, to protect her?

"I was trying to save you from the Skin-Walkers, Mitchell. I was willing to spend an eternity here alone to keep you all safe."

"Well, congratulations, because you failed miserably. We are now in more trouble than you know. Septimus came after us with a Viciseometer he stole from Up There. We traveled back to Hell; Elinor stole your records and we saw mine, which were put in your drawer. I've discovered that my mother has remarried and had another baby to replace me, and I saw my death but couldn't stop it because if I live, everything else changes."

I pause in my angry rant because Osmosis of the Dead has fully caught up with Medusa and she is throwing up into the bush. And now I feel sick with guilt, because even though Medusa should never have left us, I know she really was just trying to protect us. It's what I had planned to do at the beginning of all this. Go on alone to protect my best friends. And what Medusa was facing was way worse than what I went through. For years she's kept her life and death secret. The fact that she has now shared everything with us means she does trust us completely. She trusts me.

Elinor makes no sound as she leaves Alfarin's side and walks to Medusa.

"What is yer plan, M?"

"I want to see my mom first," replies Medusa. Her eyes are

watering. She wipes her mouth with the back of her hand. "After that, I'll confront *him*."

"Then I'll go with ye."

Elinor places an arm around Medusa's waist and supports her as they cross the road to Medusa's former house. The sun is lingering on the horizon as if Up There is watching what happens next. I swear I can hear angels laughing in the wind.

"I have a bad feeling about this," mumbles Alfarin, scratching at his face.

"Me too."

I look around the park we landed in. A rusty-looking swing squeaks, even though the chains are still. Garbage is strewn across the dying grass. Alfarin and I stare at the house. My eyes hurt with the effort as I try to glimpse anything through the grimy windows.

And then a wolf howls in the distance.

"It's just a dog," I say quickly, but Alfarin and I are already running across the street.

Another, longer howl follows us into the house. The screen door is pulled off its rusting hinges as Alfarin tugs it open with one violent yank. Whatever animal is making that noise, it sounds as if it's in pain. A caustic, rotten smell washes over me and the hairs on the back of my neck rise.

Oh, crap, not now, not here.

"Elinor, Elinor!" yells Alfarin.

I shout for Medusa, but all I can hear is the gushing of water filling an upstairs bath and more audience laughter from a black-and-white television flickering in a small room to my left. The volume has been turned up really high, and I get a feeling of dread that it's meant to block out the sounds of something else—something happening upstairs. I can hear creaking floorboards and then a muffled thump. Crooked pictures of farm animals line the wall by the stairs. They shift even more as the vibration shudders down like an aftershock. I notice a cream-colored rotary-dial telephone on a stool by the banister. The cord has been ripped out of the wall.

No one can call for help from this house.

The Viciseometer is in my hand, although I can't remember reaching into my pocket for it. I attempt to move the red needle around the numbers on the red face, but my movements are too jerky and I can't fix time properly. We shouldn't have come here. The shadows of the dead have followed us and are howling with laughter at our stupidity.

Alfarin and I crash into the kitchen and come to a skidding halt on the sticky linoleum floor. A woman is aiming a handgun directly at us. It vibrates violently in her shaking hand.

"Mom!" begs Medusa; she and Elinor are standing on the other side of a scratched Formica table. "Mom, please put the gun down." But as Medusa takes a step toward the woman she called Mom, the gun is pointed at her.

Elinor screams and puts herself in front of Medusa; her long, pale hands are raised in surrender. Alfarin makes a movement toward the girls, but then the gun is pointed at him.

"Mom, it's me," pleads Medusa, but instead of listening, the woman cocks the trigger with her thumb.

"You aren't my daughter."

Another wolf howls, and this time, it is joined by another.

They're just dogs, I keep telling myself. Just a couple of mangy old mutts that have been left outside.

"We mean you no harm, woman," says Alfarin, stepping forward. His hands are raised exactly like Elinor's. "We are here to see the man called Rory. We will deliver a message and then we will leave."

"Mommy."

Medusa has gone to pieces. Seeing her mother again after all this time has driven thoughts of confronting her stepfather out of her head. She just wants her mom.

I have no idea what to do. We're already dead, so we can't be killed again, but I have no wish to see what kind of damage a bullet can cause to a dead face.

I lean in toward Alfarin and whisper, "Can you get the gun if I get the girls out?"

Alfarin grunts, and I take that as a yes.

Then I hear heavy, pounding footsteps on the stairs in the hall. Someone is coming down.

"You can't see your living version!" I yell at my Medusa. "We have to leave now."

"Mom!" cries Medusa as Alfarin creeps forward. "You have to get away from Rory. He'll destroy you. He'll destroy other girls. He's evil, Mom."

Then the stepfather is standing in the doorway to the kitchen. For a moment he looks confused; he glances upstairs, and then he looks at the dead soul that is sobbing in his kitchen. He swears.

"Now, Alfarin!" I yell, and Alfarin throws himself on top of Medusa's mom. The gun is knocked from her hand and it slides across the floor and stops by the stepfather's feet.

"Out now!" I shout to the girls, pushing them through a single-paned glass door that leads into an untidy back garden. Spare car parts are strewn across the long grass. The howling surrounds us in the evening air as everything in this horrible world starts turning against us.

"What about Alfarin?" screams Elinor, trying to get back into the house. "We can't leave him in there."

Then a gunshot shatters time.

29. **Can't Remember**

"Alfarin!" screams Elinor.

"Mom!" screams Medusa.

Both girls make to run back into the house, but I have both of them by the waist. They're pulling away from me like a couple of puppies on leashes, and the heels of my sneakers are dragging in the dry, dusty earth. There's screaming coming from the kitchen, but I don't know whether it's the living Melissa or her mom. I wait to hear Alfarin's booming voice, but there is nothing.

Medusa's weight is easing slightly, but she's still struggling. Elinor goes completely limp as Alfarin finally crashes through the back door and into her arms.

"What happened?" I yell. "Is anyone hurt in there?"

A new pitch accompanies the growls and howls surrounding us. It's a siren.

"The police are coming!" cries Elinor. "How did they get here so quickly?"

"It's the Skin-Walkers!" yells Alfarin. "We must flee."

"My mom, my mom! It wasn't supposed to be like this!"

Medusa is getting lighter by the second. It proves easy to pull her away to the end of the garden, where we all climb over a low wire fence and run down a narrow alley lined with metal trash cans.

"Alfarin, what happened?"

Alfarin takes a quick left, then another left, and leads us back into the park where we arrived. We're at the far end, several houses away from Medusa's old home. A police car has already drawn up, quickly followed by an ambulance. Two tall, thin officers climb out, but something isn't right. Even though it's dark now, the two officers look as if they're surrounded by a dense black cloud.

The Skin-Walkers are here.

But instead of claiming us, they disappear into the house with another two men from the ambulance. They seem to lope into the house on all fours, their extra-long arms swinging in tandem with their legs.

Alfarin can't speak. His cheeks are crimson and sweat is dripping down his face. I'm struggling to hold on to Medusa, not because she's trying to get back to her mom, but because her clothes are slipping through my fingers like sand.

We hear the living version before we see her. Melissa Pallister is screaming and sobbing as she runs out onto the weathered porch of the house. A female neighbor has run out of her house and is now cradling the living Melissa in her arms. Even in the twilight, we can see the blood on Melissa's hands.

"He was shot," gasps Alfarin finally. "There was a struggle for the gun. The gun went off. There was nothing I could do."

"Is Rory dead?" Medusa sways on the spot. She goes straight through my hands.

Elinor screams. "M, what is happening to ye?"

Medusa is in shock and doesn't understand. I try to hold her hot little hands, but there's nothing but wispy vapor that swirls around my fingers like steam.

"She's disappearing!" I cry. "Time has changed. Her stepfather was shot, which didn't happen the first time around. That means Medusa's timeline has changed."

"The Skin-Walkers weren't coming for Medusa!" yells Alfarin. "They were coming for someone else in her timeline, and we led them straight here."

With a stricken look, Medusa makes to grab me, but there is nothing to hold on to as her soul starts to dissolve.

"Mitchell, help me!" she screams as tiny red pinpricks of fire start to appear on her body.

"The Viciseometer—who has the watch? We need to go back again!" I cry.

But Medusa is being swallowed by fire. It isn't the same as Elinor's death because Medusa isn't in any pain, but her face is terrified. I throw my arms around the flaming shadow of Medusa, but I can't feel any part of her.

"Stay with me, Medusa. Don't leave me!"

"Don't let me go," sobs Medusa, and she raises her right hand to touch my face. "Mitchell, don't let me go."

But she is gone before I can say another word.

"What is going on here, do you think?" asks Alfarin.

"What are *we* doing here?" asks Elinor, scratching her head.

The three of us—the triangle that is Team DEVIL—look around at each other. Alfarin is the first to start laughing. His chuckle is infectious, and it isn't long before Elinor and I join in.

"Who took us here?" giggles Elinor.

"Well, I have the Viciseometer..." I reply, pulling it out of my back pocket. The date reads the eighteenth of June, 1967. "Does this date mean anything to anyone?"

Alfarin and Elinor shake their heads.

"I think lack of food has affected your judgment, my friend," snorts Alfarin.

"Hey, maybe the recipe for fried chicken was invented in one of these houses and we're the first to ever try it out," I suggest hopefully.

We're interrupted by the sound of a woman screaming. We look over to one of the houses on the street, where a police car and an ambulance are parked. I have no idea what brought us here, and I'm in no rush to find out. I've heard dead people scream like that in Hell. You never want to find out why.

"Where are we?" asks Elinor.

"I have no idea where we are, El."

"What did ye just call me?"

"El."

"When have ye ever called me El?" giggles Elinor.

I shrug. "I dunno. It just popped into my head."

"I like it," replies Elinor rather wistfully.

"Where is my axe?" says Alfarin suddenly.

Both Elinor and I look around the park. It's Elinor who spots our backpacks half hidden under a bush near a rusty-looking swing.

We jog over, just as two men are bringing a man out of the house on a stretcher. Blood is splattered all over his chest. We can see it pulsing out in dark waves, but he's still flailing and screaming. He's saying he's sorry. The three of us stop suddenly as two tall, thin policemen follow out the door. They look in our direction. They smile at us, and for a split second I swear I see them morph into walking wolves with black, bared teeth. Goose bumps break out over my entire body, and even Alfarin shudders. The horribly injured man is pushed into the back of an ambulance—still begging for forgiveness. One of the policemen reaches into the back. There is a bloodcurdling howl, like maniacal laughter, and the screaming stops. The siren on the police car screams and they speed away with sparks of flame spitting from the tailpipes.

"Are they what I think they are?" whimpers Elinor. She's clutching Alfarin's arm.

With our line of sight clear to the house, I can see another two people on the porch. One is a fat woman with straggly gray hair. Her flabby arms are wrapped around a much younger woman: someone my age. The younger girl is really pretty, with the craziest hair I've ever seen in my life. It's the color of roasted chestnuts, and it looks alive under the beam of weak sunlight. Her hair reminds me of snakes.

The pretty girl looks over at me. My stomach flips as she continues staring. I can see that her hands are covered in blood, and I'm the one who turns away.

Alfarin slaps me on the back. "It is time to return to Hell, my friend. We can but pray to the gods that the Lord Septimus will forgive our indiscretions and will not torture us on the rack for our duplicity and thievery."

I sigh. "Have you checked the backpacks?" I ask Elinor one last time. "We don't want to leave anything behind."

"Well, the three of us didn't leave Hell with much in the first place," replies Elinor, but there is an abstract look on her face. She keeps pulling at her neck in that nervous way she does when she's worried about something.

And I feel it, too. A sense of unfinished business. It has nothing to do with changing my death anymore—I have no choice but to let go of that completely or I'll end up changing Alfarin's and Elinor's destinies. But I do have this horrible feeling in the pit of my stomach that I've forgotten something.

Something really important.

I open my backpack and take out the photo of the three of us that I've carried around since the beginning. Nothing has changed. Alfarin still has fries stuck up his nostrils. Elinor has her arms wrapped around Alfarin's shoulders, and as usual, nobody is there to hold on to me because no other girl has ever fit into our group.

I look back at the house opposite. The pretty girl is gone, although several more police cars have arrived. The policemen don't look anything like the creatures that took away that other man.

What am I forgetting? The feeling is starting to eat into my brain.

"Mitchell?" prompts Alfarin, handing me my backpack. "It is time to return to the HalfWay House."

I input the same date on which the three of us originally left but add a couple of minutes. I don't think Alfarin, Elinor, or I should meet the three devils who left Hell with nightmares that ended up coming true.

Nightmares. Why am I thinking about nightmares?

Elinor can sense my hesitance. "Are ye nervous about facing Septimus?" she asks.

"Something isn't right," I say, although the Viciseometer is starting to whistle and spit fire; it's getting impatient. "Can anyone remember *anything* about why we're here?"

"Everything is starting to blur together in my head, to be honest," replies Elinor.

"I can't remember what is real and what is not anymore," adds Alfarin gravely. "Our time among the living has passed, my friend. We must face the consequences like men."

"And women... or rather woman." Elinor pulls at her neck again; she looks really confused.

"I'll take responsibility for everything," I say. "I'll tell Septimus I made the three of you come with me."

"Three?" says Alfarin, looking at Elinor with a smirk. "No wonder the finances of the Underworld are so precarious, with an intern in accounting who cannot add."

He slaps me on the back as Elinor giggles.

"I meant two, obviously. I'm just hungry and distracted."

I give the house one last look, but the commotion and whatever happened inside are starting to draw a crowd. It's better we leave now. Alfarin, Elinor, and I link arms for the final journey. As the mirrored building of the HalfWay House comes into view on the Viciseometer, my eyes are drawn away for a split second to an upstairs window. A dirty net curtain is pulled back to reveal the girl with a mass of curly hair watching us.

I'm sure she sees us disappear into the night, but I'm not worried.

After all, who among the living would believe her if she told?

30. The Other Intern

"How did you die?"

I'm not going to bother with the saving kittens story line anymore. It was pretty lame in the first place. Of course I'm not going to tell devils the truth, either. How can I? Well, you see, I stole a time-traveling device called a Viciseometer and ended up causing my own death after my living self saw the dead version standing across the road with a Viking prince and a peasant from the Great Fire of London...

Who in Hell is going to believe that?

I'm expecting Septimus to be mad at me when I return to the office. In fact, he's waiting in the darkness for the three of us as we try to slip the Viciseometer back into the safe. Elinor is in a state of near collapse once more, and Alfarin has his axe ready to decapitate anyone from the HBI who may appear to arrest us.

Instead, Septimus is sitting with his feet up on the desk, a large strawberry cheesecake at his side and a strange expression on his face. He isn't angry. He just looks sad. It reminds me of the time my parents told me they were getting divorced. They had the same look then: downturned mouths; watering eyes; trembling jaws. I've never seen Septimus look this grieved before, and I don't like it. I don't want him on the warpath, either, but it just aggravates the feeling that I've done something I'm not yet aware of. Something bigger than a mistake.

Septimus asks us if we've seen enough. I say we've seen too much.

The combination of the safe has been changed. If that's my only punishment for stealing the Viciseometer, I'll happily take it. Septimus tells me he, too, tried to change his death on a number of occasions, but he always ended up back in Hell because living meant being back with his wife. Being married has got to be tough if you'd rather be dead. I don't think the two of them got on that well.

It's a month after our return and Septimus still won't tell me how he got hold of the other Viciseometer: the blue-faced one from Up There. I've noticed he gets perfumed letters delivered weekly, though. Elinor thinks Septimus is dating an angel. Only Septimus could get away with something as devious as that.

I keep meaning to ask him about the two angels I saw at the cemetery, but there never seems to be a good moment. Maybe I'll keep it as *my* secret. Someone once told me that everyone has secrets, but I can't remember who.

Speaking of dating, tonight I'm seeing Patty Lloyd from the library. I know I should be enthusiastic about it, but I'm really not. I don't know what's wrong with me. Hot girl, minimum third base guaranteed, and I even have Alfarin and Elinor coming along for moral support.

The devils in my dorm think I'm a hero, but Patty Lloyd just isn't my type. I want something different, someone who isn't obvious. Somebody I'm sure I've met before, but I can't for the death of me remember when. Time travel has shot my memory into a million little fragments, and I don't know how to stick it all back together again. I'm like a tall, skinny Humpty-Dumpty.

Patty meets up with the three of us in Thomason's Bar. She

immediately gets under my skin by calling the place a dump. So what if it is? It's *my* dump. Mine and Alfarin's and Elinor's and...

Well, not Patty Lloyd's.

Alfarin and Elinor are holding hands now like a proper couple. I don't think Elinor has let Alfarin kiss her yet, but the hands thing is a start, and as Alfarin says, he's waited several hundred years to get this far. Patty sits on my lap. I've faked a cold sore by gluing a cornflake to my lip, so she doesn't kiss me.

The date is hopeless. Patty doesn't even attempt to speak to Alfarin or Elinor. She whispers in my ear about finding a quiet corner where she can show me how much she likes me without kissing my mouth, but that just freaks me out. This girl moves way too fast.

Patty storms out in a bad mood after Alfarin and I start joking about slapping buttocks and cheeseburgers, and because Elinor was laughing it was obvious it was an inside joke, but I wasn't in a rush to share it with Patty. She wouldn't understand because she wasn't there.

"We'll find ye someone," says Elinor soothingly as the three of us leave Thomason's.

Time traveling has brought the three of us closer together, but we all share a strange feeling that, for me, sets my teeth on edge. Elinor thinks it may be time-sickness; Alfarin reckons his stomach couldn't cope with twenty-first-century food and all the toxins and additives in what we ate.

I don't even bother offering an opinion, but it feels as if wind is whistling through a door that has been left open. I still miss my life, desperately. I miss my little brother, too, even though I don't know him. I would have just liked the chance to know him.

Work is getting crazier by the day. Septimus is nearly in tears with the amount of money Hell costs to run and is muttering about war again. The Devil's Executive Board of Management had a meeting in the Oval Office, and even I could hear The Devil screaming about Operation H without putting my ear to the door. Then the financiers of Wall Street got involved and the stock market plummeted and Hell had another huge influx of dead because the stress killed so many people. So now I'm working at least fifteen hours a day and my eyes have black rings under them that look as if someone has punched me and then run over my face with a tank.

My eyes. My pink girly eyes are back with a vengeance, looking brighter and sparklier than ever. It is so not fair, because both Alfarin and Elinor have their bloodred eyes back, and Alfarin's beard has already grown back, too. Not as long as it was before, but give it a couple of months and Elinor will be able to braid things into it the way she used to.

Pink girly eyes and fuzz on my face that looks like the stuff that collects in a clothes dryer. What decent girl is going to go for that? I'm back in an overcrowded Hell, and instead of being the next Chris Martin, I'm still The Devil's intern.

And I'm still on my own.

Septimus announces that he's getting another intern to help me out. This comes after one of the legs on my desk collapses under the weight of invoices that have yet to be cleared. He allows me to sit in on the interviews, and the applicants get worse as the day drags on. The first devil we see thinks working on level 1 will get him closer to Up There; the second devil failed the written test (she couldn't hold a pen the right way up); the third devil had good credentials but was wearing a white shirt that had mold growing under the armpits; and the fourth devil was Brian Molewell and I will go clean the toilets on level 666 before I work with him.

Patty Lloyd was candidate number five, and by now I'm willing to revisit my death as she slips me a note that quite explicitly details what she intends to do to me on a desk once Septimus is out of the office.

Septimus thankfully ends the interview early and advises Patty she is far too valuable to the library staff to make a move into accounting.

"Are you up to one more interview tonight?" asks Septimus, before downing the triple-shot espresso the kitchens have just sent up to him.

"No," I groan. "I swear I'll work twenty-four hours a day for the rest of eternity, Septimus. Just please don't make me sit through any more interviews."

My boss laughs. "Well, this last one today looks quite promising. A young devil, about your age. Dead for forty years—perhaps she'll tell you about it. She comes with excellent references from the legal department and the kitchens."

"Great," I reply sarcastically. "Someone who can file the dirty dishes, just what we need."

"Let's give her a go," says Septimus. "She is well known for her strawberry cheesecake, which is a plus. If you could ask Miss Pallister to come in, Mitchell. Once we've seen her, I will let you run off to play third wheel to Prince Alfarin and Miss Powell."

"Thanks for reminding me," I reply. I push myself out of the chair that has been slowly numbing my ass for the last four hours.

I'm not sure which is worse these days: the albino hedgehog look with my blond hair and pink eyes, or the sad-and-alone loser look I wear whenever I'm with my two best friends. Alfarin and Elinor go out of their way to include me still, but I'm very aware it was me who joined the two of them, and they've been best friends forever. After Elinor's death... well, they're tighter than ever.

I'm about to go and get the last candidate—this Miss Pallister—when the door of the accounting office crashes open and in strides The Devil.

I nearly fall to the floor in shock, and even Septimus has to hold on to the back of his chair for support. The Devil never leaves the Oval Office—ever.

"I want to see it now, Septimus!" screeches The Devil, pulling at his goatee. "He has pushed me to the edge of reason. I want to see the virus tested now. He has sent me an invoice for the damage the cherubs have done to the Pearly Gates. He says I have corrupted them. I'll show Him corruption. He won't be whining about graffiti when I have unleashed Operation H on His foul, vile, disgusting angels. We'll be hearing their screams from here. In fact, I intend to record their agony and will release it as a free download—oh, hello, Mitchell, I didn't realize Septimus had company."

I mumble something that sounds like a cat being castrated. If I open my mouth too wide, I'll vomit on The Devil's shoes.

"Perhaps we should go back into the Oval Office, sir?" replies Septimus. He is sweating profusely.

"Yes, yes," mutters The Devil. "Well, good night, Mitchell. Sweet dreams." He skips back through the door, which automatically closes behind him.

"Take the rest of the night off, Mitchell," says Septimus quietly. He pulls out his wallet and gives me some cash. "Why don't you conduct the final interview for today well away from the CBD?"

I take the cash and nod. I have no intention of staying on level 1 longer than necessary. Septimus leaves through the connecting door to the Oval Office. I am alone. Better get this over with, I think, and I pull open the main door to the accounting chamber. It swings wide with an eerie creak. I stick my head out, look left and right, and I see Miss Pallister... or rather, I see her hair. It's mad and awesome, as if a nest of dark-brown snakes has settled on her head.

"Is Mr. Septimus ready now?" she asks with a nervous smile that shows off cute dimples.

"Miss Pallister?" I'm talking to her hair. I really shouldn't do that. It might upset her.

"Yes."

Behind me, the phone starts to ring, but I ignore it. The voice mail picks it up.

"This is Mitchell Johnson, The Devil's intern. Please leave a message after the screams..."

Mitchell Johnson, that's me. Four syllables and nothing more.